Never Letting Go

K. Wickerham

Enjoy
Ken Wickerham

Contents

26 Elizabeth

27 Coree

28 Elizabeth

29 Coree

30 Elizabeth

31 Coree

32 Elizabeth

33 Coree

34 Elizabeth

35 Coree

36 Elizabeth

37 Coree

38 Elizabeth

39 Coree

40 Elizabeth

41 Coree

42 Elizabeth

43 Coree

44 Elizabeth

45 Coree

46 Elizabeth

47 Coree

48 Elizabeth

49 Coree

50 Elizabeth

51 Coree

52 Elizabeth

1

Coree

Home always looks different when you've been away. The driveway seemed a little jankier, probably because in the city, you don't see sunken, two-track driveways. In the city, everything's on the level...except for the people. Even so, the busy sounds of the meadowlarks and the whippoor-wills, my growing-up sounds, acknowledged my return.

"Nice car," came a voice from behind the patched screen door. I glanced back in the direction of the black Lexus in the grassy two-track, a visual anomaly.

"Hey, Daddy. How you doing?"

"Doin," he said, mouth open just wide enough for sound to pass through. As always, his hip supported his elbow, which supported his arm, which held his hand and its eternal cigarette between two fingers, the long, bending ash threatening to crash at any moment. No smile, no frown, no light in his rheumy eyes.

He opened the door just wide enough for Bob and Whiskey to trot through. They gave me the once over. Evidently satisfied, they sat to be petted, gazing off, somewhere and nowhere. "The lump on Bob's side getting bigger, Daddy?"

"Hasn't changed."

"You can't get him fixed? It's about the size of a basketball, making him walk funny."

"Vet says he's too old to operate on, can't do nothin'."

I glanced from the lump on Bob to the cigarette in Daddy's hand and nodded. At the top of the cracked cement steps, I hugged him. "Daddy, you need to eat more." The two cats kept their distance as if seeing me for the first time. "Salt and Pepper look as ornery as ever, so that's good."

Daddy's old green Lazy Boy still sat on the front porch where we used to spend so much family time. I beat him to it and plopped in sideways, legs over the armrest. Bob took up a spot by Daddy. Whiskey followed me, his head close to my hand. "I know it wouldn't do me any good to suggest you slow down on the cigarettes."

"Mind your own business, little girl." He nodded out through the screen. "Tell me about the car."

"It's a friend's."

"In the money?"

I nodded. "She's a corporate executive."

"Why you have it? Why you friends with her?"

"I met her, serving...waitressing."

"And?" he raised an eyebrow.

"And we're friends."

Daddy cleared his throat.

"We're good friends. She has health problems, and I'm taking care of her for a while."

Daddy's chin rose with the tug at his cigarette, the long, precarious ash hanging on.

Salt and Pepper returned and coiled up against Bob. Their determination outlasted the big old dog's resistance, and they settled into his warm body.

"How's the modelling?"

"Not getting rich."

"You were always such a cute little butterfly."

"I'm going to go see Mommy. You want to come?"

"You go on," he said. "I'll see about dinner."

"Forget that. I'll take you out when I get back. We can take a tour of town."

"Nothin's changed."

I climbed into the Lexus feeling Daddy's stare. I couldn't see him behind the screen, but an orange spot glowed and dimmed in the shadowy porch as he drew off his cigarette.

At the end of the driveway, I glanced both ways, as if I needed to.

Our road, perfectly still, save for the faint whistle of the wind across it, formed a straight tan barrier which seemed to hold back the sea of golden yellow sunflowers in full bloom. Facing our house as they did every August, they brought it all back, brought her back. I turned away, avoiding the memories, but it didn't work. Our mailbox, just a standard, hardware-store mailbox, black, red flag, white post, standing alone by the driveway, elicited the very same tightness in my chest. "Oh, Mommy,"

I said. I saw us, holding hands by it, waiting for the bus, the first bus of the school year, our faces lit by the immense glow, the light of the sunflowers, a lifetime still before us.

***

I kneeled before her simple brass plaque, flush to the grass, brown clippings accumulating in the corners, and I talked to her in silence. Maybe she talked to me too. "Ellen Wysakee. Seeing the name in a cemetery slammed me with the realization, even after all this time. In school and in town, even now in the city, people considered me cute and bubbly, but crouching here with Mommy, I felt tired and way older.

I touched the cool of her name with the pads of my fingers. Picking the bits of dead grass out of the corners and tossing them into the wind, they drifted among the neighboring stones, big ones and little ones, lots of Wysakees. People asked if I knew this one or that one. I usually didn't. We must've been some shirt-tale branch.

The same sun that warmed the back of my neck, created a shadow on part of her name. "Mommy, things are going alright, pretty good. Aubrey got me a good job, a server at a nice restaurant, and my modelling is going okay, a bit of money here and there. I met a guy. We'll see where that goes," I said with a shrug. "Sammi's doing good too. The three of us are still together, like a family." I knew I should never have said that word. As soon as it came out of my mouth, I wanted to put it back, but words don't go back. Once they're out, they're out. Words can never go back, and the tears came.

With my elbows on my knees, I rested my face in my hands. "Mommy, why'd you have to go and leave me?" The rumble of a pickup on the highway floated over the hill, and without taking my eyes off her marker, I waited for the sound to dissipate. "Mommy, why'd you have to go and leave me? I took care of you. I tried to take care of you. I would have done anything."

I glanced around at the grass, the other stones, the trees, and I kept seeing her face, healthy, then sick and then healthy again. It always switched back and forth like that. I wiped a finger under each of my eyes. "I know. I'm at it again, same old thing. I know you'd have stayed if you could, but it's hard, Mommy. It's so God damn hard without you."

A soft breeze blew up, and I tossed more dry blades of grass into it, watching them drift and fall where the wind took them. The aroma of fresh-cut alfalfa floated in from a surrounding field. The rows of raked hay, drying in the sun brought back the old growing-up smells. "It's getting better. High school," I shrugged, "you know, a disaster." I glanced out at the big sky of the farm country and back. "It's finally getting better now. I have a new friend, a lady about your age, or what would be your age. She reminds me of you, looks like you, but she's different." I paused to think about Elizabeth. "Mommy, you were always so happy, sunshine to us all, but she's, like in her heart, she's real serious. Maybe she could have been like you, but there's some hurt in there. Maybe she needs a daughter. Lord knows, I need a mom, at least that's what Aubrey says. Maybe I can help her, do better than I did with you."

My face collapsed into my hands. "Mommy, I tried. I so tried. I would have given anything, given myself for you to live." I ran my fingers up through my hair and down around my neck and sat for a moment with my fingers laced on the back of my neck.

When a couple tear drops landed on her brass, I jumped up and ran for the car, where the scent of the vanilla air freshener and of Elizabeth herself wrapped around me. I studied myself in the rearview mirror and wiped the damp from under my eyes again. Daddy doesn't need to see me like this. He's got his own problems. My eyes lit upon the little stud in the side of my nose, the one that Elizabeth was straight-point clear on, in her usual way, that she doesn't like.

The Lexus bounced its way over the old graveyard two track and right before pulling out on the highway, I dropped it into park. Carefully holding the stone between my finger and thumb, I released the stud. Lowering the power window, I tossed it out, and they disappeared into the grassy ditch. "Happy Elizabeth?"

***

Daddy and I drove through town, past the Walmart, the Dollar General, the Walgreens, and the line of ancient storefronts that seemed to change hands every time I came home. "We don't need to go here," Daddy said, when we turned into Applebees. I ignored his protests, imagining how he'd react to the over-the-top luxury of Billie Jean's.

Despite being the finest dining in town, the potholes in the parking lot challenged the stroller of a young lady approaching us. "Nice ride there, Coree Wysakee. City life being good to you, looks like."

"Hey, Rachel, how you doing?" I couldn't have been less interested in how she was doing, but I had bringing up, so I asked.

"Doing fine. Here's my two little guys, another one on the way. Seems like every time Billy comes home on leave, we get another addition soon after. You got kids yet, or married?"

"No, and no."

"Good seeing you."

"Say 'hi' to Billy."

"Will do."

***

Our family pictures lining the hallway made me wonder who's going to take care of Daddy when he gets old. He didn't want anyone, but the cats and dogs. As a little girl, I used to walk this hall with my hands and feet against the walls, no floor needed. I'd like to think I could still do it if I really wanted to. One picture caught my eye, Mommy and me at a picnic table, her arm around her girl. I touched the picture, trying to keep the connection to her.

In my last glance, pulling away, I noticed how the swing chains hung straight and motionless in a lonely vigil, the once-bare earth underneath completely grown back.

I stomped on the gas, and the engine of Elizabeth's Lexis jumped to life down the entrance ramp. I felt guilty leaving

Daddy, but what was there to do? Mommy was the light for him, the light and warmth of the sun. No matter what I did, I didn't see how he could ever be happy again. My body sank back into the heat of the black leather seat, accelerating forward toward the city, toward Elizabeth.

2

Elizabeth

A Month Earlier

"Who'll take care of us when we're old?" I said it to an orangestriped cat which appeared atop my old mortar and field stone garden wall. It occasionally licked a paw or glanced about. If I made a sudden movement, it might take notice of me. Would we then become part of each other's worlds, both of them forever changed?

"Billie Jean's," a lively, young voice on the receiver said.

"Elizabeth Ransom here. Reserve a table for one, a booth rather, for six o'clock tonight."

"Yes, ma'am."

"I know it is Saturday, and you will be busy. Nevertheless, do not keep me waiting. I will arrive at six exactly. Make it happen."

"Gotcha, Ms. Ransom. We'll make it happen."

"What is your name, young lady?"

"Coree."

"Make it happen, Coree. I will be counting on you."

"I won't let you down."

"Coree," I said, laying the phone on the end table. "No doubt, like the cat, she just follows where the story takes her. I did that once, and I've regretted it ever since."

My thoughts drifted to Landford-Smithson, and my staff, who, no doubt, are enjoying their family time, living for the weekends for the same reasons I dread them. I sent a text. "Michael, see me first thing Monday morning. I have questions about the staffing in your department."

"Let me guess, use of personal and vacation days."

"If u r aware, why do we have to talk about it?"

"I'll be there, Ms. Ransom."

"Ms. Ransom?"

"My wife doesn't like me referring to u as 'Elizabeth.'"

"For God's sake, I'm senior vice president. Oh, whatever. Be in my office Monday morning with answers."

I laid the phone on the wicker armrest without waiting for a response, brushed a piece of lint off the white cushion, and surveyed my terrace. Swishing the last bit of mimosa around the bottom of the glass, I glanced back out at the leaves trembling on my weeping willow. Unlike me, they yielded before a stiff morning breeze. My comfortable cloister could not protect me from myself though, exiled in my memories. Is this my life then, just running out the clock? This, forever? Isn't there ever a redemption?

3

Coree

The delectable scents of oregano, basil, and onion, the reflective chrome surfaces of the kitchen, and the white-clad kitchen staff with their frantic and often crude language, fell away the moment I stepped into the dining room. Calm descended, the tranquility demanded by our patrons and their comfortable position in life.

"I got a Ms. Elizabeth Ransom in my section, booth for one."

"You better be on your game."

"Why? What's she like, Aubrey?"

"She's actually not terrible, mostly wants to be left alone, brings her work."

"On a Saturday night? What's up with that?"

"Got me. She's an executive at some corporation, always working, eating, people watching."

I could have easily missed her arrival in the bustle of the room. She could have gone unnoticed, but just when this Ms. Elizabeth Ransom stepped inside, I happened to glance over. I sucked in a gasp, a hand reflexively rising to my mouth. "Oh, my God."

"Coree." I heard the kitchen doors behind me and felt a squeeze on my arm. "Hey there, Coree. I'm getting no signal."

"She's..." I couldn't pull my eyes away as they led her to a booth. "Aubrey, she looks like-"

"Ya think? Older, definitely sugar free, but the physical resemblance is startling, isn't it?"

"Why didn't you tell me, warn me?"

"I gotta get to my tables, but Coree, listen, don't do anything stupid."

I cut straight across the dining room, a straight line to where the side booth framed this Ransom woman, two steps up, classic red brick backdrop. She dressed more for the boardroom than a Saturday night out, but straight posture and hair pinned-back tightly couldn't hide the familiarity in the depth of her brown eyes, in the mature creases in the corners of her mouth, even in the way the lines of her perfect hands rested across the grains of the perfect walnut table. I twisted the rings on my fingers. "Hey." I realized later that I didn't even use her name in greeting, as if I already knew her or something. "I'm Coree. Welcome to Billie Jean's. How about an Albarino, or Pinot Blanc, or what would you like?"

She scanned the room over my head. "Albarino."

"You alright, Coree?" Aubrey said, when we passed.

"I'm fine." I smiled. "I'm just fine. I'm perfect."

"Oh, Lord. Here we go."

"Look at this. The chefs were working on these little antipasto skewers, so snap, I made you up a cute appetizer. The cheese, olives, mushrooms, the blend of colors and textures are..." My words fizzled out watching her frown like some haughty queen in her court.

"How old you think she is, Aubs?"

"Late forties, fifty?"

Glancing across the room, I nodded, and said, "So like Mom, but like a stern, business version of Mom, older."

Aubrey followed my glance. "Well, your mom would have been older, maybe about that old."

"And this Ransom woman is so legit," I said. "She can flex it just sitting there."

"You're gonna love this soup, Ms. Ransom."

She lifted a laptop out of its leather carrying case.

"They sauteed the mushrooms with brandy and herbs. Three kinds of mush-"

"How long have you been under employ here?" Her eyes never left her screen.

"A couple weeks. My roommate's been here a long time. She got me the-"

"That will be all."

"Shot down in flames," I said to Aubrey. "But check out table fourteen. There's a guy, smokin' hot. The one with the sandy hair."

"So is his girlfriend or wife or whatever, but when did that ever stop you before?"

"Just look at him though, low key like."

"When will you ever have a real relationship, Coree?"

I turned back to Aubrey. "I don't want a real relationship, whatever that is."

"No shit. Like you can keep one."

"That's noise, Aubs."

"Well, who'll take care of you when you're old?"

I smacked my forehead with the heal of my hand. "I'm twenty-three. We're both twenty-three. It's now, Aubrey. It's right now."

My friend nodded across the room. "Maybe she can help you carry all that baggage you're dragging around."

This time, it was me who followed Aubrey's glance. The enigmatic business woman in the booth ate alone and studied her laptop.

"Check it out. Farro and fried cauliflower salad, so scrumptious, I wish I could share it with you." If she'd have just looked down her nose at me, at least she'd have been looking at me.

Luscious lines of steam twisted and spiraled above the main course. Ms. Ransom glanced at it, back at her computer, and at the halibut, never at me. No matter, because on my way back, the cute guy, while his significant other looked away, gave me a wink. My chest heaved when I told Aubrey. She rolled her eyes and said, "I pretty much hate you."

"No rings either."

"Yeah, I hate you." She side-eyed our manager. "Don't get yourself fired, Coree and don't get me in trouble. And don't make a bunch of noise in your room with him and totally depress me." Her shoulders slumped. "I'm depressed already, thinking about it."

"He winked at me, and you've got us-"

"Get after your tables, ladies."

4

Elizabeth

My skin slid against the cool of my ivory cashmere sheets in a bed no one, but me, has ever, nor will ever, sleep in, the bookend on another productive day. I considered the first half of the weekend, Landford-Smithson, of course, as always, but I did take a bit of time for gardening, and socialization at the restaurant, at least from a spectator point of view.

In the booth behind, I knew her whole story, and he knew it now too. On what was evidently the getting-to-know-you, first date, she blathered on and on and on. Conversely, the couple in the booth in front of me exchanged few words, light from the phones illuminating their faces.

Not far away, a man and woman who could have turned heads in any Parisian café cut an elegant picture. More than once, however, I observed him eyeing my server. He operated so smoothly, his absolutely dazzling consort remained completely oblivious. None of any of this for me, thank you very much. I already made a mess of my life.

The server appeared in my mind's slide show. A petite and energetic thing, she affected a charm that I usually consider annoying. Not only that, but she looked at me, no not at me, more like into me, as one might gaze into the depths of a wishing well. I approached the door, and she snaked through the busy tables in my direction, compelling me to turn.

"Ms. Ransom. Ms. Ransom."

I rolled onto my side and closed my eyes, just as ocean waves began from my sound machine.

"Thanks for coming. My name is Coree," she called, and the valet handed over my keys.

5

Coree

"Forty dollars, Aubrey. Forty dollars."

"She tipped you forty?"

"The bill was like a hundred and ten, and she just rounded it off to a hundred-fifty."

"She must like you."

I frowned at that comment, and tucked my hair behind an ear, but eyeing the bills, I said, "Let's go out after work, Aubrey. Let's spend everything we have. Let's go dancing."

***

Pounding techno beats reached out the doors of Toni's like tentacles. They mingled with the conversations of the scattered huddles of clubbers on the sidewalks. Inside the door, the relentless onslaught of music and a mixture of perfume, alcohol, and perspiration blended with an oppressive heat to nearly overwhelm Aubrey and me.

"Straight fire," I said. "Everybody's got green to burn."

"Maybe they've all got a sugar mama like you," Aubrey said.

Pulsating reds and blues from both above and below lit the frantically moving bodies jammed onto the huge dance floor. Rising around, amphitheater-like, still more humanity jammed the tables and spilled out into the aisles, filling nearly every inch of space. The two of us weaved within this undulating mass of anonymous bodies.

After dancing a few numbers and downing a few drinks, my mind and body seemed to float. Aubrey slipped off to the restroom, and a warm breath in my ear said, "Hey, cute little Billie Jean Coree."

Defenses down, I leaned right in, brushing against him before turning and coming face to face with the hottie from the restaurant. "Well, hi there. What a nice surprise."

"I know. Listen, I don't want to be too forward." He glanced around. "But there's no choice. You are so cute and," he searched for a word and settled on, "effervescent. I'm with a date, not serious, but can I get your number? I'm Grayson, and I'd like to see you sometime. What do you say?"

I glanced around. "Sure." We punched in our numbers.

"I liked watching you dance."

My eyebrows rose.

"I'm not a stalker."

"Too bad," I said, "because if I had a stalker, I'd want it to be you."

"You seem fun," he said.

"Oh, I am," I said up into him through my bangs.

"Your eyes," he said. "Your green eyes in these lights. Listen. I gotta get back. Talk to you soon." He stole a kiss on my cheek, which I again leaned into, about when Aubrey came into view.

"I don't believe it, the guy in the restaurant?"

"All cap. His name is Grayson, and we exchanged numbers."

She shook her head. "He's a smooth one, hitting on other chicks while he's on a date."

"Guys like that can do it," I said.

"Where do you suppose your sugar mama is right now, Coree?"

"Pretty sure she's home in bed resting up so she can continue to have no fun again tomorrow. Let's take a walk through this place and check out that hot Grayson and his hot date."

"Damn," Aubrey said. "She's cute AF."

"Yeah, what's he up to?"

"He's a player. He's dating her and still hedging his bets with you and who else in here? Sus to that."

"Flexing it," I said.

"How'd you like to be her, all done up for the evening, and your date is still out on the prowl, flexing it, as you say?"

"Kind of not right, is it?" I said.

"Nope."

"Well then," I said with an extended index finger. "It must be Coree's job to get to the bottom of it."

"Tell me where you go out," Aubrey said, "and I'll hang around to exchange phone numbers with him when you look the other way."

"I get your point," I said. "Depends on which end of the stick you're on, doesn't it? You don't even like men, Aubrey, and you're drooling over him." The base thudded into us. A strobe light danced on the side of our faces. "They look so trendy, the chic couple out on the scene, being seen." I pictured myself in her place, but I just couldn't do it. I couldn't be in vogue like her even if I dressed like that, and if I did, all my tattoos would show, and I'd look all extra. "Where could he even take me?" My shoulders slumped. "Where would the two of us even fit in together?"

Aubrey didn't answer, so I suspected she didn't disagree.

"Asshole."

Now she turned my way.

"Check his old-school suit. He's subtle and graceful and-"

"You're getting worked up, Cor-"

"He's living off a trust fund, no doubt, from his rich-ass parents, doing the playboy life with no consequences."

"You're building a whole life about him, and you don't even know-"

"He's like one of those princes on the Hallmark shows who want a regular girl, just a regular girl. Only, that's all bullshit. It's bullshit, Aubrey. He wants to have a night of sex with a cute little five-one, tattooed server, and he totally knows I'd be down for it."

"Chill, Coree."

"Cause he's legit and probably has a magnificent huge-ass apartment like I'll never, ever live in." I frowned. "But if I'm lucky, he'll take me there for one night."

"What's your deal?"

"Let's go."

"Wait, Coree."

I passed their table, and he regarded me with confident eyes.

Aubrey ran to catch up on the sidewalk. Shiny now from a light mist, it reflected the colors of the neon signs. "Stop, Coree." I turned and fell into her arms. "A few drinks and you go all emo. He'll call, and you'll find out you were wrong."

"I don't care, Aubrey. I don't care if he calls." I pictured that Ransom lady, sitting in her booth, quiet and unapproachable, giving me orders, making zero eye contact, absolutely zero. At least she dealt straight with me.

***

Department store sweatpants and an oversized tee shirt hung rudely from my frame in her doorway. The dim hallway light behind silhouetted me. I bet Grayson's date doesn't wear this to bed.

"Aubrey," I whispered. "Aubrey."

"Shit, Coree, you scared me to death."

"Can I sleep with you?"

"What in the world? Why? Oh, never mind." She pulled back the covers. "Come on."

I climbed in and slid over near her. "Aubrey?"

"What?

"Well..."

"What is it?"

"Well, that Elizabeth Ransom's eyes. They're just like Mom's."

"Is that what this is all about?"

"I mean brown and soulful. You remember her eyes?"

"Sure, deep and warm. But Ms. Ransom's kind of frosty. You know?"

"Her eyes though, Aubrey. People can't hide what's in their eyes."

I woke alone in a little warm ball to the words, "You better rise and shine, girl." Aubrey, leaving the bathroom light, dressed and ready for her day job, said, "Gotta make that money...until Prince Charming comes for you."

"Princes don't come for this." I hunched on the side of the bed, rubbing puffy eyes, and dragging the bottoms of my sweat pant legs down over my calves.

"What he likes," Aubrey said, "what everybody likes, is how chirpy and bubbly you are, but girl, when you go down, you go hard."

"That's what she said," I mumbled into the floor.

"There's my Coree, coming back to life."

"Sorry about last night."

"You got a lot of sides to you, little Coree Wysakee. Catch you later at Billie Jean's."

The bottoms of my bare feet swished on the cold wood floor of our hallway. I contemplated my tired face in the mirror, sleep indentations on one side. "No Prince Charming for you, biatch."

6

Elizabeth

"You can understand my concern, Elizabeth. I need to hire more personnel or risk getting backed up, making mistakes...or even losing good people by working them such long hours."

"Is our compensation competitive, Michael?"

"Of course, we-"

"Yes, it is. We both know the answer to my question. We pay our people better than competitive." I straightened a few things on my desk. "We pay them better than anyone else so we can have these high expectations."

"Still-"

"Still what? Am I not justified in my expectations?"

"Some things money can't buy."

"Like?" I knew the answer. I'd heard it too many times, so the moment I asked, I regretted it.

"Like time with their family."

The past weekend set up this Monday morning showdown. I knew it. My time alone compared to this Michael Kent, with his loving wife and family. I knew it, but still, I continued the broadsides. "So, your people want more compensation than our competitors for the same work?"

"The ones who want more family time, more time with their wives and husbands and kids-"

"I know what families are." I drummed my nails into my desk. "Michael, please get to the point."

"Well, that is the point, no offense. Like I said, we may lose some good people at the rate we..." He paused and shrugged. "Elizabeth, you don't have family."

My cheeks warmed, and Mother intruded from my past. "Yes, Libby, the other kids are playing, but you are better than them, and you will be better than them when you grow up. To do that, you will work hard."

"I'm just telling you what is going on so you'll know."

"Okay, you told me. Is there anything else?"

"Not right now."

I pulled at my collar. "Then if you will excuse me, I have work to do, and so do you." A sigh tempered his friendly, and occasionally, I suppose, even captivating eyes, and it triggered me. Slamming my hand down, I stood. "Close the door." I stepped around my desk, blocking his path, so no obstacle, even symbolically, buffered my message. "We both know what has to be done, Michael. I'm the one in the captain's chair, so I have to be the hard ass, and I accept that. It comes with the job. You'd do the same if you were in my position. Michael," I said up to him, "we must compete. Do what you have to do. Make it happen and get results."

"Elizabeth."

Mother spoke to me again, and I wanted to squeeze my ears to block out her voice, but her words became mine and mine hers. I turned them on Michael. "Why is this conversation continuing?"

"Because you're wrong."

"Is that so?"

"About me at least. If I were in your position, I don't think I would be doing the same-"

"Our strategy, at least since I've been boss, has been to pay the best so we can have the best people in the business, better than our competitors. We have that, don't we?

"Yes, we have-"

"Of course, we do." I waved my arms in frustration. "For God's sake, I know the answer. It was a rhetorical question." Sweat collected on his forehead, but it had no more effect on me than my office art of orderly city buildings, which probably began to rattle. "You're paid well. I'm paid well. We compensate our people extremely well, and dammit, they have to earn that pay with some long hours."

When I paused to take a breath, he said, "I understand your point, Elizabeth."

My temper carried me along like a wave I couldn't get off.

"Understanding means you don't agree with it."

"No, I don't, but the issue needed to be brought up. Please just consider my point. Entertain it."

I crossed my arms.

"Elizabeth, don't, at least, completely slam the door on it, you know, so it's there in however little, tiny form you can tolerate in case down the road it warrants consideration."

"That request I can grant, Michael, because you've wasted half my morning harping on it, and you continue to stand here pushing, even though a dead man could see how adamant I am against it. It's bound to attach itself to me, like a laceration from a brawl."

"A brawl you won, Elizabeth, as usual."

"I took my hits." The biggest hit being his inadvertent reminder that unlike me, most people go home to families who love them. Scrutinizing him, I said, "Use my private restroom there, Michael, before you leave. Straighten up. I don't want you coming out of my office appearing addled."

Before he left, I blocked his path to the door. "Let me see." I straightened his red and gold power tie, the first time I had done anything remotely like that since my last attempt at marriage. I inspected his salt and pepper corporate hair. "Yes, you look fine."

Michael smiled down at me. "Elizabeth, you're such a unique person."

I returned to my desk.

"You berate my idea and me as well in the process, aggressively-"

"Straight talk, Michael. It's just straight talk."

He nodded. "You respect me so much. Despite correcting me, you make sure I am fit for command, so to speak."

Where had all the oxygen gone in this room? "We have work to do. Please excuse me, Michael."

He chuckled. "Alright, alright...still, I know you care. Underneath that iron façade is a heart, a kind heart."

I waited for the door to click shut and gave him time to put distance from my office before the bottom of my fist hit the desk. Perhaps, Michael, just perhaps, the façade has become the reality. That heart you think you see has been stamped out cold long ago. By the time I entered business school, well, even my last years of high school, no one could compete with me. I had trained myself to work all day, seven days a week, and I carried it right on into my career, a twenty-five-year battle from the bottom to the top of the heap. So, even if, down there somewhere, a tiny orange ember still glows, Michael. I don't see how the fire can ever burn brightly again.

My secretary popped her head in the door. "Your 11:00 is here. Would you like a few minutes to reset?"

I blinked. "Do I look alright, Chelsea?"

"Perfect, only, maybe a little time to refocus your mental direction?"

"Good idea. Ten minutes."

She nodded and raising her phone, she said, "The clock is running." When she closed the door, the soft push of air brought a trace of Michael Kent's cologne to settle around me.

I sat rigid, eyes darting about my desk and office. There is always, always another issue landing squarely upon my desk. In contrast, Michael Kent, and the rest of my executives for that matter, certainly have issues landing on their desk as well, but he has the embrace of a loving wife waiting at home. I tried to envision her for a moment, wasting her energy on her husband calling me 'Elizabeth.' Really lady? Really? If you knew me at all, knew anything at all about me, you'd laugh at your petty insecurities, or whatever they are. Take care of your husband, and don't worry about me.

"Take care of your husband," I said to my empty office, and I clenched my fists, glancing at the clouds beyond the windows and into my past. I have issue after conflict after project with no embrace...ever.

In my so-called reset time, I just managed to get worse. Though still nearly a full workday away, making the reservation for a relaxing dinner might help me forget this annoying and unnecessary nightmare of a beginning. "Ms. Ransom here. Reserve a booth for me at six o'clock tonight. Coree is to be my server. She answered my call last time. Where is she?"

"She's not in yet, ma'am. She has a daytime job too."

I waved his words away. "I'll be there at six. A booth, Coree, and six sharp. Make it happen." I disconnected in the middle of his response.

"Two jobs." My eyes came into focus on Michael Kent's empty chair.

Three quick knocks and Chelsie popped in again. "Ms. Ransom. I just got a heads up from my girl in the lobby downstairs. Ruskin Martin is in the building."

"What?" I stood. "What is he doing here?"

"I don't know, but he headed into the elevators."

"All the way from Chicago, and with no warning." I straightened my skirt and blazer. "Get rid of my 11:00."

***

At the end of the workday, the end of the office workday, for I would be doing much more at dinner and home, thank you very much Michael Kent and your evidently overworked associates as well, I stepped onto the elevator with of all people, that same member of my executive staff. We rode silently to the parking garage below. In the time of our ride, a much too long of a ride, the weight of the surprise visit from the Chairman of the Board pressed upon me to the point that when the elevator finally pushed into the bottom, I struggled to stand.

Though only a few steps, the silent walk to the lineup of executive parking spaces, seemed an eternity and at my car, I had had enough. With a hand in front of him, just grazing his midsection, I stopped him. "Alright, Michael, give me concrete feasibility studies, complete with cost comparisons, for two years, four years, and six years going forward. Make it detailed, clear, accurate, and above all, unbiased."

"Certainly, Elizabeth." There was that smile again. "I'll get right on it. Perhaps, when we see the data, decisions will be clearer, and it'll show you're right, and I'm wrong."

I inhaled deeply to keep from lashing out at this insane comment. "Anything's possible," I said. "However, I want evidence in black and white. Make it happen."

"I will, Elizabeth. Thank-"

I slammed the door of my Lexus, and silence washed over me. Hidden behind my tinted windows, I frowned for a moment, and for some reason, thought of Mom. From the eyes of a little girl, I saw her. "Are you proud of me? I think you would have been."

I exited the parking ramp into the bright daylight, behind that same Michael Kent. He turned one way, toward his wife and family, and I turned the other, toward nothing.

7

Coree

"She asked for me, Aubs."

"Who?"

"Ms. Ransom. She asked for me."

"Big whoop."

"She's lit."

"Lit? She might be a lot of things, but not too many people think of her as lit."

I kept a sharp eye on the door and sure enough, at six exactly, she stepped over the threshold. "Hey, Ms. Ransom. I'll take it from here," I said to the host. "Come on. I'll show you where I have you." We wound through tables and across the room. "Right here. You can survey the whole place, and still have privacy to do your work. You want the same wine, the Albarino? Or I can bring you anything you like, anything at all."

"Albarino will be fine."

"Here's your wine, and I brought these little hors d'oeuvres, flatbreads with fava beans, cucumbers, and cheese. Look at 'em. Aren't they adorable?"

"Young lady."

"Coree."

She paused. "Alright. Coree. This is the second time you have been my server and both times, you selected my hors d'oeuvres without consulting me. Is this what you do? I'm sure most people would want to make their own se-"

"No, I haven't done it for anyone else. I just think you're lit."

"Lit?" she repeated, and scrutinized me. "I may be many things, but no one thinks I'm 'lit,' whatever that even means."

"My friend, Aubrey, said the exact same thing. No offense...from her I mean."

Ms. Ransom's eyes narrowed. "You two were talking about me?"

"Nothing bad. I told her you requested me, and I said you're lit."

"Lit," she said and turned back to her wine.

I tucked my hair behind an ear. "Ms. Ransom, thanks for requesting me."

"Run along to your other tables now," she said with a wave of her hand.

"Yes, ma'am."

When I returned, her eyes squinted into her laptop producing a subtle crow's feet effect that fit perfectly into her dignified façade. I waited, glancing back and forth from her eyes to the laptop. After a moment or two, without pulling her eyes from the screen, she said, "What is it?"

"How'd I do?"

Peering up over the screen into the space ahead of her, she said, "How did you do what?"

"Picking out your hors d'oeuvres?"

She turned halfway in my direction. "Fine. Select a salad for me." Her rapt attention returned to the screen. Something on it must have caused her to purse her lips.

"This is our power salad. It reminds me of you."

Ms. Ransom regarded it, eyes scanning, without moving her head.

"What do you think?"

"I'll be sure to let you know," she said.

"My favorite part is how they roasted the cashews, brown and all, and crunchy."

She took another glance at it.

"Savory." The moment that word came out of my mouth, it sounded stupid and played.

Ms. Ransom said, "Select a main dish for me," and she returned to the study of the computer screen.

"Lit," I said.

She rolled her eyes.

8

Elizabeth

All through and after the main course, a quite acceptable scallop dish with what this Coree referred to as "pasta pillows," I analyzed Michael Kent's staffing issue. In the big picture, particularly after the Chairman of the Board's surprise visit this morning, it was of minor importance, but a certain principal presented itself.

"What are you working so hard on tonight, Ms. Ransom?"

I gave my server the icy stare that crumbled all but my thickestskinned executives. To my surprise, she absorbed it with no visible effect at all. "I'm... I'm reviewing a cost analysis from one of my staff on whether we should hire more personnel in his department."

"Must be complicated. You've been at it all night."

"There are many factors invol-"

"Like what?"

I frowned at her, but answered. "Actually, there is only one issue. The rest of it is numbers and co-"

"What's the issue?" she said with a familiarity that disarmed my usual guarded demeanor.

"We feel, that is, the director of this particular department feels, we may lose good staff, because we are demanding such long hours. They do not have enough time for their families," I said, unable to hide my disdain.

"How many staff do you have?"

I glanced back at the chart. "There are fifty-seven in this particular department, however we may see fit to modify that number."

"Wow. How many departments are there?"

"I have seven directors on my executive staff."

Her lips moved, eyes momentarily drifting to one side. When her gaze returned to me, she said, "You mean you have like, like four hundred people under you?"

"Not counting support, you know, custodial, IT, and so on."

"Under you?"

"That's right," I said. "Although..." I paused.

"Although what?"

"Although." I hesitated, but the next words came out on their own accord. "Although, I was offered a promotion to CEO of the entire corporation today."

My server smiled and said, "Congrats." She gave me a fist to bump and I did, feeling awkward. "Are you stoked about it? You seem kind of chill. Shouldn't you be celebrating with someone?"

I shook my head and avoided her eye contact. "You are actually the first person I have told."

"What about your family and friends?"

I shook my head again, looking away.

"What does it mean for you, Ms. Ransom? More money, I suppose."

I shrugged.

"That's not what you're in it for, is it?"

"More responsibility," I said. "Moving to the home office in Chicago."

"That'd be hard I bet, leaving family and friends and all."

I glanced around, and back to my server, who did that thing where she looked right into me, her eyes scanning all around my face. I glanced away and cleared my throat. "Coree? You work two jobs, I understand."

She continued to stare up at me with those wide green eyes.

I rapped my knuckles on the table. "Coree, I'm talking to you."

"Oh. Yes, ma'am."

"I understand you work two jobs."

"How did you know?"

"Not important. Why, Coree? Why do you work two jobs?"

"It's the only way I can make it. Rent is crazy expensive in the city, even for the three of us."

"What is your other job?"

"I model, and a little acting, when I can get it. Gotta pay the rent, you know."

"Do you have a family, Coree?"

She shook her head. "You don't either, do you, Ms. Ransom?"

My mouth fell open. After a last glance at the numbers, I snapped my laptop shut and slid it into its case. "The bill, Coree."

She returned, bill in one hand, drink in the other. "What is this?"

"Ms. Ransom, a gentleman sitting at the bar asked me to bring it to you."

I raised my eyebrows.

"Do you see the man there in the gray suit, just there, smiling this way?"

I grimaced. "So, you've come to poke at the caged bear."

"May I join you, Elizabeth?"

I motioned across the booth.

"What's new, my dear?"

"I'm not your dear."

"You'll always be my dear."

"How many women have you used that line on, or is it just me...and Crystal?"

"Coming from anyone else, I'd be offended. However, from you, Elizabeth, well, you're just being you."

"Is that a criticism or a compliment?"

"Just words, but here's a compliment. You are still as beautiful as ever, more so."

"I am far less susceptible to flattery than I used to be, George, perhaps even immune at this point in my life." I looked away in escape, taking notice of my server watching from a distance.

"A shame. I wanted to flatter you."

"So, where is your wife tonight, George?"

"Where is your husband, Elizabeth?"

I jabbed a finger across the table at him. "You know damn well how that story played out and thank you very much for your part in it. Are we done here?"

"Same temper after all these years. It's been a long time. Can't we bury the hatchet?"

I bit my teeth and took a breath. "The hatchet has been buried, in me, for all this time. You didn't answer where Crystal is."

"Let's not talk about her. Let's talk about us."

"Is there an 'us' anymore? No, there is not."

"There could be."

"You must have lost your mind, George. You must have absolutely lost your mind. After all these years, you think you can talk to me that way, just pick up where..." I zipped up my laptop case with a violent jerk. "I got burned so bad last time. I'm still scalded. Everything just worked out wonderfully for you, didn't it?"

"Not exactly wonderfully."

"You put your life back together. My universe blew apart. I never recovered, and I never will. Evidently, you don't remember how it went down for me because you show up out of nowhere like a specter rising from the past, pointing an accusing finger."

"That's not at all my intention."

"Well, that's how it feels to have you here. George, don't open the wound again. Never mind that point. Just seeing you opens it...wide open." I felt along the hem of the tablecloth between my fingers and thumb, fighting the temptation to yank it and everything on it right off the table.

"I still have feelings for you."

My eyes widened. "You must be drinking. You have no respect for me after what happened. And by the way, I'm an executive now."

"As I recall, you were an executive then."

"A minor peon. I'm the senior vice president of Landford-Smithson, and please lower your voice to me if you don't mind."

"I still find you charming."

"Stop it."

"I'm angering you."

"What the hell do you expect?" I gathered up my purse and bag. "I'm going to be on my way now, and I did not enjoy catching up on old times

"Are you running from me or from yourself, Elizabeth?"

I hesitated. "Okay then, I'll be honest. I'm running from myself, and my past. You're just the reminder of it."

Now my little teenage sister's words came to me from the past, words that have haunted me for decades. "Don't do this, Libby. Don't do it. You'll always regret it."

"We had some good times."

I bit my lower lip and then made my admission back to her, relaying it to George. "The good times, as you call them turned into hell for me, living hell, George, and the hell I'm living in never ends." I focused back into his green eyes, a little grayer from the years. "Don't you ever consider what happened to me, the cross I've had to bear, what I carry with me every single day of my life? You act so cavalier about it, like, I guess we should just pick up here where we left off."

A family passed our booth, laughing together. I said, "Give my regards to Crystal and the kids."

"The kids are grown now, so..."

"So? There's no 'so.'" I slammed the flat of my hand down on the table, causing the silver to leap up and land with a clatter. We both glanced around at the faces turned our way.

"You loved me, Elizabeth."

"Goodbye, George."

"Oh, alright, I can take a hint."

"You can take a hint? I've given you at least five."

"I hoped you didn't mean it. Can I call you sometime, text you?"

"Shut up." I said, glancing around. "Alright, here are the straight facts. I loved you, and you know it, but honestly, right now I'm starting to hate you. You're trivializing my pain. You always did."

"We can't live bottled up in the past, Elizabeth. We have to push onward. Life is what you make it."

"I remember that old saw you used to say all the time. Now, you said you could take a hint." I noticed Coree across the room, still watching intently, not even attempting to conceal it, and I waved her over. "Thank you for the drink and for stopping over to reminisce. Goodbye, George."

With an over-sized sigh, he slid out of the booth and disappeared across the room. I took up my purse and laptop case again. "Coree, follow me to the door."

"Sure. What's up?"

I put a hand on her shoulder. "I need a buffer. I need you to get me out of here without any more contact from that man. Goodnight, Coree."

"Goodnight, Ms. Ransom."

9

Coree

"Rolling napkins! I live for this when I want to go home." I collapsed across from Aubrey in a booth.

"Good tip from her again?"

"Same."

"Mommy 2.0 throwing the green on little Coree."

I shrugged. "Not partying this time."

"Yeah, Sammi's back," Aubrey said. "With good stories, I hope."

"We talked," I said. "We talked, and she looked at me."

"Who?"

"Ms. Ransom. We talked. She asked me questions about myself."

"I don't even know what to say."

"She looked right at me, Aubrey." I peeked around our growing hill of napkins. "And she told me about her work."

"How dope is that?"

"Sarcasm?"

"More like who cares."

"Well, check this. She's got, like four, five hundred employees under her."

"That's definitely legit."

"How is that even possible? And she's being promoted to CEO of the whole corporation. She's like the real deal."

When the napkin rolls between us became a mountain, we distributed them onto the tables. One of the last settings I did was for Ms. Ransom's booth.

"Why are you just standing there, Sweet Pea? Get done so we can hit the road."

"Just zoned out. Ms. Ransom and that man, that George, sure got into it, didn't they? I wonder what it was about?"

"It must have been huge because she unloaded on him," said Aubrey.

"You know. She looks a lot like Mom, like a lot, her eyes, mannerisms, like how she moves her hands and how she moves her head, but she's different, no doubt about it.

"Yeah, your mom was so sweet, all the time. Ms. Ransom's like her flip-side," Aubrey said, with a nod to her booth. "Imagine locking horns with her."

***

"Hey Sammi."

"Hey girls. How's the grind?"

"The grind blows," said Aubrey, plopping down on our old couch. "However, Coree met a guy."

"Like that's a surprise."

"Right?" said Aubrey.

"What's he like?" Sammi said to me.

Before I could answer, Aubrey said, "You've never seen a guy like this. He is," she brought her hands against her chest, "high key, perfect."

"It's not gonna go anywhere," I cut in, sitting cross-legged on the coffee table.

"Oh, okay," Aubrey said. "Two points on that, little friend."

"And I don't want to hear either."

"Number one is, you're a hottie and you know it, Little Miss Model, and num-"

"Not interested," I said with a hand up.

"Number two," she said over my hand. It's, in your words, 'not gonna go anywhere,' because, in my words, you suck at relationships."

"Do I have a BFF or a psychiatrist?" I turned back to Sammi, but Aubrey persisted.

"Somewhere in that boy's future is a broken heart. Anyone want bets?"

"We haven't even gone out yet."

"I've seen this movie before," she said.

I rolled my eyes and turned again to Sammi who watched us go back and forth at each other. "What about your trip? What about Joey, the baseball player?"

"You know it's true," said Aubrey as we migrated into the kitchen.

"Shut up, Aub-"

"Stop it, you two," Sammi said, with a whack on the backs of each of our heads. "Both of you stop it." We gathered around our little table. After eyeing us both, she said, "In the first place, they were playing a weekend series in Toledo, not exactly party town. Still, I went there for Joey and not the nightlife."

"And how did Joey work out?" I asked. I screwed the top off a bottle, and sent it clanking across the old steel table.

"Joey worked out, but baseball? Whack. Three games, warmups before, stuff afterward. I spent a lot of the weekend by myself."

"Is he good?" Aubrey asked. "Did he play a lot?" She flicked my bottle cap in the direction of the waste basket.

Sammi watched the cap roll. "I don't know. To tell you the truth, I found the whole thing tedious."

"You got some sun," I said.

"Plenty of that and tan lines," she said, pulling up her sleeve. "Too much?"

"Oh, whatever," I said. "You fishing for compliments? You know your skin is perfect." I brushed the pads of my fingers on her forearm. "I can hardly tell the difference. You're always like copper, now maybe bronze. Whatever. It's perfect."

"Joey thinks so too."

"Of course. So?" I leaned in.

"So," she said, scrunching up her nose, "the trash can stinks."

"You mean the one spilling out onto the floor? I don't smell it," said Aubrey.

"Yeah, that one, near where the bottle cap landed." Sammi gave us a critical eye."We danced a bit, had a good time in the hotel."

"How good?" we said together.

"Pretty good. Actually, really good. Actually, really, really good."

"Way to make up for your slacker roommates," Aubrey said.

"Except..."

"What?"

"It got kind of carried away." Sammi's eyes darted to the side.

"What's the frown for?" I said. "Getting carried away's what it's all about."

"That sounds like our Coree," Sammi said to Aubrey. "Yeah well, I should have been more careful. You know?"

"Oh, that kind of carried away." Aubrey said.

"One time. You probably got lucky."

"Uh...more than one time."

"One weekend. I'm sure it'll be alright. One weekend. You got lucky."

"See, that's your problem, my friends," said Aubrey. She rose and gave the ancient fridge a firm kick. The rattle, sounding like an old pickup truck, calmed down.

"Heard it before, Aubs. Your team definitely has that advantage, but we like our side of the tracks."

"Just saying. We never have this prob-"

"Hey, Grayson texted me. 'How about a drink or lunch? What's your schedule like?'" I jumped up and danced around our little kitchen. "Oh, yes, oh, yes. Lunch or a drink? No expectations on the first round." I stopped. "Except, maybe I want expectations. But," I slid back into my spot, a knee under my chin. "What about Joey? When you gonna see him again?"

Sammi considered the floor before answering. "Did you guys do any cleaning at all? You could plant crops in here. It's all gritty under my feet." She turned her frown on us. "How can you have a relationship with a ball player? They're on the road all the time, and there's no way in hell I'm sitting in a damn ballpark, game after game, day after day."

"Does he want one, a relationship?"

"He talks like it, and well, the passion as I said, kind of got out of hand. He said stuff to me that..."

Yeah?" I said, trying to lead her along.

"Well, I wasn't expecting, kind of got me worked up."

"Guys do that," I said, "when they want something."

"He meant it." Sammi laced her fingers together in front of her. "I hope he meant it."

"You may be the brain of the bunch," said Aubrey, "but you lack realworld experience."

"Don't tell me that," Sammi said. Her dark eyes widened.

"You love him, don't you?" I said, patting her arm.

She grinned.

"Yeah, you do," I said. "What a silly grin."

"Anyway, they're on the road all the time or half the time."

"When do you see him again? I said.

"Couple weeks, probs."

"It seems all glamorous until you live it, I guess," I said. "Anyway, welcome back to the fam. We're here for you all week and all month. Can't afford to go anywhere else."

"And about that, Sammi, Aubrey said. "Can you make us dinner?"

Sammi crossed her arms. "Okay. That's another thing."

"Here we go," I said.

"I cleaned my food processer when I got home, dried...stuff on it. Dried."

"She did it," said Aubrey, throwing me right under the bus.

"My pans are dirty in the sink."

"I didn't do all of it," I said.

"I don't care who did it. Take responsibility, you two. If you see a mess, clean it up. The counter, my spatulas and spoons. It's expensive stuff, and you guys just left it out dirty."

"We're sorry, Mom," I said.

"If we get cleaning, will you make us dinner?" said Aubrey.

"Are you serious?" Sammi said. "Are you even serious right now?"

"You're the best," I said. "You're better than any of the chefs at Billie Jean's."

"Yeah, you should work there with us," said Aubrey.

She waved it away. "Not my thing. I mean, not for a living."

"Just for us, then." said Aubrey. "We'll clean. You cook."

"You two," she said, shaking her head at us.

"Yay."

10
Elizabeth

"Michael, I want to bring you into the loop on a situation I have been keeping under wraps and you are to, at least for now, do the same."

"What's that?" he said as he slid his tablet into its sleeve.

"Jack Newkirk announced his retirement."

"No kidding. That's big."

I gave one subtle nod.

"That's really big for you. Are you our next CEO? You must be."

I nodded again.

"Headed for the Windy City," he said, singsong.

I pictured Coree, this server at the restaurant, whom I had told first, before even my second in command. Tapping a pen on the desk, I said. "We will compromise at three new staff in your department."

"Fantastic, Elizabeth." Michael's wide smile brightened my office like an unwelcome trespasser.

"And you will not blab this all over the company. I can't afford hiring like this in every department."

"I'll do my best. I have to tell my people who is responsible for this, though. They'll love you."

"I do not want their love."

With tilted head, Michael said, "Elizabeth, everyone needs to be loved."

I turned, willing this meaningless parlay to go away, but he continued.

"I know you don't have a family, and I know you are uncomfortable talking about it, but like I said, under your tough façade is a kind heart."

I rose and walked to my window to escape his words. Michael and this server, Coree, unknowingly conspired to make me hire more people. With my back to him, I said, "Michael, once again, don't you have work to do?"

"Always. I'll be off then, but Elizabeth?" He paused and let the silence work the room until I had no choice, but to turn. He met my scowl with the words, "You can be as tough acting as you want, but..."

With my silence, I tried to communicate the message, "Get this over with," but I inexplicably noticed his blue eyes. Why? They have been blue as long as I have known him, but I noticed them.

"I know the real you, and I want to thank you again." He turned and left without being rewarded whatever response he might have hoped for.

My jaw tightened, and I retreated to the refuge of my desk and my work. You don't know the real me, Michael, and if you did, perhaps you would be a little less optimistic about me. I only wish I could be as optimistic as you.

I took a deep breath and slowly exhaled. Damn his eyes. Damn me for momentarily noticing something, whatever it was. Damn his wife, and damn me again for inexplicably thinking of her just now.

***

"Bring me what you think."

"Straight up. That'll be fun," Coree said. "Where do you work, Ms. Ransom?"

"Landford-Smithson Data. And why do you..." She hustled off to her tables before I had a chance to finish. I observed her scurrying around the restaurant and how patrons responded to her charm. When one diner spoke to her discourteously however, I experienced a peculiar urge to go over and set him straight.

Upon her return, she took up exactly where we left off. "Because what if you didn't come in, how would I ever see you again?" My eyebrows furrowed, but off she ran. The next time, she stopped only long enough to lay a folded scrap of pink paper on the edge of my table. I could not pull my eyes away from this curiosity, trespassing in my space.

"It's my number." The words came from the direction behind me. Appearing beside me now, she smiled at my frown, tucked her hair behind an ear, and said, "If you're sick and need-" She hesitated, a curious look at me and the pink scrap. "It's not contagious." A wave in the distance caught her attention. She looked at them and back to me. Before running off, she said, "Nothing weird, Ms. Ransom."

When she returned, she took up again. "Like if you were sick and need your dinner delivered or something, you can call me." Again, she dashed off before I could respond.

When she passed again, I said, "There is DoorDash or-"

"But now you have me." She trotted off yet again before I could respond, and her idiotic statement hung over my booth, debilitating my mental processes.

This time when she returned, I said, "Can you just stop one minute, Coree?" She finally allowed my words a stationary target, so I said, "And just why do I, as you say, 'have you?' What does that statement even mean?"

She shrugged. "It means what it means. Where do you live, Ms. Ransom, I mean roughly?"

"Somerset."

"Of course."

"Why, 'of course?'"

"You seem like you can afford it." She pushed the invading scrap closer to me with the back of her pink nails. "Text me, so I have your number too."

I stared at her like she spoke another language.

"Do it," she said.

"Why should I?"

"Because we're going to be friends," she said, and left me with my mouth open.

Working the table next to mine, she glanced at her phone and to me, eyebrows up, innocent, but insisting until Ms. Elizabeth Ransom, Senior Vice President of Landford-Smithson Data, for some inexplicable reason, did what she was told.

***

Coree became a part of my Billie Jean's routine, but one night, it took another turn, an unexpected slap in the face when she appeared before my booth.

"Why, Ms. Ransom?" Her question had plenty of weight to it, but she threw on another "Why?" to burden me more, and she flustered me with those round, green eyes.

I searched for words, finally, muttering, "I know. I forgot to request you." They were supposed to be the first five words of a longer explanation, however, to Coree, they appeared to be the only ones of importance because as I spoke, her lips mouthed, "You forgot about me?"

I was about to point out that her reaction seemed melodramatic when a voice distracted both of us. "Coree, one of your tables needs you."

I turned. "Excuse me, young man. Coree is helping me right now."

"Oh, my mistake. I didn't know she had this table."

"It is no matter whose table it is."

"I'm sorry, ma'am."

"You spoke to Coree. The apology, therefore, goes to her."

His eyes darted from Coree, looking like she had just witnessed a mugging, to mine, icy and unyielding. He chose his words wisely, saying, "Of course. Sorry, Coree. Carry on," before beating a hasty retreat into the obscurity of the crowded room.

I turned back to Coree and cleared my throat. "Do you work again tomorrow night?"

"Yes, ma'am." She stood on one foot, the other curled around her ankle.

"Before you go to whoever he says is so needing of your attention, go put in my reservation in your section for the usual time."

"Yes, ma'am."

When she turned to leave, I stopped her. "Coree, I'm sorry if I hurt you." I avoided her eyes as long as I could, but when I finally looked at them, they drew more from me. "And let me know if you have any problems from your manager there."

She gave one quick nod.

11

Coree

"Somehow, I had you figured to be the fashionably late type of guy." I plopped down at the round, sidewalk table, and tucked an ankle under my thigh.

"My parents say that about me."

Already talking about his parents. "What do they do?" I said. His oldschool, cardigan sweater, wine-colored and comfortably aged, would have worked so well for few others.

"Oh, they kick around in the art world."

"Kick around," I repeated. The comforting aroma of coffee wafting from the inside competed with the exhaust of passing traffic.

"They buy and sell art."

"And you?"

"I kick around in it too."

"Buy and sell?"

"I have a little gallery uptown."

I glanced around for a server.

"Is that the end of the interrogation?"

"Sounds interesting," I said as I waved one over.

"Except...you don't approve."

I shrugged and picked at the threads in my jeans.

He watched me and said, "Is it the art, the money? What is it?"

I noticed the name of the café in white letters over red bricks, and read it. "Go With the Flow."

"This worked out great." Grayson looked off to the buildings across the street. "You seemed so positive and fun. Now, two minutes in, I've already managed to shut you right down. She'll have a cappuccino."

"You always order for your dates?"

"You must have it. I want you to try it. I love them here."

"And yet you're drinking black coffee.

"Oh, I needed it just now, but the cappuccino here, it must be experienced."

I people-watched, and Grayson watched me until he broke the silence. "My grandfather made his fortune in banking."

"Oh?"

He nodded at me. "It's the money."

The exhaust of a passing bus temporarily won out over the aroma of coffee.

"Yes, that's it. I'm sure of it. Once in a while, I meet someone who is...like you," he paused, gazing into me until he seemed to find the right words, "who finds it off-putting."

I noted a woman near us, older, confident in her pencil skirt and blazer, and fairly open about eyeing my lunch date. "What about Tiffany? Where does she fit in?"

"Tiff-?"

"Your date at the club."

"Her name isn't-"

I shrugged. "She's a Tiffany."

He smiled. "Oh, well, she's diff-"

"How so?"

"She comes from money herself," Grayson said, "and I suppose coming from money, it isn't an-"

The metal legs of my chair screeched on the sidewalk when I rose, louder than I had intended and when people turned, I hesitated.

Grayson didn't move other than raising his eyebrows.

"You seem pretty chill," I observed. "Like over-the-top chill, like if someone ran through the, I looked up at the signboard again, The Go With the Flow Café and knocked you over, you'd just pick up your chair, brush yourself off, and finish your coffee."

"You have me down a lot quicker than I had you." Taking a little tug at his ear, he gestured to my chair and said, "Oh, sit and enjoy your coffee. We can at least have a little time together. You've turned out to be intriguing and, I know I am interesting, not to be brash, especially for a spoiled rich kid." He worked me with those eyes and dimples and I relented, just as my cappuccino arrived. "There you go. You'll love it, and if you don't, we'll find something you do love. At any rate, you can enjoy a little of the fruits of my grandfather's labors without becoming a fullblown, old money Republican."

I smiled.

"You make a tee shirt and jeans look good, Coree." We listened to the sounds of people for a while until he began the conversation again. "Do you enjoy art?"

"Sure."

"Next time we meet, let's go to a gallery."

"The next time?" I said.

"You are a little spitfire, aren't you? Your size and smile are deceiving. Yes, the next time. I obviously have to prove myself."

"If I said no," I paused to scrunch my nose at the woman ogling him again, "it wouldn't be the end of the world for you."

"I'd be dis-"

"A little, not much."

"Okay, Coree. Truth time. What's going on? The girl at the restaurant, and the one I asked out at the club...you're a lot deeper. I'm seeing it, and I'm definitely feeling it." He grimaced. "You want to be straight with me? I can take it. Why the attitude?"

I surveyed the other couples in the coffee shop, what they had in common, business people, friends, a family. A middle-aged woman and a girl my age caught my eye. I wondered about them, friends, mother and daughter? They made me think about Ms. Ransom, like if she and I went out for coffee. I turned to Grayson, who waited patiently. "I have to be on my way. I'm between jobs, my two jobs I need to pay the bills. Text me and we'll figure out the museum visit." He sat back running a fingertip across an eyebrow. "Tell you what," I said. "I'll try not to be such a bitch." The line broke him out of his reserve, producing more of a genuine smile.

Outside the coffee shop, he gave me a peck on my hand.

I touched the spot with my forefinger. "You think that shit works on me?"

"I've only got so many moves, you know."

"Thanks for the coffee." I gave his hand a squeeze, turned, and headed through the crowded sidewalk, and once I did, I smiled. Getting to know him and his art world, at worst case, might be interesting.

12

Elizabeth

"Mr. Parks," I said across my conference table. "Our companies have been doing business together for several years now. The parts your company makes are difficult and would undoubtedly cost us more if we had to change. I appreciate you not taking advantage of us."

He nodded and said, "Landon."

"Alright, then, 'Landon,'" I said as we closed our folders.

"Here I am, in town again doing business with your company. I have to eat somewhere, and I know you go to that one place all the time. It's just..."

"What is it?"

"You don't make things easy." His arms stretched to the sides in frustration. "I'm not good at this anymore."

I let him struggle.

"Elizabeth, it's a challenge, asking out a woman of your, shall we say, stature. No part of you is a damsel in distress."

"Do you find a 'damsel in distress' attractive, Landon?" The words alone brought a strong distaste to my mouth.

"Not necessarily, but I suppose a man wants to bring something to the table, strength, stability. You have all of that and so much more."

"I'll try to act more unsure of myself."

"Too late. Way too late, Elizabeth." He laughed and said, "A person has to fight through a receptionist and two secretaries just for an audience with you. And by the way, did you pick those two secretaries for their ability to intimidate, particularly that outer one?"

I grinned. "Give you a hard time?"

"You're well-protected, that vibe came through loud and clear. Seriously, what can a man even bring to the table?"

I considered it. "Looks, of course. Whatever you think of me, I'm still as shallow as the next person on that front."

"I'll take that as a compliment. I, of course, am shallow on that front too." He smiled at his witticism. "You are stunning, of course, and I don't know how you do it after all these years of deadlines, budgets, and kicking asses."

"I'm also organized, professional, and hard-working."

"Those are good too. What about passion?"

Ignoring his question, I said, "I'll make reservations. The place is called Billie Jean's, and I'll meet you there at six sharp."

"Meet me there? We're not riding together?"

"Thanks, but no thanks. Are we a couple of teenagers?"

"Let's leave from here, and I'll bring you back to your car afterwards. On the other hand, I have a charming hotel suite-"

Had I actually heard correctly?

"Or your place?"

My eyes widened. "That is not a possibility at all, in this universe."

"Of course. I should have seen that. The great and terrible Ms. Elizabeth Ransom does not let anyone in her home, her fortress of solitude?"

"I certainly do not."

"In that case, it will have to be my hotel suite."

In my office, a weeknight, and this guy is trying to get the Senior Vice-President of Landford-Smithson in the sack, making overtures. What balls. And what is more unbelievable, I'm flattered. So, Michael was right. There is still something inside me that wants kindling. Landon is working the fact that I've been driving myself so hard in the years since my second divorce. He thinks he's found the weakness he needs in a woman. What about me? After all these years, certainly, something is missing. That's nothing new. "I have work to do. I will meet you downstairs at five-thirty."

"I like it when you take charge."

He's throwing it all against the wall to see what sticks. I shook my head and said, "It's just straight talk. Out with you, Landon."

13

Coree

"Who you texting?"

"No one."

"Sus to that. Don't tell me, 'no one.' When you say no one, I know it's Jade."

"Just watch the road."

"I am watching the road. You see me?" The white delivery van ahead of me came to a stop, evidently deciding to double park. I growled and took it out on Aubrey. "I'm watching the road, and trying to get around this jerk. You need to stay away from Jade."

"We're just talking, Salty."

"Well, don't. We know what talking leads to."

"Don't worry about it."

"She treated you horrible, Aubrey. Don't open yourself up to it again."

"New subject. It went alright with Grayson?"

"It went fine."

"You were wrong about him?"

"Actually, I nailed it. He's a trust-fund baby, second generation too."

"And?"

"And he's kind of interesting."

"And kind of hot."

"So, I'm giving him a chance, but that's no reason for you to go all lonely and run back to Jade."

Aubrey deflected. "Is your sugar momma coming in tonight?"

I finally had an opening and swung back into traffic, laying a horn on the van as I did.

"You know who I texted, so tell me what's up your ass?"

I fought my way across two more lanes. "Think all these people are heading to Billie Jean's?"

"Undoubtedly and they're all going to be seated in my section, and not only that, they won't tip for shit. Now cut the crap. You're sitting on a second date with the hottest guy on the planet, who you're giving 'a chance,' she said with air quotes "and you're all sulky. On the other hand, we work at one of the best restaurants in the city, and we have to park in this ratchety-ass back alley. It doesn't inspire much optimism about life, does it?"

I climbed out and left her babbling, but when we approached the back door, Aubrey caught up, and pushed me up against the brick building.

"What're you doing, girl?"

"Why you all edged? Spill the tea."

"Get off me."

"Spill it, bro."

"Okay, okay, she has a reservation for two. Now, let me down, biatch."

"What? Who?"

"Ms. Ransom."

"Ms. Ransom? Who even cares?"

"Let me down."

"Come on." Aubrey left me standing there. "What's wrong with you, anyway, Coree?"

My last view on the outside was the smelly dumpster, overstuffed and top hanging open like a whale eating a landfill, complete with the hum of circling flies.

14

Elizabeth

I hid a smile, seeing Coree work over my date with a critical eye.

"We'll have the Pinot Blanc," he said to Coree, who shot a darting glance in my direction. "Hmm, for hors d'oeuvres, the grilled oysters."

"Are you sure, sir?" said Coree, eyeing me. "We also have-"

"Yes, I'm sure. I think I know what I want."

I flinched, but let it slide. Coree is a big girl, at least metaphorically speaking. "Do you see your children often, Landon?"

"When possible. My two boys are as busy as I am."

"Both married?"

"Yes, and doing well, both in pharmaceuticals. I'm quite proud of them." Coree checked in on us and Landon said, "Just leave us until the main dish comes." He waved her away dismissively, as I, myself probably have done many times. Watching it done, however, and done to Coree made me contemplate my behaviors.

"Grandchildren. Let me remember. Is it two boys also?"

"So far."

"Pity they never met their grandmother."

He ran his fingers along the placemat. "Elizabeth, is that something you regret not experiencing, children and grandchildren?"

"We all have to play the cards we are dealt." I glanced across the room at Coree, watching, always watching. "I've had two tries, and neither worked. It must not be fated for me."

"Don't be so quick to give up."

"I'm turning fifty in a few weeks. You consider that hasty?"

"If you think you have become old and-"

"Landon, you're throwing all your cards out on the table, the hotel, the compliments, and now we are talking about my marriage situation."

"It's not a bad strategy. I can pull back and leave only the hotel room on the table." Our eyes fixed in a silent standoff, the mere existence of which meant the chief executive had insanely, not completely, ruled out the possibility.

I broke the silence. "How is it, Landon, being a widower out on the prowl?"

"I'll let you know tomorrow morning."

Who knows? It all might have been different going forward, but for the approach of the main course, that element that makes or breaks the meal. The wine, the flirting, confident, lovely gentleman, the lonely, overworked lady, it all ran into their fate in the form of one innocent statement. "Your porterhouse will be up in five minutes."

Despite her pausing only long enough to toss out those few words, my dinner date snapped at her. "I told you not to interrupt us until our main dish arrived."

Coree retreated.

"Elizabeth, I know I live a distance away, but I would like to see you more than on these business trips." Landon continued along those lines for some time, completely oblivious to my tightened jaw and narrowing eyes. "We could meet some-"

"I did not like how you addressed our server."

"How I what?" His blathering dialogue petered out in confusion.

"I didn't like how you spoke to her." I nodded into some vague direction in the restaurant.

"Who?"

"The server. I didn't like it."

"I don't know what you're talking about, Elizabeth, but," he leaned forward. "I'm trying to talk about us here, the two of us."

I bit my bottom lip.

During and after dinner, we kicked a few work topics around, or should I say, Landon did? I ate and half listened, and noted Coree in the distance. At a pause, I abruptly stopped him. "I'm taking a Lyft home."

"What are you talking about? I hoped you could come back to my hotel for a nightcap."

"No. I've decided."

He blinked. "And when the great Elizabeth Ransom has decided, it's the end of the story, isn't it?" Coree appeared with the check. "You always show up at the worst times, don't you?"

I erupted. "Are you out of your mind?" I sensed Coree recoiling in my peripheral vision, but did not release Landon from my glare. "Don't you ever talk to her like that. Ever."

"What's your problem, Elizabeth?"

"I am dissatisfied with your tone...your attitude." I secretly agreed with him though, wondering exactly what my problem actually was.

"Oh, you are, are you?"

"Two checks, Coree," I said, still not releasing Landon from my glare.

"I'll take mine here, and he will pick his up at the front desk. Thank you for the evening, Landon. I'm going to stay and catch up on my work as is my routine." Coree withdrew, and I dug for my tablet.

"This is crazy. All because of some server. Who even cares?" I completely ignored him and logged on. Landon finally turned away, but fired off a parting shot. "This explains the two failed marriages." I almost returned fire, but maturity brings with it some wisdom, and with the war over, any more skirmishes would simply be wasted casualties on either side. I had work to do.

Landon sulked away, paid at the desk, with, I'm sure, more frowns at the impossible, Ms. Elizabeth Ransom. Within minutes, I pushed him out of my mind and clicked away at my keyboard. In fact, I became so productive that when Coree appeared out of nowhere and asked, "Will there be anything else tonight, ma'am?" I looked up to a mostly uninhabited room.

"Oh...Oh, I got caught up in my work. Yes, I will need a Lyft. My ride is gone. Can you take care of that?"

"Certainly." In a moment, Coree returned. "Ms. Ransom, my section is empty, and my friend, Aubrey still has two tables going. Can I drive you home?"

I frowned. "What a preposterous idea."

"Why?"

I hesitated.

"I have plenty of time to take you home and come back. You ready to go?"

"I-"

She trailed off through the restaurant calling back, "Meet you out front then. I have a blue Chevy. I'll pull up to the front like the valets."

15

Coree

"Looks like your date didn't work out."

"It's alright. My better judgement became clouded."

"Not disappointed?"

"Not in the least. Life goes on. I am not in the market for a relationship anyway."

"As soon as he ordered those oysters, I'm like, 'This won't last long.'"

"I hate oysters."

"Aware. Were you tight?"

She sighed and said, "Just a business associate."

"His loss."

"I don't know whose loss it would be. I suppose you'd have to send a woman up to his hotel room, like a control group in an experiment, and we could compare notes in the morning."

"Is that a joke?"

"I meant it to be. However, it could have some scientific merit in an idiotic sort of way."

"Is that what he wanted, you to go up to his room?"

She waved my question away.

"He was cute."

"He's too old to be cute."

"Whatever you would call it."

She waved that point away too.

"You date a lot?"

Ms. Ransom peered over the crack stretching across the length of my windshield. The silence in my car would have been awkward if it weren't for the rattle somewhere in the dashboard and the other one somewhere in one of the back doors. She finally said, "Not too often. I've been down that road already...twice."

"Marriages?"

She nodded without turning my way.

"Kids?"

Ms. Ransom ignored that question and said, "Perhaps, I'm meant to be alone."

"Don't say that. It's sad. Who'll take care of you when you're old?"

I noticed her flinch and glance over my way. "It's not the life I planned for sure, but-"

"You planned your life?"

With an ugly, sarcastic melody to her answer, Ms. Ransom said, "No, I did not plan my life...exactly, per se." She raised an index finger. "I'll tell you this, if I had been given the opportunity to plan it, I sure as hell would have done a better job."

"It looks like you're doing pretty well."

"I suppose it does have that outward appearance."

I tried another tack. "Anyway, I think we all need someone to tuck us in once in a while."

"I don't know if I agree with that or not," Ms. Ransom said. "Probably not."

"Doesn't matter if you agree with it. It's true."

Ms. Ransom glanced my way again as if viewing some novelty act.

"I think that's a pretty respectable metaphor. I'm proud of it." I smiled out at the city lights.

"At this point in my life, I'm awfully picky about this tucking-in business." Her stony facade gave away nothing.

"That's the second time I've seen you on a rampage. You're scary when you're pissed, no offense, cause it's kind of impressive."

"I will not tolerate rudeness."

"Actually, he was rude to me. Guests are like that sometimes." I fingered my rings at the top of my steering wheel. "I can handle it. I'm a big girl, metaphorically speaking."

"I had the power to stop it, and I did."

"I'm just glad you're flexing it on my side. My friend, Aubrey says I have relationship issues, but I've seen you shred men twice now, pulverize them."

She waved my comment away again and said, "I appreciate the ride, Coree."

"Sure. I liked hanging out with you." We crossed a four-way stop, and I found myself and my little Chevy out of place, rattling along among fortress-like homes, guarded by stately, mature oaks.

"Hang out with me," she said to herself. "Why would you," she paused and raised a hand, "or anyone, for that matter want to, as you say, hang out with me?"

"You're lit, Ms. Ransom."

She looked out the side window. "Lit, I'm sure I am not."

"Lit comes in a lot of different forms."

Using two hands for emphasis this time, she said, with force, "I turn fifty soon. Turning fifty is not, as you say, 'lit.'"

I glimpsed over at her hands. They looked fifty, but a good fifty, a cared-for fifty, perfectly manicured nails, in a natural tone, confidence without swagger. "A person turning fifty can be lit."

"And can a person, however old you are-,"

"Twenty-three, almost twenty-four."

"Can a person twenty-three, almost twenty-four even think a person forty-nine, almost fifty is lit?"

"Or interesting, whatever. Sure. Now that I know you better, I think the word is legit. You are definitely, undoubtedly legit. Legit AF."

"Whatever on earth you are talking about, thank you, I'm sure," she said, with another wave of her arm.

Swinging into the driveway, my headlights flashed across symmetrical rows of flowers, strictly organized according to height and color, troops guarding the palace. An orange form's bright yellow eyes reflected back. "I see your cat on the front porch."

"I don't have a...oh, damn."

"What's up?"

"My car is still at the office. I forgot about it. I told that Landon man we should take separate vehicles. He had me considering his hotel." Ms. Ransom covered her mouth.

I laughed. "I didn't think you were a nun."

"I should have stood my ground. Damn him. He's the bad date that just keeps on giving. I'll have to take a Lyft in the morning. Damn him and damn me for not anticipating it."

"I've got my daytime free tomorrow. I'll give you a ride. What time?"

Ms. Ransom turned to me with a frown.

"What time?"

"I leave...I usually leave at exactly, um, at seven-thirty."

"I'll pull in five or ten minutes before that. Are you always punctual?"

"Always."

"Snap. Me too. You can count on me, Ms. Ransom." She climbed out, and I yelled, "This is sort of a metaphorical tuck in."

Without turning, she raised a hand in acknowledgement.

I waited for her to close the door before backing out.

***

"What's the point of that?" Aubrey said when she climbed in. "She's what, fifty?"

"What's the diff?"

"You're going to latch onto her, aren't you?"

"Already did," I mumbled out the corner of my mouth, but to Aubrey, I said, "I just go where the story takes me." I didn't mention the morning pick up to my friend.

"You so need a shrink."

"Because I'm nice? You're texting again."

"Jade's coming over."

"Great," I moaned. "Absolutely great."

"Don't be coming into my room all crybaby in the middle of the night, little one."

"Oh no. She's spending the night?"

"We'll see."

"We'll see? We'll see? I know what that means. Everyone knows what that means. It means... don't keep Sammi and me up."

"Put on headphones."

"And it means we'll have to pick up the pieces when she lays waste to you again."

"Not this time. She's changed."

"Receipts needed."

"Telling you."

"You need therapy, Aubrey. I'm not the one. My being nice to a woman vs. you running back to a girl who destroyed you, physically and emotionally, ripped your heart out and threw it away, not to mention-"

"I don't need a lecture, Coree."

"Then don't give me one." I frowned out at the empty road, fingering my rings at the top of the wheel. "All those butt wads that were in front of us on the way to work are home in bed already."

"After giving us shitty tips."

"Except for my sugar mama."

Aubrey laughed with me and slapped me on the leg.

"Save it for Jade, biatch."

***

Sammi's black and white tuxedo cat, aptly named "Old TV" stretched out happily on the bed between us while we stared at whatever was on the TV screen. I said, "I wish she would be more patient, and particular, and not go back to Jade. We both know how it's going to play out."

"All three of us know how it's going to play out, Aubrey too. You know, it wouldn't hurt for you guys to clean out his litter box when I'm gone."

"Jade knows more than any of us. She'll get what she wants and crush her again. Whatever. Aubrey's gotta learn."

"Like the rest of us," Sammi said.

"Yeah? How's it going with your baseball player?"

"FML. They're on the road another week. Who knows what they're doing, or who they're doing it with? Like I said, how can you have a relationship? Did you hear what I said about the litter box?"

"What's he like?" Both of us petted Old TV, who stretched his front legs and back legs in opposite directions to become the impossibly long cat.

"He's so cute-"

"Duh. He'd have to be cute to have a shot at you."

"And so built-"

"Duh again, so are you. Black or white?"

"White, but-,"

"Snap. Call your hook up Old TV too. Black and white. Get it?

"I get it, Coree, and he's not a hook up, and can you please stop interrupting me?"

I slumped my shoulders and ran a hand down Old TV's back. Sammi had been the one Black girl in our high school, from the one African American family in our town. Despite how tight the three of us were, we never talked about the special challenges Sammi must have faced. Probably, for my part at least, I was just too shallow, or caught up in my own problems, but maybe Sammi just possessed all the attributes to succeed, attractive, though evidently not enough for any of our country boys to ask her out, intelligent, though not above bonding with those of more ordinary academic abilities, like Aubrey and me, but mostly, Sammi was a natural leader. Aubrey and I did stupid things, occasionally broke the rules. Sammi didn't do stupid things and didn't break the rules, and sometimes she even made the rules. We pushed the boundaries. Sammi looked on, shook her head, and reigned us in. But now here was a guy in her life, a special guy.

"You know, just to prove I'm not all shallow, besides being cute, he's incredible in bed too, and I mean incredible."

"Looks and sex both. If that doesn't prove Sammi isn't shallow, I don't know what does." I nodded to the closet. "Not really into cleaning litter boxes."

"Or anything else. Don't you guys smell it? It only takes a minute, and it's not nice to my Old TV." She ran a single finger over the top of his head.

"One day there's gonna be a whole-sale ass-kickin' around this place."

"Oh, Sammi. You been saying that for years. No doubt you could do it, but you love us too much."

"Keep pushing me. You two just keep pushing me." Her voice lowered. "Let me just tell you one thing. He's just so sweet to me and says all the right things, but he's so good in bed that I think he could get away with being a jerk, and I'd stay with him, just to sleep with him every night. You ever have a guy like that, Coree?"

"First part yes, but the second is a deal breaker. You treat Coree Wysakee like crap, you can hit the road and hit it right now."

"Oh, little friend," Sammi said and frowned. "I so call BS on that. The road behind Coree Wysakee is littered with great guys who've treated you like a queen, and you still up and dump their asses."

"Heard it before."

"Hey, what's this? Aubrey says you've got a crush on some old lady."

I shook my head. "We're friends. Aubrey doesn't understand chick friends."

"A new mom, then?"

"Can you not? I hate it when you guys say that stuff to me." But, I thought, "Maybe," to myself. "Anywayyyyy, back to you. Joey is so good he could be a jerk to you as long as he put it to you every night?"

"Of course, here's the thing. I'm not getting it every night, and I never will, because he's on the road, playing stupid baseball all the time."

"Life's so unfair, but you don't need him anyway, Sammi. You're gonna graduate from college pretty soon and start making the green like my Elizabeth."

"Your Elizabeth?"

"Just a figure of speech."

"Your Elizabeth," she repeated. "You like her, don't you?"

"Yes, I do," I said, "and we're going to be friends, and if you guys don't like it, or think I need therapy, then it's whatever to both of you."

"It's all good, Coree. It's your life."

"That's right. It's my life. Anyway, you'll be out of college soon and all, so if it doesn't work out with him..."

She frowned. "Yeah, but I want it to work out."

"You in love?"

"Maybe," Sammi said.

"With a white guy?"

"What's a matter with that?"

"Nothing. It's just, that's all I've ever dated, and it always goes south."

"Going south got nothing to do with their whiteness, Coree. Matter of fact, it's got nothing to do with the guys at all. You just play catch and release."

"I'm not playing with them."

"However you want to say it. You're always all up into 'em 'til they fall for you. Then you find some trivial-ass reason to give 'em their walking papers."

"Sounds began emanating from Aubrey's bedroom. Old TV's ears twitched and Sammi cranked up the TV.

***

At the appearance of my car, the orange shape bounded off the porch and into the shrubbery. In a secluded corner, protected from the morning mist, I set out the bowl of kibble I'd pilfered from Old TV's stash.

The chime of Ms. Ransom's doorbell rang deep and melodious like a church bell. "Are you ready to have a great day?" I said. Though not invited, I followed her in, all the way into her kitchen. "You like a chilly house, don't you? It's like winter in the country in here."

She ignored my comment and sized me up in my jeans and tee shirt, I guess.

I sized up the terrace behind her. "It's beautiful out there. Is that where you have your executive parties?"

She followed my gaze. "Um, no."

"And this kitchen. You got everything. My roommate, Sammi would love this. You like to cook too?"

"That was the plan."

"What's that mean."

"It means..." Elizabeth frowned. "It means what it means." She scanned all her latest, best, and most expensive gadgetry and threw a purse strap over her shoulder. With a computer bag in one hand, and a brief case on the other shoulder, she said, "Ready for combat. Let's go."

The strap of her laptop case turned one lapel of her navy power blazer under. I straightened it for her and said, "Now, you're ready."

Ms. Ransom blew me off. "How did I ever look after myself?"

My answer, "You don't have to worry about that anymore, do you?" prompted furrowed eyebrows from her.

16

Elizabeth

"I live in an apartment uptown, only about ten or fifteen minutes away, with my two friends and a cat."

Coree said it as if I had inquired, so I politely asked a follow up. "Do you like your roommates?"

"I love them. They're my best friends from high school, even before that. One of them had an overnighter last night." Coree sang, "Awkward." We turned the TV up. "You know how it is, being single."

Looking out over the long windshield crack, I previewed, in my mind, the challenges awaiting, and checked the beginnings of a day's assault of emails on my phone, while I politely asked, "Do you have a boyfriend?"

"Not at the moment, but funny you should ask. I met a guy one night, at Billie Jean's actually, and we had coffee, going out again soon."

I nodded.

"We'll have some laughs, but it's not going anywhere."

"Why not?"

"He comes from a super-rich family, and he's super gorgeous." After I didn't question deeper, Coree answered anyway. "Aubrey, my friend at the restaurant? She says it's on me though, thinks I have commitment issues." Again, Coree answered the question I didn't ask. "I'll admit it. I find it annoying when they start clamping on. You know what I mean?"

"I suppose."

"Yeah, you know what I mean, Ms. Ransom. I've seen you shred guys in the restaurant...brutal."

"You evidently find it amusing."

"Now I do. Now that I know I'm safe from flying debris."

"You say you met him at Billie Jean's?"

She nodded. "And ran in to him later in a club."

"I'm going to take a guess here. Sandy hair, dimples."

"Snap." She tucked her hair behind an ear. "How did you know?"

"I noticed him."

"How could you not, right? And his date."

"He had eyes for you, though."

"He did? His Tiffany is ravishing."

"You are not exactly a plain Jane, Coree."

"Why, thank you, Ms. Ransom." She pulled her left foot up under her driving leg.

"And you evidently have qualities she doesn't...qualities he finds attractive." I looked over. "Perhaps he likes your tattoos."

"Yeah?" Coree dragged up one sleeve of her oversized tee shirt to reveal a crawling vine. "You like it?"

"It is...interesting."

"You think that's lit, check this out." Driving now with one knee, she yanked the neckline of her tee shirt down with both hands nearly to the point of flashing me right there in four lanes of rush-hour traffic. An intricate, multi-colored butterfly spanned across her chest. "Now this is legit, isn't it?"

"Uh...pretty legit."

"I have a smaller butterfly down here." She indicated in the middle of her chest. "But I don't know you well enough to show you."

"And we're driving. There is that too," I said, my eyes darting around at the angry commuters.

"You know what else?" When I didn't respond, Coree said, more insistent. "You know what else, Ms. Ransom?"

I indulged her. "What?"

"I designed them myself."

"Is that so?"

"I drew out what I wanted, and the tattoo guy put them on for me. See, my dad calls me his butterfly sometimes."

"You can't ever get rid of them, right? Do you think you will ever regret them?"

"Maybe, but I figure since I made them myself, they're just one more part of me, permanent-like. It just becomes part of the stuff you carry with you...I don't know...like maybe...like maybe emotional baggage."

"On the inside." I said.

"Exactly," Coree said, while swerving across lanes, prompting angry car horns. When she settled into the lane she had sought out, she pulled down her shirt again with one hand and glancing at her artwork, she said, "Maybe I went a little overboard, but I've done that before, and I just have to live with it. Know what I mean?"

"I do."

"Life slaps you around, doesn't it?" Coree said.

"That's a way to look at-"

"But what's done is done. I mean, you can't live your life with regrets."

"I disagree." The words spilled out of my mouth before I knew I had uttered them.

Coree glanced over. "You're right, unforch'. I'm carrying around a suitcase of my past shit all the time. If I'd just let it go, life would be easier, wouldn't it?"

"I have two suitcases and a steamer trunk," I said, before raising a hand to my mouth.

"No shit?"

"No...shit," I said to her, but also to myself.

Coree reached over and gave my hand a couple taps and said, "We should just blow off work, call in, and go shopping, buy some stuff." She glanced at me. "Bet you don't do that though, do you, Ms. Ransom?"

I shook my head. "What about the nose piercing?"

"What?" She touched her nose.

"The nose piercing. Is that permanent?"

"No. I could take it out if I ever change my mind. You like it?"

"No, I do not like it." A motorcycle roared by. "Tattoos, I have always been lukewarm to. Nose piercings, I do not like at all. The entrance under the Landford-Smithson logo there is fine. I'm going to give you a twenty for gas and your trouble, Coree, and you will not argue with me."

"In that case, I won't. No lie, Ms. Ransom, when you get powerful with your swag like that, you're impressive. Maybe I'll see you tonight."

"It is possible."

I stood alone in the elevator. A handsome, young businessman, who I'm sure worked for me, somewhere down the line, ran for it, but I let the doors slam in his surprised face. What is going on with that girl? The doors opened on my floor, but I stood inside thinking and the doors closed before I snapped out of it. She is interesting though. She is a breath of fresh air in my life.

Barely off the elevator, Chelsea met me and accompanied me down the hall with her full-on assault, reviewing my morning schedule.

"Michael, are you ready to have a great day?" He shot me a bewildered stare. "And is it necessary for you to wait in my office, before I even arrive?"

"Yes, it is, so you can't avoid me."

"I need to talk to my secretaries about that." While I unpacked, I said, "Alright, let's have it. Chelsea, where's my-,"

"Here, ma'am."

Coffee in hand, I studied the manilla files in Michael's hands.

"I have selected people for the new positions, Elizabeth. Would you like to review them?"

"Why should I? It's your department. However, anyone can clearly see you have four files there, and we agreed on three additional positions. Either you are carrying an unrelated file with you, of the exact same color and size, or you hope to push another eighty-thousand dollars on me, far beyond which I agreed. Say it ain't so, Michael."

"It's so."

I sighed. "You always do this. We don't have money to throw around and we agreed, etc, etc, etc."

He looked like a guilty boy, a guilty forty-year-old boy.

"Stop the pout, Michael. I've seen it before, wasn't impressed. Now explain."

"Please take the files and have a quick look at them. Of all the candidates, four stood way above the rest."

"But of course."

"Hear me out. The others, I would not have hired, no matter how much we needed personnel, but four stood out. Why don't you review them and decide on which one to knock out?"

"Or?" I said. "I know you have something in mind."

"Now that you mention it. I would like to hire the fourth on a provisional basis."

"They are all on a provisional basis as long as I'm around. You are too, for that matter."

"Understood, but a strict sixty-day trial with a review of not only the person's performance, but also our costs."

I opened my laptop. "I'm going to be watching your department's productivity like a hawk."

"You always do. You watch everything and everybody like a hawk."

"Like an eagle. I better see improvement in a progress report, improvement which can be specifically attributed to these hires."

"Of course."

"Oh, and I don't ever want to see your face again, Michael."

He laughed. "That's going to be a hard one. Remember the quarterly infrastructure review meeting at ten?"

"I don't have time for that." I collapsed into my chair and repeated into the ceiling, "I do not have time for that."

"You're entertaining today, Elizabeth."

***

Ten minutes into said meeting, I had selected the fourth associate and passed the files on to Michael. Thirty minutes in, my eyes had poured over every face and every inch of wall. Forty minutes into the droning, I picked up my phone and texted, "I'm dying in this meeting," adding a row of sleepy face emojis.

A text almost immediately shot back, "Pretend to go to the bathroom, and I'll pick u up around the back door. Shopping time. LOL"

I gawked at my phone. What just happened? What the hell just happened? Why did I just initiate that exchange of texts? As I considered it, a pain in my abdomen caused me to involuntarily gasp. I waved Michael's glance off as it dissipated.

17

Coree

"Coree Wysakee?"

"Yes?"

"This is Sharon Blaze." I yanked the booming voice away from my ear. "Greg Wiesberg gave me your number. We're shooting right now, at this very moment, and I need another person, a certain look. He said you have it. I know it's short notice, no notice at all really. Can you come?"

***

With all the shots in, except mine, they took me straight to makeup and on to the cameras, no chilling around, and soon enough, I found myself hustling along to her office. "You look and act exactly like your name," I said.

"Yeah?"

"Red hair and," I borrowed Grayson's word, "effervescent." Despite Sharon Blaze wearing heels and being, what some might call 'curvy,' I trotted along in my black Chucks to keep up. Inside her office, the perfume which had trailed her, now caught up and overwhelmed. She took a call, waving her free hand around, while reaching about the little room and printing my check.

The call, the check, and whatever else, all came to simultaneous conclusions, and she abruptly zoned in across from me. "I have a shoot on Friday, a little, neighborhood paper. It's all lined up, but let's get you in for a couple shots. It wouldn't be much, a bit of spending money. How 'bout it?" She drummed shiny red nails on her desk. "You have a look I like. What do you think? Down for it?"

"Sure."

"Good. I noticed your ink. There's a couple shots I want you in, your girlish charm, contrasting the tats." She touched her hands to her own chest while nodding at mine. "I'm glad Greg sent you my way. You have a certain quality-"

"A high school girl?"

"Bet you get that a lot, don't you? Gotta make that money though, right?" She rubbed the invisible cash in her fingers. "Friday will be older shots, and I'll definitely find some other stuff for you down the line. I'm starting to cave. Let's grab coffee? I gotta keep it going, gotta full day, a lot of loose ends to tie up. You coming?"

I snuck my "yes," into Sharon's rapid-fire approach to conversation.

"You're twenty-three, Coree?"

"Right. Almost twenty-four."

"Great. Good age for your look."

"In some ways."

"I mean, it's about money. It's all about money. You can still do this teen work for a while and older stuff too. Take me. I'm going on thirty, and I look like it." Her arms waved around in a wide reach. "I'd have to do my age, which would limit me. I don't think I could do MILF stuff yet." Her reverberating laugh shook her body, her bracelets, and her dangly earrings. "And that business of sitting in a chair with your feet scrunched under your butt. Sorry Coree, but you sit like you're in a junior high school desk, you're going to get some young assignments." Sharon exploded into laughter again.

I laughed too, but couldn't even hear myself over her. "How long have you been in this, Sharon?"

"Oh, a few years. I've worked for other people, but I'm out on my own now, and I've got more work than I can handle. I'm going to have to expand beyond a one-person show at some point." She shrugged. "A lot of work, but the money doesn't always go with it."

"Never seems to."

She tossed her red hair back. "You have to consider the fringes though, in any job, don't you?"

"For sure."

"Exactly. Like the travel. We did a shoot in Rome recently, fun, fun, fun. The food, the wine, the warm weather, the models."

She let out a roar of laughter again. "We were doing a shoot in front of this fountain. You know, Rome has all these fountains. Anyway, I arranged the shoot, and I slipped backwards." Her arms flailed wildly, reenacting her lost balance. "I fell right in, dress completely soaked, clinging right to me."

Sharon tossed back her orange hair again. "You meet so many stellar people. Like you, I'm going to like you, Coree. I can tell already. When you walked into the studio, you caught my eye and now here we are in a café. I do like you." Her chair scraped across the cement as she pulled closer.

"I like your energy, and now I'm liking the whole package. You're super cute and exciting."

After a siren passed the café, echoing off the building fronts, I said, "I just came to this place the other day, for the first time." I read the sign over her again. "Go With the Flow."

"Must mean something," she said. "Alrighty then, Friday, nine, probs." She made a texting motion with her hands. "I'll confirm." Sharon Blaze stopped abruptly and took a breath. "I'm going to find you more work, Coree Wysakee. Stick with me. In the meantime, Friday shoot."

I sat in my car, recovering from the Sharon Blaze assault. Before starting it, I texted, "I had a shoot today. Thumbs up emoji. R u coming to Billie Jean's tonight?"

"I don't think so. I'm not feeling well."

"I'll stop over on my way home and tell u about the shoot. CU." I didn't get a return text, so after a while, I texted, "U want me to bring food?" Still no reply, so I texted again. "I'm bringing food."

***

Before entering the house, I filled Landon's cat bowl. I gave him the working name of her unwanted date. She didn't like the man, but I liked his name. After I rang the bell, I felt the vibration of a text. Ms. Ransom's entry combination. "Snap. I'm through the castle doors."

18

Elizabeth

"Leah, pardon the late hour, but I have a job for u." When I finished the text, I laid the phone on the empty coffee table. The side of my index finger slid softly, back and forth across my upper lip. "Well, Landon, that was a costly dinner for you. You will never talk to her like that again. I guarantee that." Hearing the door open, I turned.

"Hey. How you feeling?"

"Just some stomach cramps."

"You hungry? I brought soup, a pasta salad, and bread sticks. I'll set up the salad here on the coffee table and be right back with the soup."

"I didn't ask for food," I said to Coree's back, though by the time she returned, I munched on a bread stick.

Coree threw herself onto my high-backed chair, sitting sideways, her feet hanging over one arm. She kicked off her high tops and let them fall beside the chair. "An agent called me this morning, a shoot for a clothing store, and she needed a high school girl. That's me. Makeup, shots in, check in hand, worked out great. No waiting around, no probs." I sat, watching, and listening to her like a court jester had somehow slipped into my house and draped herself over my throne. "The lady wants me to do some shots Friday too, a little unexpected green. So, tell me about your pains, just usual monthly stuff, more serious? What's going on?"

Why am I telling you? "Not monthly stuff, I said, using air quotes for her words. "I don't know."

"You going to get it checked out, or isn't it that serious?"

Again, why am I telling you? "I'll wait."

"You lift something heavy?"

"No. I've had a few little pains now and then. They seem to be getting worse."

"We went to this sidewalk café," Coree said, examining her toenail polish, each nail a different color. "A cute little coffee place called, 'Go With the Flow.' Second time I've been there now. You and I'll have to check it out sometime."

"Coree." I managed to wedge only her name in before she plowed on.

"Hey, wait. You're not pregnant, are you?"

I deadpanned that absurd suggestion.

"Grayson and I are going to go to an art gallery."

"That's a good place for a date."

Coree nodded. "Not a lot can go wrong there. I've only been a couple times before. How about you?"

"I've been a few-"

"Maybe we could go sometime."

"Coree." I couldn't hide my perplexed stare.

"What?"

"Why? Why me? Don't you have friends your own age? I know you do. I'm sure you would have more fun."

"I have friends my own age, lots of friends, but I like you too. Don't you like me, Ms. Ransom?"

"Of course, I like you." My eyes searched about the room for an escape from this idiotic conversation. "You have my house code. If that doesn't mean something, I don't know what does." I shook my head. "Tell you what. Go ahead and call me Elizabeth."

"Lit. Then maybe, you won't talk to me like I'm a little kid."

"That's ironic, because you're sitting there sideways and barefoot in my Italian-leather, high-back chair." I might as well have made that comment to the wall.

"Photo shoots are usually fun," she said, as if I had just asked her about it, "unless the director is a jerk." She stopped and considered me. "Ms. Ransom, Elizabeth, are you a jerk to your people?"

"I am demanding, and I keep a certain persona about me-"

"No shit."

I blinked at her comment, in my house. "So, sometimes, I wouldn't be surprised if they, some of them, might perceive me as being, in your words, a jerk. They have a job to do, and my job is to make sure they do it. I have to kick a little butt once in a-"

"Damn, you have charisma, power charisma," she said, but scanning around, she quickly shifted course. "Your house is...quiet, no sounds at all unless you make them yourself. In our apartment, the wood floor creaks in certain places. I know where they all are, but I still step on one once in a while. You can hear the whoosh of water in the walls when someone above flushes or takes a shower. Sometimes you can even hear the couple next door arguing. The quiet here reminds me of our house growing up."

"Where is that?"

"Richville. You know it?"

"I've heard of it."

The pain shot through my stomach again.

"Are you alright, Elizabeth?"

"I'm okay." But I wasn't okay.

"Can you walk? I mean, not right now, but does it hurt when you walk?"

"Only when it hurts."

"That makes a lot of sense."

"It's just that, when these pains come, they just come."

"How often?"

"Perhaps three or four today?"

"We need to get it checked out."

"'We,' I emphasized, "don't need to do anything. I'm far too busy right now. There are too many projects going on. The quarterly earnings report will be out soon. Besides this, I'm perfectly healthy."

Coree's eyes met mine with surprising resolve. "Well, you can't drive in this condition. It's not safe, and I don't see anyone else around to help you. Call your doctor in the morning and make an appointment."

I shook my head.

"Do it."

"Maybe I'll do it at some point if you quit badgering-"

"You know what? I don't believe you." Her words carried an attitude, and attitude stood out for me because it so rarely pointed in my direction.

"I'm going to call right now and leave a message that we'll be there in the morning."

"Impossible. Tomorrow...well, there is just too much-"

"Gimme that phone." She grabbed it off the coffee table before I could even think about reaching for it.

"Hey, you got a text here from a 'Leah.' It says, 'taken care of.' Who's Leah?"

"Don't worry about it."

"Shade."

"Oh, it's one of my secretaries. It doesn't matter."

"How many secretaries do you have?"

"Two"

"Why do you need two?"

"Coree, you can't even imag-"

"What did she take care of?"

"Just never you mind."

Coree turned her attention from me to the phone again. "What's your doctor's name?" she said, scrolling through my numbers. "Here's a 'Dr. Lewis.' Is that him?"

I nodded and mumbled "her." She typed the number into her phone.

"Coree, you seriously need to butt out."

"Hello, this is Coree Wysakee, calling on behalf of Ms. Elizabeth Ransom. She's having abdominal pains. We're gonna be there the moment your office opens. Thanks." She turned to me. "It's done, Elizabeth. I made it happen, as you say. Call your secretary, one of your secretaries," she said with a sing-song voice, "and tell her you'll be in late. They'll probably get more done without their bossy boss anyway."

"You do not tell me what to do." I gave her the deep-freeze glare, but I might as well have given it to the fireplace.

"You want me to call her too?"

"Okay, okay. Give me my phone back, and I'll text her."

"What's her name?"

"Chelsea."

"What about Leah?"

"Not under her job description. Give me my phone, Coree." I rose, but a pain shot through me, and forced me back down.

"TSC," Coree said. "Here you are, alone in this big house. Where the hell is everyone?"

I shrugged. "There really isn't-"

"You're all alone in this big, cold house, and oh, we need to get you to emergency."

"No."

"Yes. We're going. I don't know what's going on with you, but we can't wait for the doctor tomorrow."

Coree sprinted up the stairs, and returning with a little bag, she grabbed her high tops off the floor. Once she had me in my car, she ran, still barefoot, back up to the front porch. "What now?"

"I'm feeding your cat, before we go."

"My cat? I don't have a cat."

"You do now. I named him Landon.'"

"Landon?"

"Yep. This particular Landon looks a little broad in the beam though. I think Landon might be pregnant. Maybe Lily, or you can think of another name while we drive."

"I don't need a cat." I looked out into the night in frustration.

"You know Elizabeth, I'm realizing you need a lot of things you don't think you need."

"One thing I don't need is a bossy little girl telling me what to do. That's for sure."

"Evidently, you do. What if I hadn't stopped over?"

"I'm sure it would have gone away."

"Oh, okay. My dad's word for that is 'applesauce.' I call it BS. Elizabeth, your car's like silent inside. Mine rattles like a washing machine. It's chill in here, but a little eerie, like your house."

"I like sil-"

"You need an air freshener in here."

"It smells-."

"It doesn't stink or anything. It just doesn't have any smell at all. You could have some nice clean scent in here, you know, vanilla or something."

I turned toward the side window.

***

"Coree, you don't have to stay with me," I said after hours of being fussed over by nurses and technicians, hauled to various imaging, and answering the same questions to various doctors.

"No probs. I stay up late anyway, and I'm not working...or dating tomorrow."

About one in the morning, the doctors came in for what Coree referred to as, "the word up."

"We are going to be admitting you, Ms. Ransom. Is this your daughter?"

"She is a friend."

"Would you like her present for our discussion of your situation?"

I frowned at Coree sitting cross-legged in the chair next to me. "It's fine. Go ahead."

One of the doctors, a woman easily young enough to be my daughter, said, "First of all, I don't want you to panic or overreact to this, but you have a tumor or tumors..."

"We need more tests," another doctor cut in.

"...along the walls of your uterus."

"Go on," I said, but then added, "Please tell me you were the most brilliant student in all your classes."

She smiled. "I may have been. I'm duty here tonight. The resident specialist will be here tomorrow, well," with a glance at the big wall clock, she said, "actually today."

"It wasn't a criticism. Actually, it was a complement. You are so young looking."

"Can we stop this chatter and get to the point," Coree said. "Is she going to be okay?"

The doctor looked at Coree, back to me, and finally back to Coree. "We need more tests, lab work, and imaging."

"Can't you give a straight answer?" she said, pulling a knee up under her chin.

"Coree, stop it," I said.

"Oh, God." She jumped up and ran out of the room.

My chin in my hand, I said, "Go on, doctor. I'll deal with that later."

"Come in here, Coree," I texted. "The doctors left. Where r u?"

When she returned, I motioned the chair next to the bed. "Listen to me now. I want you to take my car home. Drive carefully and do not be distracted by this. I'm a big girl. Believe me, I've been through a lot in my life."

Coree pulled her hair behind an ear and followed my words, mouth open and wide green eyes.

"Come back after a good night's sleep."

19

Coree

I found Landon, and sure enough, the name had to be changed for she indeed sported an expectant tummy. With a dish towel from the kitchen and a tote from the closet, I made a comfortable bed for her on the front porch and set out to explore Elizabeth's house, immediately falling in love with her terrace. A sunroof allowed an inspiring view of the trees above and the stars beyond. The surrounding three walls of glass must have created an ambiance of light in the daytime, bouncing off white, upholstered furniture. Aside from one recliner, the furniture all looked factory-fresh. Next to that one recliner, a bottle of neutral nail polish, a note pad, and a wireless charging station lay on a white marbletop end table. I found myself drawn to it. I sat, only on the edge of it, but I felt the power. A pair of Elizabeth's shoes, some brand I'd never heard of, maybe Italian, waited for her, as neat as a store display. Channeling my inner Goldilocks, I yanked off my black canvas Chucks and slid into these black leather pumps. Perfect fit on my feet, but not perfect for my MO.

Comfortable-looking and well furnished, the guest rooms, like much of her furniture, were decorated in neutral colors and designs, and appeared to have never been touched by any life form. In contrast, Elizabeth's room glowed in yellows, whites, and golds. Though made perfectly, I could pick out her regular spot in the bed, slightly indented, next to an insane Tiffany lamp, another wireless charging station, and a sleeping sound machine.

I pulled the bedding back, climbed right in, and curling into a little ball, I found myself surrounded in her scent. Before the sheets even warmed up, I jumped out, bounded down the stairs, and out the front door.

Leaving her basket in the closet, I pulled the cat to me, into my warmth, feeling under her neck to see if she purred. She did, a minute vibration. "Now Lily, you have to be a good girl for a few hours until I can get you a litter box." She studied me with round yellow eyes, and I knew she understood. As our spot warmed, her motor roared, and we succored each other's worries.

***

"They think I might need to have a hysterectomy."

"Will you be fine after that? I mean that's bad enough, but are you going to recover? They said you had-"

"Just stop," Elizabeth said. "Yes. They are quite optimistic."

"I'm sorry I ran out. It was just too much for me."

Elizabeth frowned. "This is kind of about me, isn't it, Coree?"

I nodded at the floor. "How do you feel? I mean about the whole thing, the whole sitch? How are you coping, like mentally?"

"Not going to lie, at my age, with no children, it's a gut punch."

"Maybe Landon won't want you anymore." I laughed at my wit.

Elizabeth didn't laugh. "There is that."

"Is it urgent?"

She shrugged. "Fairly soon. I'll be able to come home a few days, get work affairs in order."

I furrowed my eyebrows.

"Don't get worked up. I can afford this. I'll hire a caregiver or a nurse."

"No. No to both of those. I'll move in and take care of you."

"Coree, that's kind of you, but you don't have to."

"Well, where's your family? They should be here."

I shrugged. "There's not really anyone who-"

"Then, that's it. I'll move in and take care of you and your house."

"Oh, here we go."

"No, not 'here we go.' That's the way it's going to be. It's the way it's got to be. Don't argue with me about it."

"I don't want to impose on you."

"We're friends. It's not imposing, and it's settled."

"Young lady, you don't boss me around."

"Don't call me 'young lady.' It's condescending. I'm telling you the way it's going to be, and that's the end of it. I'll take care of you."

"Do you even know who you are talking to, Coree? Do you know who talks to me that way? Exactly no one."

"That shit doesn't fly with me right now, so chill." We both noticed the doctor watching from the doorway. I retreated to my chair and pulled a knee up under my chin.

"It appears you have the support you're going to need."

"She thinks," Elizabeth said, shooting me a side eye.

"You lost. Take it like a big girl."

"I didn't lose, and furthermore, I don't lose."

"It's whatever."

"Ms. Ransom, I have a lot of information here for you to go over. Tonight, you'll be released, and you'll visit the surgeon tomorrow to learn about the procedure and ask questions. We have concerns about operating with your high blood pressure, but we can't wait long."

"High blood pressure?" I said it to both the doctor and Elizabeth. Is she safe to drive, work, and carry on as usual in the meantime, because she'll try to?"

"The pain can come on and-"

"That's what I wanted to know. I'll take you to work and pick you up, and don't roll your eyes, Elizabeth."

20

Elizabeth

My eyes lit on something attached to one of the vents and I pointed an accusing finger at it. "What is that?"

"That...is an air freshener."

"Did I tell you to put that in my car?"

"Not exactly."

"It was a rhetorical question. I know the answer. No, I did not tell you to put that in my-"

"It's vanilla."

"It's not-"

"It smells epic in here."

I frowned at the offending object.

"Don't you think?"

"It is my car."

"I'm aware, and are you aware that I did a nice thing?"

After one more glance at this young girl who could barely see over my steering wheel, but who would not give any ground, I looked off through the side window. "I had planned to go visit my father on Sunday. He lives in a nursing home."

"And now you need me to drive you."

"I didn't say that."

"Duh. You didn't have to."

"If you are busy, I under-"

"Let's do it."

"Can you stop interrupting me, Cor-?"

"High blood pressure, huh? He said you have high blood pressure. That's funny because I recall you telling me you were in perfect health."

"My job comes with a lot of stress, I suppose, to say nothing of having conversations with you, Coree."

"Maybe you better be more straight with me. Try that."

"I can't believe you talk to me this way."

Coree turned on the radio and began running through stations.

I turned it back off, something she evidently found funny. "What?"

"You always get your way?"

I looked over at her as if to see if she was real. "What you call 'getting my way,' I refer to as independence."

She laughed. Coree actually laughed at me, before saying, "You can't have it. Maybe I'll give it back to you in a month."

The soft hum of the road covered the grinding of my teeth.

"If looks could kill," she said, "I'd be dead, and the car would go rolling off the road with you bouncing in your seat, screaming. Maybe the car would stop because Ms. Elizabeth Ransom commanded it to."

"You think it's all so funny, don't you? I don't know how we got to this point so fast."

"I'm just going where the story takes me. I'll drop you off at work tomorrow and pick you up later."

I glared straight ahead.

***

Coree walked to the door with me and when I shot her a questioning glance, she said, "I'm staying over again. Come on upstairs. I want to show you something." I wondered, with some trepidation, what on earth she could have to show me in my own house.

"First of all," she said, "I slept in your spot."

I spun around.

"This big house freaked me right out and with you gone, I guess I needed the security." Her little circle of an indentation still showed in the bottom sheet.

"You did not even make my bed."

Coree followed the line of my stare and smirked, but I just could not pry my eyes off my most personal of spots being completely violated.

"I'll buy you some new sheets and a mattress too if you want." When I raised my hand to my mouth, she said, "Oh, come on, Elizabeth. Are you serious? Chill. It's a bed. If you're shocked by that, come look in here."

"Is it warmer in here?"

"I turned the thermostat up. Your house is too cold."

"I find it feels refreshing on my skin," I said, "and why am I justifying how... It's my house."

Coree opened the closet door and pointed into the dark corner.

"What is it?"

"It's Lily and three kittens, all girls, I think. It's hard to tell at a day old."

"In a wicker basket lined with one of my Delorme tea towels."

"We couldn't leave them outside starving, could we? In the rain?"

"It hasn't rained in-"

"It might though. She's such a good mom, and she lets you pick them up. I named them Aubrey, Sammi, and Little Coree. If you don't like the names, you can change them."

"Those cats are laying in, what, two-hundred-dollars, more, worth of bedding."

"Here, this little orange one looks just like her mom. It's 'Little Coree.'"

She laid it in my hands the same time a pain forced me back to the edge of the bed. "Here, put it back," I said.

"Oh, yuck." Coree laughed and pulled her tee shirt up over her nose. "Lily farted. Mama cats stink it up sometimes to drive off visitors."

I sat at the edge of the bed thinking of everything I had lost, but Coree rambled on.

"We had lots of kittens, growing up." She finally paused. "You alright, Elizabeth?"

With a flat smile, I said, "At least someone can have babies."

Coree sat beside me and looking up, said, "You don't let it out much, do you?"

I tried to think of a suitable response.

"How come?"

"Will you bring me a pair of pajamas from that dresser and excuse me a moment."

"Nice subject change."

Sliding within my cool cashmere and cotton sheets, I whispered to my room, "Nothing beats your own bed." The distant and familiar sounds of my neighborhood comforted me. Occasional, faint trilling sounds emanated from the closet. Though unfamiliar, I found them comforting as well.

My eyes flashed open, startled at the silhouette of a figure in my doorway. "Coree. What on earth? You scared me to death. What are you doing?"

"Elizabeth?"

"What?

"Can I sleep with you?"

"Can you what?"

"Can I sleep with you? Nothing weird. I won't bother you. I'm stressed out in this big house."

"How old are you again?"

"I know. Aubrey says I'm a baby."

"You sleep with her?"

"Once in a while, when I'm having a bad time."

I frowned in the dark. Before I had gotten the words out of my mouth, the shape of her little figure darted low around the end of the bed. "I cannot believe this is happening and don't even think about me tucking you in. No one, other than me, has ever, ever been in this bed before and now-"

"No one?" Coree giggled. "Elizabeth, you gotta get out more."

"Enough. You be quiet if you are going to be in here."

"Yes ma'am." She giggled again. "By the way, there's a litter box and food in the closet too."

"Good to know, but I have my own bathroom and kitchen."

"You're funny, Elizabeth. Low key."

I clung to the edge of my bed, facing away from my new little friend, yet, when I woke up in the morning, I felt her back pushed against my own, a sensation I found unwelcome, prompting me to rise earlier than usual.

21

Coree

"It's going to be different this time. She wants it to work. I know you're rolling your eyes. I can feel it right through the phone, but she's different this time, Coree. She's changed."

"Receipts needed."

"She's really trying."

"I don't want her to hurt you again, Aubrey."

"She loves me, and she's changed. She wants to prove it to you too."

"You don't screw over my BFF and expect me to forget it right away." I turned sideways, back against the door, legs stretched out until the treads of my Chucks pressed flat to the passenger window. "Jade's scary."

"You'll see."

"Has she been staying over every night?"

"Not every night."

"Oh, whatever. It's every night."

"Coree, you've been over at your Ms. Ransom's every night."

"That's totally different, and you know it." I waved my arm as if Aubrey could see my annoyance. "First, she's sick, and I'm taking care of her. Second, it's not a romantic relationship, at all. And third, unlike Jade, Elizabeth's nice to me, most of the time."

"What do you mean, most of the time?"

"Alright, all the time."

"Too late, you said, 'most of the time.' What's up? Spill it."

"She can be aloof sometimes. You know how she is in the restaurant? Well, that's her, a lot of the time, authoritative, confident."

"You thought she would be all warm and fuzzy for you?

"Stop it, Aubrey."

"Be your mom?"

"Aubrey, please stop."

"I mean, you talk about Jade...what are you going to do when she dumps your whiny little ass? Tells you she doesn't want an annoying Klingon?"

"She's not like that," I said.

"How is it different than how you talk about me and Jade?"

"It's a lot different. We're not queer, and Elizabeth's not abusive."

"Jade never hurt me."

"Bullshit." I said. "Stop covering for her."

We sat quiet for a moment. "Anyway, what are you doing today, with the Ms.?

"Right now, I am sitting in the parking lot of a Senior Center in Newburgh while she visits her dad."

"Sounds fun."

"A bit of a drive, but I spend more time with Elizabeth this way and get to know her more."

"Back to her."

"I like her."

"Sounds like it."

"Will you get out of my head, please?"

"And you get out of mine."

"Truce for a while?"

"A while."

"In the meantime," I said, "What's going on with Sammi?"

"She's up in my ass about Jade too, you'll be pleased to know."

"Yes, I am. You should listen to her, to both of us."

"We had a truce."

"How's the other issue going?"

"Not yet."

"Is she freaking out?"

"A little."

"And Joey?"

"They talk all the time."

"Oh, Aubs, I went home to visit Daddy."

"Yeah? How'd that go?"

"Nothing's changed in Richville," I said.

"Never will."

"I ran into Rachel Simms in the Applebee's parking lot."

"Hate that stuck up bitch," Aubrey said.

"I know, right?"

"How's the homecoming queen?"

"Two kids, third in the oven. Putting on weight."

"Good."

"Here's something," I said. "She saw me with Ms. Ransom's big, black Lexus."

"Lit. She can shove that vision right up her stuck-up ass."

"Shade."

"I'm liking your new momma right now."

"Oh, she's coming out the door. I gotta go."

"What up, girl?" I said.

"Nothing."

"Something is. I could feel the edge the minute you stepped out the door. All the flowers about wilted when you passed."

Elizabeth said, "Why are their tread marks from your shoes on my win-?"

"This is a nice place. Your dad must be rich." The arcing sprinklers thumped against the side of the car as we passed the manicured lawn.

"You'd think."

Elizabeth gripped her thighs and stared straight ahead.

"What did he do?" The sound of my question died a quick death in the quiet interior, and the faint hum of the road soon swallowed it.

Elizabeth's sighed, giving vague evidence of life.

"Want to talk?" I asked.

"Not really."

"Back to silence," I said, my sarcasm shriveling on the vine as well.

A few more miles of road passed, and Elizabeth inhaled, as if to speak, however she let even more miles drag by. Finally, she inhaled from deep in her diaphragm, paused, and said, "I pay for him to live at that 'nice place.'" She only released the grip on her thighs long enough to wrap air quotes around the space her words occupied.

"That's nice of you."

"Yes, it is. It is nice of me. It's very nice of me."

"I detect some 'tude." We climbed a long gradual hill doing a slow pass of a semi with huge, colorful fruit on the side of it, grapes, apples, pears, pretty droplets of condensation clinging to them.

Elizabeth inhaled again, paused again, glanced at the fruit, too huge and colorful to ignore, and said, "I pay for him to live in that comfort, and safety, and...oh, whatever." She waved away the subject with a swish of her hand in the direction of the giant fruit.

I wanted to talk, to share our story, our experience, like Aubrey and Sammi and me, but the irritated Ms. Ransom made me hesitant to pry and turn her guns my way. "I talked to my friend Aubrey while you visited your dad. She's in this relationship with-"

"I pay for it," she said as if I wasn't even talking. The angry-looking grill of a red pickup truck took up most of my rearview mirror. "All of it." Stealing a quick glance over, I caught the classic clenched jaws that I had quickly come to know. She never took her eyes off the road in front of her, yet probably saw little of it.

"This tailgater behind me needs to-"

"Don't you think it would be nice if he would show a little interest in me?"

I could not find a suitable response, if one existed out there some place.

"I sat in there for how long?" She glanced at her Rolex. "For an hour and a half, I sat in there listening to him go on and on about Jo and Allison, all about their children, his grandchildren, every trivial detail and minutia about their lives for an hour and a half." Elizabeth paused, and again I glanced at the silver grill filling my rearview mirror, now following on the exit ramp. "I'm going to have a hysterectomy Tuesday, a hysterectomy, Coree. Ask me about it, how I am feeling. It's a pretty big deal in a woman's life, isn't it?"

I may have been only twenty-three, but I knew when to lay low.

"Ask me about my job. CEO, Dad, CEO of a huge corporation. Ask me about," she waved an arm trying to bring something forth before adding, "the new cat I apparently have. Anything, ask me anything. I'm never going to have kids, except..." I glanced over, and she halted abruptly. She fell silent again for a block or two and finally hit the dashboard with the bottoms of her fists before resuming squeezing her legs. "Pull over. Pull in here."

"What? Where?"

"Right in here. Over there, by that table."

"You alright, Elizabeth?"

"No."

I drove us over to the back corner of the McDonald's parking lot, and Elizabeth busted out before I even dropped her Lexus into park. With me in hot pursuit, she booked it over to a picnic table where, sucking in breaths, she bent over one end of it, clenching it with both hands. I stood beside and behind her trying to anticipate what was going to happen.

After a moment or two, she looked back at me, a twisted, semblance of her face. "I raised those girls," she said, then yelled down at the table, "I raised them. I was only a girl myself, and I raised them. No one ever asked me if I wanted to. It's just, 'Elizabeth, you're the mom now.'"

Is this what they call a nervous breakdown, or maybe an Elizabeth Ransom temper tantrum, times ten?

"I didn't know how to be a mother. I just wanted my own mom." She spoke to the empty space in front of her. "I didn't know why she left me, left us, nothing. How do you think I felt, Dad? You never talked to me about it, never asked me how I felt."

The muscles in her arms twisted like ropes. She seemed to have become someone else, talking to someone not there.

"How do you think I felt? You ever think of that? No. Just do it, Libby. Just do it all. Just suck it up and do it all. I was only ten, for God's sake, only ten, Dad."

I wanted to go to Elizabeth, to comfort her, but I didn't know the right words. The cars in the drive-up line just kept on, not noticing us, dealing with their own lives.

"And now it's like, okay, let's just forget about everything you gave up for us. Oh, and by the way, why'd you have to be such a bitch? And I didn't know anything about life either, still don't, because I never had any time for it, no time at all, so I totally made a shit of that. And here I am, this wreckage, and no one gives a shit about me." She squeezed the table edges in her hands and yelled down into it, "No one gives a shit about me."

"Elizabeth, I care about you. I don't even know what you're talking about, but I care about you. I care a lot about you. You don't even know how much I..." She leered back at me, all wild-eyed and stomped back to the car, leaving me stranded with my words.

When we pulled back out into traffic, I took her hand in mine. She flinched and yanked her hand away. "What are you doing?"

"Just trying to comfort you."

"Well, don't."

I brought my hand back to the wheel, and remembered Aubrey's words, "...when she tells you she doesn't want an annoying Klingon." I sniffed a couple times and, feeling Elizabeth's glare, wiped under my eyes.

"Stop that crying, Coree. You stop that crying right now."

"Well, I can't just shut it off, Elizabeth." My voice felt screechy. I wanted to say, "Not everybody has ice water in their veins," but thought better of it.

After yet a few more blocks, she sighed, and reached over. I glanced down, maybe needing to see it to believe it, our hands together. They were the same size, hers maybe an older version of mine, what mine will look like, what Mom's would've looked like. We rode the last couple miles that way.

The garage door rumbled down behind us, and when it thumped bottom, the silence within the already quiet car became almost overpowering. "Elizabeth, can I ask you something? Do you want to tell someone about these things in your life, talk about it?

We sat in silence for a few moments, still holding hands, me looking up at her, Elizabeth looking straight ahead, otherworldly. Finally, she said, "That wasn't me back there. I don't know what happened."

"Elizabeth, that was you back there."

She looked up at the ceiling a moment. "I guess I'm under a lot of stress right now. It was a rare breakdown in the steel. It won't happen again."

"You don't have to go through this alone. I'm here for you."

"What does that even mean?" she said.

"It means, you're a few days out from major surgery, life changing surgery," I said, "and I'm right here with you."

"You know, Coree, they have these brochures, if you want to call them that. They explain all about it. They have all the answers, but they can't really give the answers, because the questions are all your own, your own unique, personal life. How will it feel? How soon can I go back to work? Will I be depressed? Will I ever feel like dating again?"

I nodded slowly.

"Will sex be okay?" She shrugged. "I haven't had sex in so long...does it really matter?" She glanced at me with a sheepish grin. "I actually considered sleeping with Landon. Perhaps I should have, my last time. They said I will feel normal again. Too funny. As if Elizabeth Ransom is anywhere near normal now about intimacy. The way he treated you though. That was a deal breaker, a deal breaker on all fronts.

"I can take care of myself."

Elizabeth surprised me by saying, "I'm not so sure."

"What do you mean? I can. I can take care of myself. Always have, since..."

Elizabeth let go of my hand to wave the subject away. "Landon said, my behavior explains the two divorces."

"Well, he's wrong," I said. "You came to my defense, even though I didn't need it."

"So maybe I am capable of caring," she said.

"Maybe," I chuckled. "But, anyway, you can tell me these things. Tell me anything. I won't judge you. Maybe it would help you to talk."

Elizabeth became rigid. "You can't say you won't judge someone, when you don't know what it is you might be judging."

"I hear what you mean, but I care about you. I'll listen and support you. I mean how bad can it be?"

Elizabeth softly slid the side of her forefinger back and forth against her lips a few times while staring blankly ahead, perhaps at the past, perhaps at our friendship. She took a deep breath, patted my hand, and said, "Let's go inside."

"Evidently it can be pretty bad," I mumbled as I climbed out.

22

Elizabeth

Chelsea met me at the elevator door. "How are we feeling Ms. Ransom?"

"Fine. Where's my day schedule?"

"In your office."

"What is it doing in my office? Why are we wasting this time walking down the hallway?"

"I thought you might want to slow down a little. You know?"

"No, I don't know," I said.

Chelsea took my hand and whispered, "Please slow down, ma'am. You're going to hurt yourself."

"Unhand me. I am not an invalid."

"Ms. Ransom, we have all the time in the world."

She closed the door and took a chair in front of my desk.

"What is this about?" I said, watching her.

"Before the executive staff arrives, can we review how this is going to work, in your absence?"

"You have-"

"You will be out of contact for a couple days."

"One day max and do not interrupt me, Chelsea"

"Coree says it will be two days at the absolute minimum, but probably more like four or five."

"Coree says?" I raised my voice. "Coree is not the boss of me."

"Ms. Ransom, you have an excellent staff. You built it. Landford-Smithson is not going to fall apart in your absence. I'll be in contact with Coree several times a day."

"Does she think she is going to run Landford-Smithson now, besides running me?"

"She'll be my liaison to you, like a personal assistant, and she'll travel back and forth between you and us as needed. It makes sense, doesn't it?"

"Yes, but my recovery will happen faster than you think, Chelsea, faster than you think."

"I'm sure it will," she said.

"Do not roll your eyes at me."

"Ahh, our girl is feisty, sounds like," said Michael Kent, arriving first.

"Yes sir," said Chelsea, with more smile than I thought necessary.

"I'm not, 'our girl.'" The rest of my staff arrived, seating around my conference table.

"Good morning, everyone. We have much to cover. As you know, I have a contact person Chelsea will go through to keep you posted on my progress. I will be expecting updates just like always. I may not answer them right away. Nevertheless, I want to be kept in the loop."

"Really?" said Director of Marketing, Dianne Dunning. "Elizabeth, as the one person at this table who has been through what you are about to go through, I can tell you, it is not going to be easy."

"Is that right?"

"It's not a minor surgery."

"And I am no weakling."

"No one is saying you are, but we are capable people. I often go days, sometimes weeks, without even talking to you, all of us do. This will be one of those times."

"I hope so."

"You doubt me, Elizabeth? My people won't even know you're gone. There will be zero effect on-."

Michael waved a hand. "Can we move on here? No doubt Dianne's sales and marketing force will continue to be hard at work and no doubt your leadership means more than being here cracking the whip every single day, but we're digressing. Whatever you think about when you'll be back, you suggested we need to make contingency plans for your absence for up to a month or more. It's best to be prepared."

"Thank you, Michael. Perhaps I have lost some of my coherence already." My staff politely chuckled at my extremely rare attempt at selfdeprecating humor.

At the end of the meeting, the last person to pass, Dianne Dunning, surprised me by taking my arms in her hands and saying, "You'll be fine. Elizabeth. Listen hon, we have that timeshare on the ocean in Florida.

It's just sitting empty right now. When you're better, but not back to us yet, you should use it for a little refresher."

"I don't know what to say."

"Just say you'll think on it at least. You never take vacations, but it would do you a world of good just to get away."

"I hate it when people play on my heart."

"You like to act like you don't have one, Elizabeth."

"It might not be an act."

23

Coree

"Thanks for waiting." My voice echoed on the marble walls, and I scoped Grayson out as I approached. "That herring-bone jacket makes you look like a college professor, hands all in the pockets."

"Too conservative?"

I shrugged. "It works for you. You're forty, right?"

"Thirty. Take it easy."

"Just playing you."

"You fifteen then?" he said, nodding at my usual outfit. "I think you actually could wear anything and make it work. I mean, tee shirt, jeans, high-tops and there you are." He chuckled. "I'm going out with a model. How cool is that? Is it glamorous, having everyone fawning over you and snapping pictures?"

"Not as glamorous as you seem to think, at least for me. Today, I modeled winter coats, the kind high school cheerleaders would wear, but I got a check."

"So, I'm going out with a cheerleader then?"

"That's a hard no, Gramps, but I guess that's my look. My agent says I should own it."

"Sure. Why not?"

I studied his enigmatic smile and said, "Evidently, you like it, Grayson."

"I'm not looking for a cheerleader."

"You sure? Cause we could skip the art and go back to your apartment."

"You're joking, right?"

"I think so."

"You're funny, Coree. I like you."

We walked into the gallery, the only sounds, the echoes of his footfalls on marble. Grayson said, "That's when you are supposed to say, "I like you too, Grayson."

"Tell you what, I'll let you know at the end of your art appreciation class."

"So, this is my tryout?"

"A restaurant server and part time model with a high school education dating a college professor. We don't have much else in common. I'm pretty sure I know where this is going, just a matter of how soon we get there."

"You say the quiet part out loud, Coree, but I'm just happy to hang with you."

"K."

We stood in front of a huge red and orange canvas, much taller than me. "This is a Mark Rothko," "What do you think?"

"What should I think, Grayson?"

"I mean, first impression, do you like it?"

"Sure, it brightens up a room."

"Second impression?"

"A four-year-old could've made it."

"Ahh, it might seem so at first observation, but there's more to it, to all of these." Off we soared into the intricacies of Rothko, Jackson Pollack, Mondrian, Kandinsky, Picasso, and on and on.

"Grayson, this is fun, so interesting, especially after being the subject in the morning. They seem so simple, but there's much more to them and there's much more to you."

"Thanks, Coree. So, are you liking me yet?"

"Don't rush me."

"I'll remember that." He tugged at his ear and smiled. "When do you model again? Is it often?"

"I got a shoot for Valerie's Closet coming up. You know it?"

"I think so...kind of an avant-garde type of place, risqué?"

"I don't know what it is. This agent set it up. She said she's making up for the kiddie shoots."

"Pretty sure it will. You might want to check their web site. Have you ever been in a shoot you were uncomfortable with?"

"Once in a while there's weirdos hanging around, but mostly, like any other business, everybody's got a job to do."

"It sounds fun."

"You meet different people, wear different clothes. It's never the same, but the money's undependable. I just go where the story takes me. This new agent is all up into me, though. She says she is going to get me a lot of work. Sus."

"I want to watch a shoot sometime. I'd like to see how they construct the pictures and layouts. It's really a form of art, isn't it, in the end?"

"Spose, making ads people want to look at."

"Maybe I can meet more hot models there."

I laughed. "It's not about being 'hot,' Grayson."

"Well, you're hot."

"Thanks, but it's about having a certain look. I have a look they want for certain products, and they think resonates with certain markets."

In the huge echoing foyer, I took him over to one side, ostensibly to ask about a piece of art, but when we got there, I put my hands on each side of Grayson's waist to get a feel of his form, his temperature. "Jury's in. I like you, but listen, my friend is having surgery. I won't be available for a bit, but I'm down for another art lesson if you are."

"Absolutely."

"I found this fascinating and you're a good teacher." He wrapped his arms around my neck when I stretched up on my toes to kiss him.

We passed through gold doors, so heavy they nearly took both of us to push open. "I'll see you, soon I hope, Coree." We shared one more kiss in front of the marble pillars, before he turned one direction for his BMW, and I turned in the other for my Chevy.

24

Elizabeth

As provisional director of operations in my absence, Michael and I discussed issues privy only to the two of us, long into the afternoon, so many contingencies I found uncomfortable to let go of. The two of us remained at the long conference table, and when I straightened my papers and laptop to rise, he asked, "Anything new on the promotion?"

I shrugged. "The timing is awkward.

"With your impending absence?" he said. "But that shouldn't be an issue, should it?"

"I hope not, just a little forced time off."

"What's their timeframe, if you don't mind me asking?"

I rubbed my fingertips against my forehead.

"Are you stressed? It's a big step, a big move."

I glanced at the pictures of my sisters, their families and Coree passed through my thoughts.

The intercom caused me to jump. "Ms. Ransom, Mr. Landon Parks is on the line."

My eyes refocused, my mind following. "I'm not taking calls from him, Chelsea. You know that."

"He's a little insistent."

"Get rid of him."

Michael raised his eyebrows.

"He's-"

"Chelsea, if you can't handle it, have Leah do it. That will be all."

We sat for a moment, letting the dust clear until Michael said, "I understand his contracts have been terminated."

"That's right."

"That could be costly, getting a new supplier."

"Couldn't be helped," I said, waving it away.

"When will your promotion be public? Everyone will be happy for you."

"Will they really be happy for me, Michael?" I said, nodding toward my door.

"Of course. Why would you even ask that?"

"Because, you know how I can be."

He furrowed his brows. "We're all grownups here, Elizabeth. They respect you and what you've done...what you do every day of your life."

"Every day," I repeated more to myself.

"No one gives more of themselves to Landford-Smithson."

His words echoed in my head. What a great headstone I'll have. "Elizabeth Ransom, She Loved her Corporation."

When he rose to leave, I rose with him and did the unthinkable, I hugged him. "It'll be fine," he said, holding me. "Everything'll be fine." I held on too long. My life crashed inside me, like a sink hole giving way, snapping at my secretary, my trivial argument with Dianne, melting down in front of Coree, the surgery, and driving my people so relentlessly hard, always driving them so hard that the board of directors has rewarded me with my life's achievement. What a cruel irony. I have sacrificed everything in my life for this, and now I have nothing else.

My thoughts culminated in a moment of unexpected weakness. Holding a man, for the first time since... I couldn't even remember. How utterly pathetic. The feeling of solid masculine arms elicited unexpected sensitivity inside me. I pulled back to face him, inches away, and my eyes fell headlong into his. Placing a hand on the warm skin of the back of his neck, I pressed my lips into his, a kiss not intended, and one that never, ever should have happened. My body against his, I became aware of his arm around my waist, and the delicious feel of being pulled tighter. I did one unthinkable thing after another. First the hug, then the kiss, and now my mouth opened to his, my tongue searching. I pressed hard, and was not disappointed. All the pent-up years released into that one kiss, that press against his body.

I feared pulling away, having to open my eyes, for losing the long-lost passion unleashed inside me, for losing his taste and his smell, but I also feared our reactions. Where do we go from here? What are we now?

Eventually, of course, we did part. His patient blue eyes displayed the same desire surging within me, but I averted my own. "I'm sorry, Michael. I'm so sorry. I don't know what happened to me. I-"

"It wasn't all you, you know."

"I initiated it. I take responsibility for it."

"Elizabeth, you're a human being. Human beings have needs...even you."

I understood what he meant because if he would have pushed my raging vulnerability, we might have done it right there in my office, damn Landford-Smithson, damn the surgery, and damn my tortured life. I lowered my head and said, "Please excuse me now before I make even more of an ass of myself."

Touching a finger to the bottom of my chin, he rose my face till our eyes met again, and he gave me a last quick kiss, which I did nothing at all to avoid. "Good luck tomorrow. We'll all be thinking about you. I'll be thinking of you." His blue eyes gave me one parting shot.

At my desk with my face in my hands, I said, "What have I done? What in the world have I done? My subordinate, my direct subordinate, ten years my junior, married, a wonderful wife, children. As if I don't have enough problems, I bring more upon myself. What in God's name is wrong with me?"

Chelsea stuck her head in the doorway to ask something and, without looking up, I said, "Please leave me for a few minutes."

My appeal had the opposite effect intended, and she ran to me.

"What's the matter, Ms. Ransom?" Are you alright? You want me to call help?"

"No, no. I'm alright. I'm just having...I need some alone time to regroup." Nowhere in this existence at that particular moment, however, could I even envision what a regrouping from my current insanity would look like. What happens now? How am I supposed to discuss policy, give him directives, talk business, when that one provocative moment of our lips pressed together, our eyes gazing into each other's, and our bodies pressed against one another, washed it all away, covered everything, like a huge debilitating wave? All these years destroyed in one moment. And

I felt Michael against me, his arousal. Thank God, he couldn't feel mine. The room became oppressively warm.

"Coree, I need to go home."

"What? What's going on?"

"I need to go home. Right now."

"You alright?"

"I have to get out of here. I'll meet you downstairs."

"You having pains?"

"No. I did something stupid, epically stupid. I need to get out of here now. Please come for me." I held the palm of my hand against my forehead a moment before pulling it back and smacking my forehead with it.

"I can't wait to hear about it," she said.

"I don't think I can tell you."

"That bad?"

"You have no idea."

"Lady, I've done some pretty stupid things in my life. I'm like the queen in that department. Pretty sure I can beat whatever you did."

I pushed around the gold revolving doors, and the sun temporarily blinded me until I escaped behind the veil of my tinted windows.

"What's up?"

"I don't want to talk about it." In my mind, I could picture rows of faces at the glass watching Ms. Elizabeth Ransom, senior vice president, escaping her disgrace. The reality hit even harder. The glass building reflected me, my car anyway, the car which contained the senior vice president, the senior vice president who inexplicably lost control of herself today.

Coree glanced over. "Pretty sure you do."

"No," I mumbled and stared into the palms of my hands.

"Don't make me beat it out of you."

"I deserve a beating."

"Wow. That bad. See, now you have to tell me. You can't leave me hanging like that."

"I'll take this to the grave."

"Oh, bull. How bad can it be? Security didn't escort you out." After a block or two, she said, "Let's grab take out at Billie Jeans' since you have to start fasting pretty soon."

I nodded.

"What do you want?"

"You decide. I'm sure I'll screw that up too."

She laughed at me. Coree straight up laughed at me, yet again. When we pulled into the parking lot, she said, "Change of plans, let's go in and eat."

"Someone might see me."

"Oh, stop. No one knows what you did. I don't even know. Plus, it's still early. Hardly anyone's here yet."

25

Coree

"Do you realize I've never eaten here before, I mean as a guest, during open hours?" I squeezed Elizabeth's arm. She pulled away from my grasp. "Aubrey's here. We can sit in her section." I touched her arm again. This time she didn't yank herself away like I carried some contagious disease.

"Hi, Aubs. Ms. Ransom is having her Last Supper." Seemed like a good joke there, but the two of them gave me nothing but silence to work with. "I'll have Merlot, and she'll have a double scotch."

Elizabeth looked away. "No alcohol allowed tonight."

"Oh, yeah. Bring us tea, Aubrey. How am I going to pull the good stuff out of you if you can't drink?"

"You're not," Elizabeth said.

"Yes, I am."

"No, you're not."

"What if I tell you one of my darkest secrets?"

"No," she said through clenched teeth and looked off into space.

When Aubrey brought pasta pillow hors d'oeuvres, I said, "Elizabeth here, Ms. Ransom, did something stupid and won't tell me what it was. I said I'd tell her one of mine if she did."

Aubrey laughed. "You're the queen. Tell her about Josh and Danny."

"Shut up, Aubrey."

She walked away chuckling. "Enjoy," she said in a sing-song voice.

"Josh and Danny?" repeated Elizabeth.

"I don't want to tell you about that...or, we make a deal and trade stories?"

"I don't think so."

Though we ate mostly in silence, I enjoyed the Elizabeth experience, people watching Billie Jean's. "Dinner tastes better when you share it. Don't you think?"

She totally ignored what I thought was a great observation, but peeked under the table.

"What are you looking at?" I said.

"You seemed taller. I looked under to confirm my suspicions. You are sitting on your legs, your feet, in Billie Jean's of all places."

"So?"

"I used to sit like that," she said, "a long, long time ago."

"Try it again."

Elizabeth ignored me.

"You don't allow anything arbitrary in your lifestyle, do you? It might be good for you, doing something silly. Elizabeth, how come you talk so formal all the time, was not, do not?"

"They are called contractions, and my mother did not allow them."

"That's kind of over-the-top control isn't it, if that doesn't offend you, talking about your mother?"

"Yes. It is over-the-top control, and I could not care less what you say about my mother, at all."

I raised my eyebrows to that, but went on. "What's the big deal about contractions? To me it makes you sound all serious."

"That's me, serious little Elizabeth Ransom."

"Serious little Elizabeth Ransom? What's that mean?"

"That's what kids used to call me, but not anymore, evidently."

"No?"

She patted her mouth with her olive-green napkin, and still covering her mouth, she said, "I kissed Michael Kent."

Mid swallow of tea, I coughed. "What? What do you mean?"

"I kissed him. Pretty easy to understand, isn't it?" she said, straightening her silverware.

"Well, not really. What do you mean you kissed him? Why would you do that?"

"Because I'm out of my mind."

"You mean like kissed him on the cheek?"

"No, on the lips."

"Why? Why would you even do that, Elizabeth?" I sat up higher on my feet, almost standing on my knees.

"You already asked me that. I don't know. It's one for the ages and Coree, please sit down in your seat. I feel like I brought my toddler to dinner."

I tried to sit down, but it was too exciting. "What did he do?"

"Oh, he kissed me right back," she said, shaking her head, fingertips of each hand to each temple. "We held each other and kissed."

"Why?" I said, blinking.

"I don't know, I tell you." She hit the table causing the silver to rattle.

We glanced around, but no one noticed, what with the place being nearly empty. I regrouped and said, "That's pretty wild, girl. How was it?"

"That is not the point. That is not the point at all, Coree."

I laughed, but picked at the edge of my placemat, searching for a way to broach the next question. "Low key observation here, but is he married?"

Elizabeth reached over and swatted my hand away from the placemat. She gazed up at the prisms of the chandelier above and began counting off on her fingers, "He certainly is married, with children. He is my subordinate, my direct subordinate, ten years younger, and..." She picked up her napkin and threw it down on the table again. "I can never go back there."

"Because of a kiss?"

"Because of a kiss?" she repeated in a mocking sing-song tone.

"Have you guys been doing anything else?" A tray of silver exploded onto the floor outside the kitchen door, and we both jumped.

"No, we haven't been doing anything else." She said it in an icy tone that could have taken down an entire combat platoon. "I'd like to think it was just a case of my hormones freaking out under pressure, and I latched on to the 'big strong man,'" she said with air quotes.

"And his response?"

"As I said, he kissed me back alright."

I fiddled with my rings. "Lit."

"No, Coree. It is not, as you say, 'lit.'"

Elizabeth grimaced, and I reached over to take her hand. My bright pink nails said, "Here I am." Her neutral shade shouted back, "Selfdiscipline."

"It's alright to be human and hey, you're not yanking your hand away from me, so we're making progress." I pushed it by lacing my fingers into hers. "Elizabeth, I'm going to miss you when you're in the hospital."

She nodded, one small nod, looking at our hands.

Aubrey appeared when Elizabeth had excused herself to the Ladies room. "Holding hands at the table, Coree?"

"Aubrey, it's whatever. She's under a lot of stress."

"Just playing you, girl. I can imagine, what with surgery tomorrow and all. Hey, where's your nose stud?"

I touched the spot. "Elizabeth doesn't like it."

"Oh. Elizabeth doesn't like it... and just like that, it's gone."

"Don't be salty. How's Jade? Never mind. The crashy look on your face tells me all I need to know. Still in the love boat."

"To spill the tea," I said, in the car, on our way home, "my boyfriend at the time, Josh, well he and I were torching it up pretty heavy one night, in more ways than one, and his friend Danny came over...and let's just say the rest is history. Now you know one on me."

"You mean?"

I nodded. "You see, Elizabeth, your stupid kiss is kind of trivial, isn't it?"

We rode the rest of the way in silence.

When I climbed in bed, she sighed and rolled away from me to the far edge. A moment later, Lily jumped in between us. "How the hell did this happen?" she said to the far wall. "It used to be my bed."

"Just like that, you're a mom." And while we laid there in silence, that made me think of my own mom, and then Josh and Danny, and all the other crazy things I did, and people I did them with, and thinking of Mom again, I soon became dewy-eyed. If you would have been there, Mommy, I wouldn't have done all that stuff. I tried to take care of you, make you better, but you left me. You left us.

"What are you crying about, Coree? Stop it. Stop it right now."

I rolled away from her and faced the wall. Clutching handfuls of sheets, I pressed them to my mouth. "Elizabeth?"

"What?" She answered in her usual no-nonsense tone.

"Elizabeth, I'll take care of you."

The only response was Lily's purring between us.

"Let me help you, Elizabeth."

A few long moments passed until she said, "Sure, Coree."

***

"So how did you and our sister become such close friends?" asked Jo. I scanned the waiting room artwork and the gold-trimmed furniture, wondering how it helped all the sick people get well. I couldn't see a huge difference between this artwork and some of the pieces in the museum, although much of that attributed, no doubt, to my ignorance.

"I'm her regular server at Billie Jean's, if you know the place."

"Sure, we've been there, once or twice when we've visited," said Allison.

"And when she foots the bill," said Jo.

"Right? She's in there at least three times a week. We sort of hit it off and became friends."

"Elizabeth never did take the time to cook," said Allison, who had a rounder face and body than her sister's. She had warm eyes and an equally warm laugh.

"Three times a week," Jo repeated, eyebrows up. "How much does it cost to eat there?"

"You could drop fifty without a problem, a hundred. I know I couldn't ever afford to eat there. Actually, I ate there for the first time yesterday, as a customer. Elizabeth took me."

Jo eyed me. "Is that right?"

"Of course, she's on her own," said Allison. "Imagine if Jeremy and I and the kids went there." She raised her hands in mock surrender.

"How many children do you have Jo?"

"Three. We both have three. Elizabeth could have had children too. She made choices."

"Jo," said Allison.

"Just saying."

"Well, don't."

Jo turned to me, an eyebrow raised. "So, a server and an executive. That's quite a combination."

"It's not a combination. We're friends."

"I suppose. It's not her usual friendship though."

"She doesn't have a usual friendship, Jo," said Allison, who turned to me. "Our Elizabeth always had acquaintances, colleagues, rather than what the rest of us might call friends."

"Yeah?"

"Growing up, when her own friends were dating," Allison said, "Elizabeth studied. Like she'd come to watch us play sports with her homework, and I suppose her efforts created this world all her own."

"Still," said Jo.

"Stop," Allison said.

"She didn't have to-"

"Stop it," said Allison. I watched her eyes nervously dart from Jo's to me and back to her sister. "When Jo and I had children, Elizabeth doted on them, still does, showering them with expensive toys. She's even created college accounts for each of them, six college accounts. She's made a lot of money, and she's been generous, extremely generous, wouldn't you say, Jo?"

"Yes, Allison," she agreed, not taking her eyes off me. "So, I understand you're watching her house while she's in the hospital?"

"And her cat or cats. She has kittens."

"Interesting."

26

Elizabeth

"Look at the flowers. Your staff must love you," Coree said.

I shrugged. "If they like me this much, perhaps I can drive them even harder."

"You're joking, right?" Coree walked around feeling the white daisy petals between thumb and forefinger and stroking across the top of the tight, but delicate roses. "I mean, I hope you're joking. You said it with a straight face though."

"I'm not sure."

"What about that Michael Kent? Did he send a huge bouquet?"

"Please don't. I feel so ugly and weak, like, what's affection?"

"I like the pictures too. Must be from your nieces and nephews. Children's art is the best," she said, before biting her lip.

"Everything alright at home?"

"Just fine. Lily and the girls are doing great. Their eyes might be open by the time they let you out of here."

"I suppose you're sleeping in my bed."

She nodded. "Right in your spot, and there's not a damn thing you can do about it."

Even my eye roll hurt.

"Tomorrow, I have a shoot. I don't know how long it'll take. It's for a place called Valerie's Closet."

I turned my head. "Valerie's Closet? Hmmm."

"What?"

"Do you know about the place?"

"No. Grayson said to look it up, but I didn't yet."

"So," I said, "look it up."

"TSC," she said, eyes on her phone.

I just stared at Coree until she gave me the translation.

"That shit crazy."

"It's none of my business, but be careful. Don't...don't do anything that will...close any other opportunities. You understand?"

"This new agent has promised me a lot of work."

"Nevertheless, if it doesn't feel right, it probably isn't."

"Yes, Mom," Coree said.

I winced a little and pushed the painkiller button to my IV.

Coree took my hand and kissed it. "On another subject," I said and took a breather before pushing ahead. "My little sister is, shall we say, suspect of your motives."

"My motives?"

"Why we are friends?"

"Oh?"

"I told her you think I'm lit."

"No, you didn't."

"No, I told her to mind her own business."

Coree did that search thing into my eyes. "Elizabeth, I don't have any...motives, other than I like you."

"I think there is more."

"What do you mean?"

"Do you have some neurotic need to take care of people?"

I shrugged. "Elizabeth, it's not that I want to take care of people," I said it with air quotes. "I want to take care of you."

"And how does one account for that?"

"I want you to be better. You think everything is transactional? You think I want something in return for taking care of you?"

I studied her a moment until heavy lids fell again. The lonely beeps of the monitors were the only sounds against the silence until she said, "What's the worst thing that can happen to a twelve-year-old girl?" With effort, I pushed my eyelids open to see my bubbly, young friend had become pensive. "Daddy still hasn't recovered. I don't think he ever will or even wants to."

A nurse fussed around me for a few moments, checking tubes. When she left, Coree said, "I just turned twelve when it started. She was gone before I turned fourteen. I did everything I could...fed her, washed her, combed her hair, dressed her, read to her. I think in my mind, the more I did, somehow, I could keep her. Daddy 'bout pulled his hair out, frantic, but I kept on. I skipped school all the time to be with her."

The bed moved, and I looked to see Coree's face pushed into the coverings on the side. "I did everything for her, everything...and I still lost my mother."

The damn pain meds...they helped the pain, but I wanted to communicate, so I motioned for her to come near. "What did you read to her?" I mouthed.

"What did I read to her?"

I nodded.

"Well, I read a lot of things. The one I remember most was *Charlotte's Web*."

I managed a wan smile.

"You know that book?"

I nodded.

"Mom read it with me lots of times growing up. At first, she read, and I listened. We always stopped and talked about each of the illustrations. As I learned to read, we took turns on paragraphs and when I got better, pages." Coree slid her hand underneath mine, and lifted it a little, as if to examine it. Her pink nails stood out among our white skin. "In her last days, I read it to her one last time. I don't know if she heard it. I'd like to think she did. Do you remember the part when the little baby spiders fly away, calling 'goodbye?'"

I nodded again.

"Mommy loved that part." Coree burst out crying, burying her sobs into the white blanket on my legs. I managed a weak stroke of her hair. When she calmed, I moved the back of my hand to her mouth hoping she would kiss it and she did.

27

Coree

"So, the shoot. I had a great time and met some interesting people."

Elizabeth peered over her reading glasses.

"Your disapproving look is coming back."

"I can think more clearly without all the pain meds."

"Hey, Lily misses you."

"How can you tell?"

"When she's not with the kittens, she sleeps in your spot."

Elizabeth groaned. "That cat is sleeping on a blend of high threadcount cashmere and Egyptian cotton-"

"And she's happy."

Elizabeth groaned again. "It's going to be all hairy. Those sheets are hundreds and hundreds of dollars. I'm also going to bet you haven't been making the bed."

"You sound like our Sammi. Come home, so you can lay down the law."

"I hope work at Landford-Smithson is going better than my house."

"Chelsea is sending some documents up this afternoon, but don't push yourself. You know, Elizabeth, you have nice hair. It reminds me of my mom's. You shouldn't always keep it pinned up."

"Maybe Michael would like it down."

"Hah. Now you're laughing about it. Is he hot, Elizabeth? Is this Michael Kent hot?"

Elizabeth made a noncommittal shrug.

"About the photo shoot. Let me just say this. They had some wild clothes and some wild models I hadn't met before. You thought I had a lot of tattoos? You should've seen a couple of the models, lit up. I don't know where they came from. Well, actually, I think I do. In the dressing room, we talked a bit. Some were vanilla like me, but some had experience, and I mean experience, sex shots and videos, danced at clubs, and so on. They were all super nice though. I see the look you're giving me, but it paid good money."

"Nevertheless."

"And she says there is more work next week."

"With all your clothes on?"

I nodded. "Regular stuff."

"So..." she hung that powerful little word out there for suspense with eyes over her glasses. I tried to prepare for the shot I knew Elizabeth was about to fire. "You exposed yourself in pictures in front of these strangers?"

"Not much, a little, not too much."

She shook her head, eyes beating me down.

"Elizabeth, it's just business."

"What did you show?"

"Just my top a little on a couple shots. They wanted my innocent look, but with the naughtiness, you know, my tats contrasting with the...."

Elizabeth looked away.

"You're not happy with me, are you?"

"It's your life."

"I don't think a couple tit shots are gonna ruin my career."

She sighed. "It might close other opportunities, and I don't like it."

"What do you know about modelling?"

"I know about life, Coree. I know about life. And is that all you did, a couple of," Elizabeth hesitated, looking like she just bit into a lemon, "tit shots?"

"Mostly."

She shook her head and cleared her throat while I twisted at my rings. "Does this Sharon Blaze have your best interest at heart?"

"What do you mean?"

"She's making money off this stuff, isn't she?"

"Of course, she's making money. We're all making money. Money's what it's all about." Elizabeth had an instinct for when to let quarrels pause for fermentation, and I was all too aware I couldn't go toe to toe with her. I pulled my hair back behind my ear. "This feels like arguing with my mother."

"Well, what would she say?" Elizabeth's eyes bored into me. When I didn't answer, she asked again. "What would your mother say, Coree?"

This is what a boxer must feel like when a hard punch blasts in by surprise.

"Answer me," she said.

Damn. This was worse than my mom. And yet, it took me back to the last time my mom got into me, throwing tomatoes at the chickens. I not only wasted our garden tomatoes, but it was mean to the chickens, and I sat there on the front steps with my head down listening to her. It was at the beginning of her sickness, and she never reprimanded me again after that. Did she know already? Did she not want to be remembered for disciplining me? But now that Elizabeth was taking me down, I realized it is part of love, part of being a parent, and it had been so long since I had that. I'd just run wild ever since. Elizabeth shredded me, made me feel shame, and yet somewhere deep inside, I embraced it. I pulled it close to me and held it tight.

Elizabeth rapped her open hand on the bed rail to get my attention.

I glanced up at her and back down at the floor. I had no answer, none that I knew she wouldn't destroy. Is this what she does to her employees?

"I want to see these pictures."

I glanced up through my bangs.

"Actually, I don't want to see them, nevertheless, I feel I should find out what is going on."

"You think you're going to start telling me what shoots I can do?"

"Mind your tone to me, Coree." She gave me that over-the-glasses withering look again, and I studied the linoleum again, noting every speck of dust.

"I've never seen any of your professional work. Bring them in."

My shoulders slumped. "Fine."

"I'd also like to meet this Sharon Blaze person."

I glanced up. "Seriously?"

Her eyes shot me right back down.

"Alright, alright, alright," I said. "You can come watch sometime. Maybe you can model. Everyone has a look. You can be the disapproving-mom look."

Elizabeth ignored my comment. How can someone be so talented at ignoring? She obliterates me with her lines, but my own words seem to melt in thin air on their way back to her.

"You know, I'm not as inexperienced as I look."

"I'm not interested in that." Elizabeth peered into her laptop screen as if I was about the tenth most interesting thing she had going in her life at that moment.

"Well, too bad. I'll tell you. I'm twenty-three, almost twenty-four."

Clicking laptop keys, she said, "I guess you have all the answers in life, then."

"I didn't say I was proud. I've done some stupid things. I'm talking to you, Elizabeth. Can you at least pretend to listen to me?"

She looked at me, and now I wished she didn't.

"Well, don't be like that. I just...it's just that..."

"Go on, Coree."

"Well, I want to tell you that after my Mom died, I was depressed and alone and the older I got, the wilder, partying, sexually active, you know?" Elizabeth's knit brows, eyes peering over her glasses, were not an easy audience, either disapproving or uninterested, maybe both, or maybe something else entirely. "I just wanted you to know. I was lost. Feeling alone, I had nowhere to turn." We sat in the quiet, serenaded by the beeping monitors, until I looked up to her and said, "It sounds like you had some bad times yourself."

She nodded and said, "Different."

"Do you want to talk about it?"

"Not really."

"You keep it bottled up until you about blow apart like you did that one day."

Elizabeth nodded.

"You gotta play the cards you're dealt," I said. "Can't show weakness."

"What's that acid tone for?" Elizabeth asked.

"My daddy. You sound like him. He's like, 'Talking about it is for weaklings.'"

"He's right."

"No, he's not right, Elizabeth. He's wrong. I needed someone to talk to. Look at me. I'm a mess. We're both a mess."

"Speak for yourself. I'm surviving."

"Is that what that was in the back of the McDonald's parking lot the other day, surviving? I thought your head was going to spin right off your body. How often does that happen?"

Now Elizabeth broke eye contact.

"I guess you're right though," I said, shaking my head. "You're surviving." I scrutinized her while she ignored me some more.

The incessant beeping of the monitors filled in the background until Elizabeth said, "I am transactional."

"What?"

"I am what you said, transactional."

"Why are you telling me that?"

"Because you are helping me, taking care of me, and the first thing I considered is what do you get out of it."

I tucked an ankle under my thigh.

"It's a bad way to try to construct a social life. Maybe that's why my social life is pretty much nonexistent." Elizabeth waved it away and said, "but it is what it is."

"It is what it is? That's a stupid saying, stupid AF. 'It is what it is' is the stupidest saying there is."

"It fits."

"'It is what it is' is for lazy people, people too lazy to change. You're a lot of things, Elizabeth, but you're not lazy. You make it happen. That's your life."

"Maybe I'm emotionally lazy, then."

"Would you help me if I got in trouble, Elizabeth?"

She blinked.

"At least you could lie and say yes," I said.

"I'd like to think that I would."

I imitated her. "I'd like to think that I would."

Elizabeth frowned. "Okay, you made your point."

"What point?"

"I'm a mess too."

"I mean, it could be worse," I said. "You're sitting on buttloads of cash, a great house, and a great job."

"Coree, you are helping me with my physical issues, and I am grateful, as grateful as I am capable of being, but if your ulterior motive is to help my...mental or social problems, you can forget it."

I tilted my head.

"I'm fifty. What you see...this is...well, it is what it is."

"So, you're just going to run out the clock, live out a miserable life, alone in your mansion until it's time to pack it in."

"It's not a mansion, and I'm not miserable."

"But don't you have hopes and dreams? We all do. It sounds like you want something out of life. Don't give up on them."

"You have no idea what my hope is and how utterly impossible it is to attain." The sudden ice in her tone startled me. "No idea."

"Maybe you could tell me. Maybe I could help you."

Elizabeth looked away.

"You so resist revealing yourself. Well, don't give up on it."

"I might as well just run out the clock." She picked at the edge of her bedding.

"A team runs out the clock when they're winning, not when they're losing."

Right when I made my good point, my roommates burst into the room. "Elizabeth, this is Sammi, my other bud. She's an overachiever like you," I said with a laugh, "and dating a minor-league baseball player."

"Along with everyone else, probs," she sulked.

"Not going well?" I said.

"Not seeing him much."

"What about the other thing?"

Sammi made a sour face.

"What's the 'other thing?'" Elizabeth asked.

Aubrey's eyes darted from person to person. "We should be cheering your friend up, not bringing her our problems."

"What's the other thing?" Elizabeth repeated, eyes boring into Sammi above her glasses.

"Watch out. Elizabeth's in her mom mode today," I said. "Combine it with her board room demeanor, and she can take us all down, easily."

"You're late, aren't you?" she said to Sammi.

"Damn. She is sharp," said Aubrey, and Sammi herself, now took an interest in the linoleum.

Aubrey tried to lighten it up with her usual stupid response. "See, I keep telling you guys. Jade and I never have this problem."

Elizabeth regarded her in confusion.

"Aubrey likes to throw her queerness in our faces when the straight life fails." I glanced over and noticed Jo just inside the door.

"How's my big sister?"

"Getting stronger. I didn't know you were coming up."

"I wanted to surprise you, but it looks like you have plenty of young admirers."

28

Elizabeth

"So, what's this all about? Why are these young girls hanging around you?"

"First of all, mind your tone to me, little sister."

"I won't. Who are they? I listened from the doorway. One's late on her period. One's a lesbian, and who knows what this little Coree is into, hanging on you."

"I practically run a corporation. Don't you think I know what's going on in my life?"

"Maybe being sick is making you let your guard down. Libby, I don't want them taking advantage of you."

"Oh lord. Listen to you. Little Jo doesn't want me to be taken advantage of. What a laugh."

"What's that supposed to mean? And I'm not little."

"You know exactly what it means."

"Just because I didn't finish college like my over-achieving sister, who no one can ever hope to measure up to anyway."

"Finish college? You barely started before you...oh, whatever. Just don't lecture me, little sister."

"I hate that when you call me little sister. It's so condescending."

"It was meant to be. Remember your place."

"Dammit. I drove an hour to come see you, and this is what happens."

"Don't come up here telling me what to do."

"Yeah, that's the first rule of talking to Elizabeth Ransom, isn't it? Don't ever tell her what to do."

"If you know the rule, why are you breaking it?"

Jo frowned. "You're lucky you're sick. I'd tell you what I really think of you right here and now."

"Whatever," I said with a wave of my hand.

"Libby, can't you lighten up for one minute. Why..." A nurse came in to check vitals forcing us into an intermission. "You always have to push us around, bully us. We're your sisters."

"My little sisters," I said, with heavy emphasis on the "little."

"Why? Every time. You say that every time. Can't we just be sisters?"

"Maybe we could have in another life, but we," I channeled Coree's words, "all had to play the cards we were dealt, didn't we?"

"We're grown up now. We got through it. Just because you're so much older than us, doesn't mean you're some surrogate mom, at least not anymore."

"Yes, it does. It is what it is." I realized that this time, I used the phrase that Coree referred to as the stupidest ever, but I doubled down on it. "It just is what it is, Jo."

"Are you kidding me? Tell me you're kidding me. I'm married with three children. You're not my mother."

"Did you come up here to brighten my day or take me back down memory lane? Evidently the latter, so here it is, clear and simple. I didn't ask for what life laid on me. I didn't have a choice, did I? Well, you wouldn't know. You were barely walking."

"Like forty years ago." Jo threw up her hands. "I can't believe this. We're going to rehash this yet again, and right here in the hospital? I cannot believe you."

"Believe it, Jo. You can't even afford to save money for your kids to go to college."

"What has that got to do with it? I can't believe this," she repeated, looking around the room as if all the hospital technology had answers to our family issues. "Why do I even come up here to see you?"

"Because you love me...like a mom, and you know I'm right." But as my patience thinned, my face heated. "By God, if I felt better, I'd be out of this bed and give you something you'd surely remember."

"I'm forty," she said. "Are you out of your mind?"

"I don't care how old you are. Don't you show me attitude, Jo."

"You haven't changed one bit."

I waved her off again.

"From the snotty, domineering teenager who bossed us around."

"I raised you two." I pointed at Jo and wherever Allison was, an hour away. "My whole teenage years and beyond raising you two. You're welcome. How many dates did I have? Zero. How much time with my friends? Zip, and you call it bossing you around. You're welcome."

Coree popped in, eyes darting back and forth. "Sorry. I think I left my phone." She tucked her hair behind an ear. "Yeah, there it is. See you tonight." She flitted out of the room as quickly as she appeared.

"Nice ink," said Jo with a side eye.

"I talked to her about it."

"No doubt you did." Her eyes narrowed and she sucked in a breath. "That reminds me of another happy childhood memory. I'm sixteen. I talk Dad into letting me get a tattoo, just a little, tiny one, and out of the blue, you come home, find out, and just veto it, nullify the whole damn thing right out of hand, as if you're in charge, as if it's any of your business. Remember that, Elizabeth?"

"I certainly do. You were too young, much too young."

"You weren't my mom."

I peered over my glasses at her.

"And you're not my mom now, in case you need a reminder."

"You were my responsibility. Do you honestly think Dad was going to take charge? Do you?"

She threw up her hands again. "I got one later. You couldn't stop me forever."

"You did a lot of things I couldn't stop you from, but I couldn't supervise you twenty-four-seven, even though I didn't go to the university of my dreams. If you remember, I commuted so I could raise you two."

"It's all coming out now, isn't it? Death bed admissions."

"You wish."

"Of course, I don't, but you could at least treat me like an adult. The young men at the store call me 'ma'am' for crying out loud. If I have to have the bad, I'd like some of the good too."

I glanced at Coree's empty seat. "Everybody needs a mom."

"You're my sister."

"Please." I peered over my glasses again.

"I hate it when you look at me that way. You have no right to make me feel like whatever it is you are doing."

"It's been nearly forty years."

"When someone else gave birth to me, not you."

"And she walked out on us, passing you on to me, and Allison too." I pointed at Jo. "You think I asked for that? Do you? I did what had to be done and did the best I could. No one asked me what I wanted."

"We should be on a TV show about toxic sister relationships."

"It's not a toxic relationship. It's the shit life gave us. I've had to do my part. You and Allison have to do yours."

"Libby, you've turned into everything you hated about Mom."

That comment used to knock me off my game, but now I channeled Mom's words, whether I wanted to or not. "Just behave. It's simple. That's all you have to do. That's what I've always told you. Just behave."

"What is wrong with you?"

"You're my baby sister. You can always come to me."

"And sometimes I hate you, Elizabeth."

I let that sit there, let her words hang in the air, weigh her down, with the beeps in the background, before continuing. "I'll always be there for you, Jo. You know that. Always. No matter what. Unlike another person we know or did know. I always was there for you, and I always will be."

Jo's gaze dropped to the linoleum, the third person I had driven to it today, and I took some perverse pride in that. She whispered, "I know," the sign that I had finally bludgeoned her into submission.

"If that husband of yours ever screws up-"

"Like you did with Raymond?"

"You drop that right now, girl."

"Sorry, Libby."

"If that husband of yours ever screws up...again. I'll be there for you...and the kids. You know that. You never have to worry, Jo."

"I know," she said, still studying the floor. "And I'm grateful for that. Allison and I both are, but..."

"But what?"

"No disrespect, Elizabeth." Jo glanced up at me without raising her head. "It just seems weird. They aren't your usual company, and I just want to make sure they are, what do you say, on the up and up."

"For not wanting me to be your mom, you sure are possessive."

Jo sat perfectly still, hands folded in her lap, eyes down.

"I have it under control," I said, and I stretched my hand out to her.

"Always, big sister," she said and kissed the back of my hand.

"That's right, 'always.' Now, if we are through with all this," I said, with a hand moving back and forth between us, "Tell me about the kids? What are they up to?"

Her face lit up. "Let's see. Thomas is busy with the junior high basketball team. You should see him. He looks so serious out there in his little uniform." Jo became animated. "Do you think you could come up and see him play, Elizabeth, I mean, when you're better? I know it's a long way, and you're busy and all, but it would mean a lot to him and to me."

I paused and smiled, "Sure. Send me the schedule."

"Oh, great. Of course, Samantha is eleven, going on eighteen. You know how it is."

"I know." I glanced again at Coree's empty chair.

Jo took my hand. "Libby, I just want you to be better, healthy and all." She kissed my hand again and rose to leave, but paused. "Elizabeth, don't get angry again here, but as I've said before, and I'm just saying this because I love you, I don't think you're ever going to be happy until you deal with the other issue."

I sighed and said, "I hear you. You know I hear you, Jo, but it's not that easy. It's not even close to that easy."

"Elizabeth, you have the power, the connections."

"I know, but then what?" I shook my head. "No, it's too big of a risk. I could lose everything."

"Like what? You don't have anything now. Libby, if you don't ever take the risk..."

I nodded. "Jo, if I had listened to you a long time ago, I wouldn't be stuck like this, but now, well..."

She gave me a little smile. "I had to say it."

"Understood."

29

Coree

"I marked where all the signatures go. She'll figure it out. How's she doing?"

"Saltiness coming back."

Chelsea and I smiled at that.

"How long have you been Ms. Ransom's personal secretary?"

"Over two years now."

"And you're not a whole lot older than me, I'm guessing."

"Pushing thirty."

"Course, we're from different worlds," I said, indicating her appearance. Chelsea possessed an aura all her own or somewhat similar to Elizabeth's, tall, fit, dark hair pinned back, make up done so expertly it didn't look like make up at all, contrasting with me in my usual outfit and face clean. Her lipstick so perfectly matched her complexion that I decided sometime I must ask her about make up.

Chelsea returned the glance at my tee shirt and jeans, so completely out of place at Landford-Smithson, I half expected security to come and toss me out the back door, but she surprised me with her comment. "Occasionally, I wish I had the freedom someone like you has. We all have our place though, don't we?"

"I just go where the story takes me. You could do that, Chelsea. How about blowing this pop stand for a while and getting coffee?"

Chelsea shook her head before I could even finish saying the words. "No. No, I couldn't do that." She motioned to her conference table. "We can sit for a few minutes." With her perfect grammar and articulation, her perfect hands, posture, and power suit, she reviewed the papers for Elizabeth

"You guys' swag blows me away." I ran my hand along the satin surface of the table. "You got a better office than a lot of apartments. This table alone is epic."

Chelsea sat back, a leg smartly crossed, hands laced on a knee. I couldn't tell from her expression if she thought I was a dimwit or a bimbo or what. "Chelsea, Elizabeth will be homebound for a while, not for long, she says."

"Of course."

"Right? Her birthday is coming up, and I want to surprise her with a party at her house. I'll have my own friends there. Would Landford-Smithson people come?"

"Sure, but I don't know anyone who's actually been in her house."

"That's just crazy, but whatever. I wasn't sure if they would come anyway. She can be pretty rigid."

"I haven't seen that side of her," Chelsea said, no expression.

"Wow. You got the same dry sense of humor as Elizabeth, but I didn't know her reputation here well enough, like if she had terrorized everyone."

"It's a love/hate relationship. She runs this place and everyone in it pretty tight as you can imagine, yet she also takes care of us. We know she has our back...if we don't let her down."

"Then, let's do it. If a dozen people from here come, you and Leah and maybe her executive staff?"

"Sure. I'd like that." She lowered her voice. "Leah won't come though."

"No?"

Chelsea raised her shoulders and gave Leah's door a side-eye. "She supposedly works for me, but Elizabeth sometimes gives her special assignments that I'm not even privy to. Actually, I don't think anyone's privy to them, just her and Elizabeth. When Elizabeth moves to Chicago, Leah will follow her in a heartbeat."

A knot formed in my stomach. "When do you think that'll be?"

"You'd have to ask her. You know how she is. Everyone's on a needto-know basis with Elizabeth, but the clock is ticking, right?"

"Right," I said. My mouth dried right up, and my eyes darted around as if the ramifications of what she just reminded me of zipped around the room like lightning bugs.

"Anyway, I can't go with her. I have a husband here. Actually, I might as well go, he's so annoyed at me for working so much."

"Leah would follow her to Chicago," I said, "but not come to her house? What up with that?"

Chelsea shrugged. "The others will come." She walked me toward the door, and we passed back through Leah's office. The outer secretary herself glanced up at me, just eyes over her computer, then to Chelsea, and back down.

Walking down the hall, I said, "Damn! You have to bust through two secretaries to get to her, not even counting the receptionist at the end of the hall. No wonder she sports a major 'tude."

"She's the real deal." At the elevator, Chelsea said, "Coree, let's have that coffee sometime."

"Yeah?"

"Yeah. I could never be like you, but maybe I could get a little of your influence to rub off on me."

"I kind of feel the same about you, Chelsea," I said.

I stood alone on the elevator thinking. I never had a sibling, certainly not an older sister, but I decided that if I did, I would want it to be someone like Chelsea. She so had her act together, goal-oriented, a solid relationship. It wouldn't hurt for a little of all that to rub off on me as well.

***

"The sun. The lawn. It's so perfect."

"I think it's called an outfield."

I frowned. "Whatever, Grayson. I've never been to a game before, but look at you."

"What do you mean, 'Look at me?'"

"Oh, I don't know, the yellow polo, sweater sleaves tied around your shoulders?"

"Children, we're here to have fun," cut in Sammi.

"It's whatever," I said to him. "Maybe they'll think I'm here with the team owner's son."

A vendor bellowed out, "Red hots. Get your red hots," and I ordered us all hotdogs and beer.

"How lit is this?" I said, a little too loud, because people turned and raised their beer in agreement. Through a mouthful of hotdog, I said, "Have you ever been here, Grayson?"

"Not here exactly," he said motioning around us. "Up there." He pointed to the air-conditioned boxes above.

"Figures."

Sammi elbowed me, a little too hard, I thought.

"Sorry, Mom," I said.

"She seems tough," whispered Grayson.

"Sammi's the whole package," I whispered back.

We stood for the national anthem, and I felt Grayson's arm slide around my waist. Glancing up at him, I tried to read his eyes. The damn smile and dimples dazzled me though, and I told myself to keep control, but why should I?"

"Joey hasn't gotten any hits, but he made a couple nice plays," I said, as if I knew a nice play if it landed in my lap. "He looks built."

"He is, Coree. How's Elizabeth doing?"

"As well as can be expected. Thanks for helping me settle her in."

"It's cool. When you were upstairs, she talked with me a little about my," she motioned out to the field, "my sitch."

"Oh?"

"She said if I needed someone to talk to."

"That's something. I wish she would listen to me."

"I'm sure she does, in her own way."

I waved that one off.

"Coree," Sammi whispered into my ear. "Elizabeth said something about acts of passion that get us in trouble, get us all in trouble."

"So?"

"Has Elizabeth had acts of passion?" We both made the same funny face at each other.

I turned to Grayson. "We settled her in downstairs, cats in the closet, me in the room next door."

He nodded without responding.

Sammi whispered in my ear again. "He's the quiet type, isn't he?"

After the game, entering the nearest exit tunnel, I noticed, a few rows up, a girl sitting, happy as a clam, holding a homemade poster with glitter and hearts. It read, "Hi, Joey Thomas." We passed through the tunnel and into the stadium concourse without Sammi noticing it.

"I'm going to go over by the locker room and say hi to Joey before he gets on the bus."

"See you at the car."

Grayson opened the door of his BMW and we stood within it. "When are we going to another museum?"

"You tell me. You're the busy one, with your Elizabeth."

"She's home now and improving. Listen, I'm having a surprise birthday party for her. Just a short affair because she is kind of weak.

Can you do me a solid and stop by?"

He looked down at me, paused, and said, "Sure."

"Great. You can put in an appearance and be on your way, in case you have a date with your Tiffany."

"I want to be with you, Coree, just you, just you and me." He made his move, standing there within the open door of the car. His words, BS or not, pulled my body to him as much as his arms ever could. The line of cars snaked its way out of the parking lot behind us while we shared a moment kissing. His hands traced down to my behind, and he whispered, "I want this."

"Literally or metaphorically?"

Grayson scrunched his eyebrows.

"I mean, is my behind just a metaphor for the whole me, like you want me, or do you literally just want that specific part of my body?" I thought it was a clever comment and a set up for Grayson to make a clever response, but he just smiled.

Sammi rode in silence, but I had to break it, if only to lend support. "Tell me what happened."

She shook her head and averted her gaze.

"Tell me, Sammi."

She groaned. "I'm so stupid. I'm so stupid, stupid, stupid."

In the Ransom driveway, she finally spilled the tea. "Coree, I stood there outside the locker room door, players spilling out here and there among the relatives, wives, girlfriends. A couple reporters asked questions. I just stood there like a girlfriend...not. Across from me, my eyes lit on another girl, white, younger than me probably."

"Blond?"

Sammi turned to me.

"We passed her on the way out. I didn't have a chance to tell you. Sus. I was afraid to tell you, Sammi. I'm sorry."

"She had a poster, all glitter and hearts and shit."

I nodded.

"What if he came out the door, right at that moment? What a train wreck that would have been. I melted back into the crowd. Sure enough, when he came out, they hugged and talked. He gave her a little kiss and left for the bus. Coree, I'm so stupid."

"I'm sorry, Sammi."

"This girl turned and walked right toward me, passed right next to me, close enough to touch, not even knowing me, or that I might even be carrying his baby."

"You don't know that."

"Hell, she might be carrying one too."

"I'm sorry, Sammi."

"A cute young white girl. I'm so screwed. A cute young white girl."

"I don't know what to say. I mean, I don't want to say the wrong thing here, but...I mean..."

"Say it, Coree. Go ahead. Get it out there."

"Well, do you think she's got an advantage because she's white? I mean, I don't know how it works."

"I don't know how it works either," Sammi said, "at least with Joey."

"Well," I stumbled over my words, not knowing which way to go. "Sammi, you've got it all. You're smart, like really smart. You are dropdead beautiful. I don't know how she could compete with you."

"She's white, Coree."

"Joey wouldn't be like that, would he? He couldn't be. You love him. You wouldn't have loved him if..." I stopped and thought about it while she looked away out the side window. "Have you told him you love him?"

"Not exactly, in so many words. Figured he'd be able to tell."

"Oh, okay," I said. "You're giving men a lot of credit on that one."

"What am I supposed to do, lay it out for him?"

"If you love him, tell him, maybe before you lose him."

"You could be right."

"It's possible, but then again, I've blown every relationship I've ever been in, so what does Coree Wysakee know?" We both laughed at that.

"Can I talk to your Elizabeth?"

"My Elizabeth? Sure. I suppose I can share her. Aubrey thinks she's all hard ass."

"She is all hard ass, but maybe I need a strong shoulder to cry on."

"She's a strong shoulder, for sure, but don't go crying to her. Elizabeth doesn't go in for crying. She'll get right into your shit if you start crying. You know, Sammi?"

"What?"

"Well, you're our alpha, you know, around the three of us, but Elizabeth... well, don't tell her I said this, but when I went back to her hospital room for my phone? Remember?"

Sammi nodded

"I eavesdropped outside the room for a while, listening to her talk to her little sister and let me tell you, she ripped that woman a new ass hole."

"Her little sister's not that little."

"No shit and she's like forty. She tried to flex it, tried to stand up to Elizabeth, but by the time they were done, Elizabeth had her blubbering and apologizing, and even begging her to come visit her children. Elizabeth's the boss in that family, and she takes no shit. She wields a hammer. They have some issues."

"What family doesn't?" said Sammi.

"Right? But she's the boss." I dropped to a whisper and picked at my rings. "It's like something happened to her mom."

"What do you mean?"

"I guess up and left."

"You mean walked out on her husband and her kids?"

I nodded. "Elizabeth took over like when she was ten or something. I tried to ask her about it, but she froze me out."

30

Elizabeth

"My house. All those people in my house, the sound seemed so unfamiliar. Coree, girls, thank you for doing this, but I'm worn out."

"Elizabeth, what time were you born?" asked Coree. "Do you know?"

"I don't."

"Ask your dad."

"Why?"

"It's just fun to know...the exact moment. Ask while you still can. The time you were born tells about your personality. Maybe we can find out what's going on in there," Coree said, pointing to her own temple.

"I don't put anything into that theory."

"You want to hear something else freaky?" Coree said.

"I'm sure you'll tell me whether I want to hear or-"

"You and my mother have the same birthday. What's the chances of that?"

"I think we can figure it out. That'll be one in three hundred and sixty-five."

"No, I mean same year too."

"Weird," said Aubrey.

"Agree," I said.

"Hey, what did you think of my new agent?"

"Sharon Blaze? I didn't talk to her much, but I put a face with the name. I'll get with her."

"Elizabeth, you don't need to."

I cut Coree off with a hand. "Drop it for now. And who was that Jade person?"

"That's Aubrey's friend, her very good friend," Coree said in a singsong melody.

Elizabeth nodded.

"What did you think of Grayson?" Coree asked.

"He was like some glamorous movie star from the sixties, back when men were reserved and dignified."

"And how did you think it went with Mr. Kent?"

"Fine," I said, glancing at Sammi and Aubrey.

"What's going on?" asked Aubrey.

"Nothing," I said.

"Ohhhh, okay. That kind of nothing," Aubrey said.

"He saw me with my hair down."

"And I bet he noticed," said Sammi.

"Don't tell her that. Don't encourage her," Coree cut in. "All your executive staff made an appearance. You're such a bad ass, but they like you," said Coree.

"They respect what I do. I don't know if I would go as far as to say they like me, and anyway, they are bad asses themselves."

"They like you," she continued. "At least Michael does. I watched him. I watched his eyes." I smiled, but Coree stomped on my smile. "You need to stop this business, though. When you get back to the office, be the grown up in the room."

"Yeah, Coree," said Aubrey. "You're such a great example."

"Shut up, Aubrey."

Aubrey laughed. "Enjoy." She and Sammi carried dishes to the kitchen.

Coree said, "I overheard one of your people mention a time share in Florida. You going to take her up on it?"

"Dianne Dunning, and I certainly am not."

"Why not?"

"I don't take vacations, and I'll be running the company from home."

"You should get away, get some sun."

"I am needed here."

"Oh, crap to that. They won't let you go back for two weeks. Do a long weekend. You could use it. What's the difference between virtual meetings from down there or from your house?"

"Stop it. I told you-"

"A long weekend, two or three nights, and I'll take care of you, everything."

"Coree, when I tell someone-"

"Please." She interrupted and fell to her knees next to my chair, taking my arm in her hands. "I'll take care of you. I told you I would. It would be so good for you and fun for us."

"Part of having children is...them begging for things?"

Coree lifted herself up and right in the side of my face, close enough to feel her breath, she said, "Elizabeth, I'll take care of you. I'll do everything. I'll never let you out of my sight. You don't think I will?"

"It's not that, and will you please get away from me? Get out of my space."

"Not until you say yes."

"You are being annoying. If you get away from me and stop your badgering, I'll consider it."

"Yay."

"But it will, would be a working weekend."

"Will. You said, 'will.' This is what being a parent is like, Elizabeth. Harp on them until they give in."

I sighed and waved her away, but she wouldn't be waved away.

"I'll look for flights. Hey, what about the other girls? Please, Elizabeth. You already have the whole place. It would be nice for them."

"You said you would take care of me, Coree. Now you are turning it into spring break."

"I won't do anything with them. I told you, Elizabeth, I'm going to take care of you." When I sighed, Coree yelled into the kitchen, "Girls, we're going to Florida." They popped their heads into the living room. "We're going to a timeshare in Florida for a weekend. You guys down for it?"

"Oh, yeah," said Sammi.

"If you can't go to work, how can you go to Florida?" said Aubrey.

"They can't tell me what to do."

"Not Elizabeth Ransom," Coree said.

"And Coree will be taking care of me. With you two along, she can have a break now and then." Coree hugged me. "Get off me, Coree."

"Oh, Elizabeth. Stop it," she said. "Everyone needs a hug once in a while. You do nice things, you get hugs, Elizabeth."

"That's why I don't do nice things."

"I can't believe this," said Aubrey. "I've never been to Florida."

"Coree and I did that spring break down there," said Sammi. "Good times. Coree was totally out of control."

"Can you guys shut up about me in front of Elizabeth? Besides, what happens in Florida, stays in Florida."

31

Coree

We were up, high cap, on the way to the airport, four girls headed to Florida, actually three giddy girls and a dour chaperone in a wheelchair. Loading our bags onto the gold, trolley, something caught my eye. "What's on your forehead, on the side there?" I said to Aubrey.

She pulled her hair over. "Nothing. I banged my head in the shower."

"Let me see."

"No. It's fine."

Her darting eyes told me all I needed to know. "Jade. She's at it again."

"No. I told you Coree-"

"Enough." I said. "Don't you lie to me, Aubrey Smith." I grabbed her shirt collar. "I know you're lying."

Sammi jumped in to pull us apart. "Shut up, you two. You're making a scene right here in the airport."

"What's going on?" demanded Elizabeth.

We stared at each other like a couple of boxers before a match.

"What the hell is going on?" Elizabeth said. "We're not going on a plane if you two are going to act like this."

Aubrey broke the gaze and looked down. I said, "It's nothing. It's all good."

"Don't insult my intelligence," said Elizabeth. "When we get through security and settled in, we'll get to the bottom of this. I'm not getting on a plane to spend the weekend with a couple of lunatics."

The first chance she had, Sammi got right into our faces. "Don't wreck this for us, bitches."

We picked a spot far from any other flyers, Sammi sitting between Aubrey and me. Elizabeth, in a wheelchair, faced us. "Talk," she said. When we hesitated, Elizabeth said, "Back to the car. I'm not putting up with this. I should have listened to Jo about you kids."

Sammi said, "Aubrey is in an abusive relationship."

"Shut up," said Aubrey.

"Girl, don't you ever tell me to-"

Elizabeth shut down Sammi with a wave of her hand and turned to Aubrey. The loudspeaker around us echoed off flight information and those piercing eyes bored into her. "Speak."

Aubrey looked down. Without pulling her guns off Aubrey, Elizabeth said, with a wave of her hand, "You two go for a walk."

We jumped up, more than happy to leave Aubrey to Elizabeth's fury.

"Way to throw the shade and run," I said to Sammi. "Did you know?"

"Who knows what's going on in there? They make so much damn noise. It's hard to say what is...well, it's awkward AF."

"And she just goes back for more, the neurotic need to be shit on."

We drank eight-dollar coffee, looked at fifty-dollar tee shirts, and observed from a safe distance.

"See you there in a minute," said Sammi, disappearing into a restroom.

They sat quietly, no conversation, so I approached and said, "I checked the weather down there, and it looks like it's going to be nice."

"Isn't it always nice there?" said Aubrey, who looked like a wilted house plant.

"Can I get you coffee or something, Elizabeth?" I said.

"Sounds good."

"May I go with her?" said Aubrey.

"Well, let's see," said Elizabeth. "Can you two not get into a brawl in the Starbucks line?"

"We're good."

"A round for all of us," said the returning Sammi.

"Well, Aubs?"

"I'm sorry, Coree."

"I'm sorry, too. You know I care about you. What happened with Elizabeth?"

"Can you imagine being stuck between her and Jade?"

"Why? What happened?"

"She made me spill the tea. When she heard, she got all pissed and made me call Jade and break up."

"Made you? I mean I'm glad, but how'd she make you?"

Aubrey shrugged. "You know how she is. Remember when you first met her, at Billie Jean's, and I said she reminds me of your mom?"

I nodded.

"Well, maybe her looks, but when your mom got mad, you could still feel the love. When Elizabeth gets mad, it's all like, 'Do what I say and do it right now.'"

"And you did it?"

"I left a message. That's the chicken shit way to do it, right? But Jade's at work anyway, and Elizabeth wanted immediate results. 'Make it happen,' she said. I probably won't hear from her till we touch down. The shit'll hit the fan, but I'll be in Florida, afraid of Ms. Ransom. Back home, I'll be scared of Jade."

The long coffee line crawled forward until Aubrey said, "You're right, Coree...about Jade. I mean she has a lot of good qualities. For one-"

"Don't go there, Aubrey."

"Just saying. She's intense."

"I said don't go there."

"Alright, Coree." Aubrey chuckled. "But she can be scary too, like you said."

I nodded. "Jade has that look in her eye sometimes." A couple high school boys in the line made eye contact with us. "What'll happen when we get back?"

Aubrey scrunched her nose at the boys, then me. "I'm not going back. I'm staying in Florida the rest of my life." We inched up a few places. "Or if I'm extremely lucky she'll find someone else. Either way, Aubrey'll be back to no one." With four cups in four hands, we headed back. "Coree, what's the deal with your agent, Sharon Blaze?"

"What do you mean, 'What's the deal?'"

"I mean, does she have a partner?"

"What do you mean. Aubrey?"

"Did the oblivious bus run over your ass or what?'"

"My Sharon Blaze? You mean my Sharon Blaze?"

"How many Sharon Blazes are there? Yeah, your Sharon Blaze. The one who has a crush on you."

My drinks both slid out of my fingers and when the cups hit the white marble floor, their full contents sprayed out in brown lines in front of us.

"Come on. Let's give them these two and go back for more."

"Wait. Are you telling me?" I called, running after her.

"Your gaydar down?"

Seeing our mood when we returned, Elizabeth frowned. "Is this the way it is around you three? I feel like I'm in the bipolar funhouse at the carnival."

"Elizabeth drops these funnies when you least expect it," I said to my friends' confused faces.

"So, back to my question," Aubrey said, but the sight of an unhappy janitor mopping up my mess momentarily distracted us. "People are such slobs," Aubrey said to her. "What's the deal with Sharon Blaze?"

"I think she might have mentioned a significant other. I didn't pay attention."

"So, pay attention, would you? She seems fun."

"She's all kinds of fun. Loud, energetic, funny. When she laughs out loud, like she does, her curvy body nearly busts out of her tight clothes."

"I noticed."

"And she has great clothes and shoes."

"I noticed that too."

"You think she has a crush on me?"

"Doesn't everybody? You didn't think she gave you all this work because of your talent or looks, did you?"

We laughed at that.

32

Elizabeth

Just inside the door of our rental, the light of the sun blasted through sliding doors, lighting up the opposite wall, the furniture, and now us. Beyond those doors, stretched a gray wooden deck with surrounding rails, on which rested a cedar-walled hot tub. Down a half dozen steps, across fifty feet of hot, white sand, the ocean awaited, and the girls, armed with sunscreen, towels, and blankets, piled out.

Sammi and Aubrey stepped out into the Florida sun, but Coree turned to me, "Let's get you to the bathroom and we'll relax on the deck."

Looking out at the ocean, I said, "I'm sorry you have to stay with me, Coree."

"Wow. Who's in there? Who took over Elizabeth's body?"

We emerged onto the deck to be blinded by the bright white sun and deafened by the caws of seagulls. Drinking tea and people watching, I asked, "Why doesn't Sammi model?"

"She has other plans. Besides being beautiful, she's smart, and she's almost done with college, but to be honest, she doesn't have "the look."

"What's 'the look?'"

"There's all kinds, but I have one of them, something unique, agents and businesses see. It's subjective. I just go with the flow, what gets me some green."

"The first time you were my server, I'm afraid, I didn't look at you at all."

"Totally aware, Elizabeth."

I wondered how many other people I'd subjected to my indifference. "I observed your Grayson watching you, though. Remember, with his, what do you call her?"

"Tiffany."

"His Tiffany, but still eyeing you."

"He wanted a little kinky side action," Coree said.

I grimaced at her description of herself that she gave with such a casual laugh.

"It's my look, barely legal."

"Barely legal," I repeated. "I don't like it." I could just make out the sound of waves lapping in the distance.

Coree rose and leaning over the railing a little, pulled off her oversized tee. In her cheeky bikini, I had more of a view than I cared for.

"Everyone has a look though," she said out to the ocean. Looking back at me, she said, "Don't you think? You know, what categorizes them."

"I suppose."

"You suppose?" She turned to me. Below her breasts, barely concealed in little yellow patches of her bikini top, the bottom tattoo she told me about, stood out now on display. Leaning back on the railing, she supported herself on her elbows. "You're so powerful, Elizabeth, so damn powerful. The endorphins swirl around you everywhere you go. If you flexed your power swag, you'd have more action than you ever knew what to do with."

"I don't have time or interest in action."

"Just making a point. Everyone has a look, including you. What's going on with Michael Kent?"

"He's a long, long ways away," I said and looked as far off into the ocean as I could.

"I think you get off on bossing him, Elizabeth."

I rolled my eyes.

"How does he handle it?"

I shrugged. "He takes it in stride."

"Yeah, and then you held him and kissed him and what does he do? He kisses you right back. He gets off on your power, like I do. I mean, I don't 'get off ' on it. It's legit though. Michael, he gets off on it."

"So, you are saying when I take charge and be the boss-"

"Yep. You're turning him on."

"No way."

"Yep. Nice job, boss. Way to excite the help."

"Don't say that."

"I did say it, and I'll tell you what else. I know lots of guys my age who would kill, absolutely kill to go out with you."

"Guys your age? Are you actually suggesting that I go out with men, guys your age, like twenty-five years old?"

"Why not?" Coree said.

"Umm, I can think of lots of reasons."

Coree laughed. "I can too, but seriously, younger guys have a different outlook than your Landon."

"He's not my Landon. I burned that bridge...to the ground."

"I mean, he wants to be the boss," Coree said, "but I know you gotta be the boss."

"That wasn't even the point with that."

"Well, what was the point?"

"The point was, he was rude to you."

"Thanks for the intel."

"And the rest of the point is, I will not allow that."

"Wow. Thanks. I've got a power mom in my corner."

"Evidently," I said, both to Coree and to myself.

Aubrey and Sammi splashed, dots in the distant waves, and the sun warmed my skin. I considered sunscreen, but for a while at least, I wanted the full onslaught, the full vitamin D.

"Elizabeth, why don't you like me?"

"What are you even talking about? I like you."

"You tolerate me, only...I don't think you really like me."

"I just told you I gave that Landon his walking papers because of you, Coree. Keep up. I like you...at least as much as I can like people." The smell of a nearby grill wafted to us on the breeze.

"I want you to think I'm special."

I blew out a deep breath. "Okay, here goes. Coree, I like you, and I think you are special."

"You say it like we're in the boardroom."

"That's the way I talk."

"I bet not always. I bet you've talked with passion."

"I'm not going to talk to you with passion."

"Glad to hear that." She sat, cross-legged beside my chair and took my hand. "Elizabeth, I'll take care of you. Don't you worry about anything."

"Coree, I'm not worried, and I'm not dying. This is routine. It's not pleasant, to be sure, but I'm going to recover."

She murmured something inaudible.

I stroked her hair with my other hand and said, "Oh, Coree." I felt the youthful freshness of her cheek when she pressed the back of my hand to it. We watched the ocean together. What am I going to do with this little mud lark when I am better, when I have work to do, and then I move to Chicago? She asks why I don't like her. Hell, I don't even like myself. How can I like her?

The minute we entered the timeshare, they had claimed their spots. Two rooms, two beds in each. Aubrey chided Coree. "You can sleep in Elizabeth's room, in case you need tucking in.

"Shut up, Aubrey. I need to be in there to take care of her."

"What did we talk about at the airport?" I said.

"Sorry, Mom," said Aubrey.

"She's not your mom," said Coree.

"Lord, Sweet Pea. Get some help already."

***

We tried a Jamaican restaurant, and between the Spicy Mahi Mahi and the Spicy Jerk Chicken, Jade blew up Aubrey's phone in a searing assault. I asked to read Jade's texts, and as soon as I had her phone in hand, I dropped it in my bag.

"What are you doing?" Aubrey spluttered.

"Enjoy Florida. Let her sweat."

"Well...It's my phone."

I ignored her.

Aubrey frowned. "When can I have it back?"

"We'll see," I said.

Sammi said, "Ghosted Jade."

***

"They have a Salvadore Dali museum here," Coree said, sitting crosslegged on her bed. You know the melting clock and all."

"*The Persistence of Memory*," I said over to her face in the faint light of her phone.

"What?"

"The name of the painting is *The Persistence of Memory*."

"Let's go. It'll be extra credit for Grayson."

"If you are up to helping me around."

"Cool Beans." Coree startled me and yelled through the wall. "Hey guys. You want to go to the Salvador Dali Art Museum tomorrow?"

"Yeah. We're in Florida. Let's stay inside."

"Let me help you out to the balcony, Elizabeth. There's lightning way out there on the ocean. I think it's coming our way, and there's light twinkling on the shimmering water from the city lights."

I had to picture Coree's view from our balcony in my mind because I drifted off to sleep.

***

The Dali Museum exterior, like stepping on a balloon, blue, glass geodesic sections appeared to push out to one side from the weight of the concrete encasing it. Coree took the first of many selfies of the two of us in front. At the bottom of the open oval stairway, we took another. After elevatoring to the top, we admired the city skyline and distant wave crests, through turquoise triangular glass sections, which turned out to be huge up close.

Atmospheric Skull Sodomizing a Grand Piano , the first canvas we viewed, carried a title which demanded explanation. From there we began our exploration into Dali, dreams, and the subconscious. "If I had these dreams, I wouldn't share them with anyone," I said.

"This piece, this *Apparatus and Hand,"* she said. "Look how the woman, a small woman stands sort of in the shadow of this large robotlike person." Coree's enthusiastic words echoed off the white, marble walls. I picked up on her tone more than the content, and watched her gestures.

33

Coree

"I'm going to send Grayson pics one by one until he guesses where we are," I said.

Elizabeth nodded.

"Don't look this up," I texted when I started him with a rare Dali cubism painting. "Just guess where I am."

"Spain."

"Yeah, okay. I jetted off to Spain on my grandparent's inheritance."

"Don't be salty, or I won't play."

"You'll play. U like me too much. I'm still in the country and that's clue number two. Elizabeth, take my pic while I pose like this girl in..." I stopped to read the title. "*Girl with Curls.*" I posed the same way, pulling my loose shorts tight around my behind, one cheek higher than the other, just like the lady in the painting. Elizabeth indulged me and took the pic with a predictably sour expression.

"It's what he wants, Elizabeth," I said, tucking my hair behind an ear on one side.

"No doubt," said Elizabeth.

"You've had three clues. Your fourth is that they are all by the same artist."

The next painting, *Bouquet,* I sent just a part of, a cropped white rose. Any more and he might have figured out the artist and then maybe the museum. "Clue five."

"U have me completely stumped. R U in town?"

"No. That's six."

"How about u? R u with Tiffany? Please say u r not still in bed, and she's asleep next to u while u text with me."

"Would u be jealous?"

"U want me to be jealous, Grayson?"

"Yes, I would."

"A jealous woman could never find contentment with a man like u."

"I guess that's a compliment."

"Oh, whatever. U know u r gorgeous. I know it. Everyone knows it, so drop the BS. If I'm going to compliment u, it's not going to be on your appearance."

"My $?"

"Whatever, again. Maybe your sense of humor."

"I'll take that, then."

#7, *Wonders of the Abyss,* was from a special exhibition the museum had of high school art, Grayson picked up on it right away. "R u at a school?"

"No, and that's 8."

34

Elizabeth

Coree wheeled me through an exhibition of middle and high school art from the area. "I could never in a million years do anything like this," I said.

"Your talent is bossing people around."

I frowned.

"At least you're great at something."

We stopped in front of *Secure*, an ink on paper portraying the head of a girl with dozens of eyes that looked out into the world around in teenage insecurity.

"Is it you?" I asked. "Or was it you?"

"No," Coree said. "I know how it works. I know the world treats cute girls differently. People have always smiled at me. I got used to it at an early age, and I learned I was supposed to put on a façade when times got bad." She absently took my hand for a moment while regarding the black and white drawing. "After Mom died."

"Come around so I can see your face when you talk to me," I said.

"Of course. I'm doing pretty well most of the time, once in a while not."

"Like when you stand in the doorway at night and scare people out of their wits."

"I don't always like the night, but what about you, Elizabeth. Was that you at all?"

I shook my head.

"Ever?"

"No."

"You were always an alpha, even before your little sisters came along?"

I watched my own fingers work in my lap, and Coree twisting her rings.

"What?" she said.

I laced my fingers together, working them. "My mother."

"Tell me, Elizabeth."

I shook my head. "Too long ago. Too many things have happened."

"I was an only child too," Coree said. "What was it like for you? How did your mother treat you before the others came along?"

"My mother..."

Coree tilted her head. "Tell me, Elizabeth."

"She pushed me, relentlessly." I looked up at the ceiling, as if to find the words or the strength to say them. "I was little."

Coree found a bench where we faced one another at the same level.

"I was nothing but a little girl."

"Did you love her?"

"I worshipped the ground she walked on...and then she left me."

"Left you, Elizabeth?"

"Us. All of us, my father, my sisters...she left."

"What do you mean she left?"

"She left us." Elizabeth's tone became icy. "How is that so hard to understand?"

Coree's lips parted. She hesitated and said, "Well, it is. How does a mother leave her children?"

Her question jolted me, but I recovered and said, "You'd have to ask her. She never gave us a chance. We never heard from her again." I stared off into space, uncomfortable confronting these words. "I was her star. She drove me, relentless and uncompromising, and I loved her for it, pleasing her. Then she just disappeared...out of my life."

A woman, maybe a teacher or a mom, seemingly supported by the little cluster of children around her, floated by us like a cloud in the sky.

"Everything changed...everything, except me. I remained the harddriving, cold little girl she created, and her leaving only succeeded in making me colder still, bitter. Made for the boardroom," I hesitated, "lost in the bedroom."

"You miss her?" I said. "Like I miss mine?"

"I miss the idea of her, not her."

"Are you grinding your teeth, Elizabeth? It's so quiet in here, I think I can hear it. You're angry at her, aren't you?"

"Of course, I'm angry." Taking a deep breath, I said, more evenly, "Who wouldn't be?" I thought about it and said, "I don't ever want to see her again as long as I live...but, like I said, I miss the idea of her."

"I miss everything about my mother."

"I want this conversation to be over now, Coree."

"She must have had good qualities. Look how you turned out."

"Look how I turned out?" I furrowed my eyebrows. "Look how I turned out?"

"What?"

"Even as a little one, I kept my room spotless, pushed in school, even preschool. Gradually that pushing became me, I suppose, pushing relentlessly to be the best in every class."

"I believe it." We resumed our progress, now more absently glancing at pieces.

"And if I let up for a moment, which I didn't, she was right there behind me, with her thumb on me. If anything, someone should have encouraged me to have fun, but what parents do that? Off I bounded into a life of overachieving and isolation."

"And the sisters came along, Alison and Jo?" Coree stopped my wheelchair but still pushed the conversation.

Having Coree behind me, out of my eyesight, made it easier to open up about myself. "They weren't like me."

"Who is?" Coree became animated. "Hey, check this out. This is lit. This Dali Museum has a display of junior high kids' paintings of their room done in the style of Vincent Van Gogh's painting of his room. Don't you wish you would have done this, painted a picture of your room?"

"I have no talent."

"Doesn't matter how technical it is, the memories would be worth having."

"Whatever. I have no childhood memories I want to revive."

"Elizabeth, that's sad."

We passed paintings of room after room after room in all the individual styles each student brought to their own. Coree stopped in front of one in which she said the color combination reminded her of a Mark Rothko.

"Did Grayson teach you about Rothko?"

"Yes. Do you know about him, and his style?"

"Allison had a poster print of his in her bedroom, oranges and reds. I remember the bright splash of colors."

"Sweet. We should redo your whole house in modern art."

I ignored that comment.

Crossing over the threshold and back into the exhibits of Dali, Coree had the last word, albeit silently, and she thought, walking behind me as she did, I did not notice. While her eyes were down on me, I watched the two of us in the reflection of clean glass windows, and easily read the words which her lips formed.

35

Coree

I glanced down at the woman before me, hands folded in her lap, even recalling the familiar scent of those hands from the deck the night before. I mouthed, "I love you, Ms. Elizabeth Ransom." I had to say it, though she didn't need to hear it or know I said it. As we turned to move on, I noticed our reflection in the glass of a huge display frame, and I also noticed her eyes studying me.

"What is it?" he texted.

"Number seven and my answer to your question is number eight. It's a young person's painting of her bedroom. It's inspired by Van Gogh's famous bedroom painting, but I think it has Rothko in it as well, don't u think, the colors?"

"Sure, but how am I supposed to win if u send me unknown art?"

"Number nine. This one might get u on track." I sent *Beigneuse (Female Nude)*.

"Aha! Dali. I don't know the piece, but it's Dali."

"Well done. It's a painting of me. LOL"

"I'm not into a body consisting of a pink blob with a hand, a nipple, and no head."

"So particular."

I sent him, *Geopoliticus Child Watching the Birth of the New Man* for number ten and *The Discovery of America by Christopher Columbus* for eleven. Elizabeth and I stood before it, she sat, I stood, before the monumental painting which took up most of the wall. We used an app on our phone which made the many different parts come alive, moving in vivid color.

When I sent him *The Disintegration of the Persistence of Memory,* a sequel to Dali's original masterpiece, which modernized the theme, we had made it up to seventeen. "R u in Florida? At the Dali?"

"Snap."

"I've never been there."

"It's legit. I didn't know art could be this deep. We r reading all about every painting. U should come here."

"What if we fly down together, and u give me a tour?"

"I can be the teacher?"

Grayson sent a thumbs up emoji

"Sounds like a plan. I require a skyline view of the city from the hotel room."

"We could have just flown down for the day, but I like your idea better."

"What happens in Florida, stays in Florida." I texted.

"Coree, I won't want it to stay in Florida."

"Here we go," I thought, but I said, "What about Tiffany?"

"Stop with the Tiffany. It's not even her name."

Elizabeth said, "I see the smiles when you text. You're beginning to like him, aren't you?"

I nodded. "But I don't want to. There's no future, just a now."

"That's relatable," she said.

"How is it relatable?"

"My life."

"Really? The Senior Vice President of Landford-Smithson, making a shit-ton of money, and you have no future?"

"There's more to life than work, career."

"I know that, Elizabeth," I said, laughing, "but I didn't think you knew it."

"As you know, I won't be having children."

I patted her shoulder. "Now you have me."

Elizabeth took out Aubrey's phone on the elevator ride down. "Look at all the texts."

"There's gotta be dozens," I said. "Jade must be blowing a gasket."

At ground floor, a couple politely stepped aside for me to wheel Elizabeth out. He wore a perfectly cut, brown Armani. His charming smile, sparkling blue eyes, and copper, brown hair pulled back in a man bun, all fell right off the cover of GQ. No doubt, a Maserati waited in the lot. The woman had in beauty what Elizabeth had in power. She not only had beauty, but stood comfortably within it with her deep tan, straight black hair, and a sensual, confident face. To present her perfect proportions, the tiniest white dress barely reached her thighs, a neckline plunged to her navel, and a halter showed off her flawless back.

I took all that in, in the short moment of our passing, but the sound of a throat clearing from the elevator caught my attention, as did the clicking noise of the door being held. "Excuse me."

I turned.

"Do you model?"

"Yes, some." I don't know why I qualified it with 'some.' Perhaps to humble myself before her perfection. "Up north. I'm just down for a weekend."

"I thought I recognized your look. What's your name?"

"Coree." I didn't know if my girlish smile would work with her, but it's what I had, so I pulled it out of my quiver.

A nod to the man prompted him to reach into his sport coat, for she certainly had no place to hold anything. He handed me a rosecolored card, holding it stylishly between the tips of his fore and middle finger. I took it between my forefinger and thumb. "Call me sometime. You have one of those interesting looks, don't you? You're down right now," she said glancing at my casual attire, "but, one can easily see it. Until then, cute little Coree." She nodded to the man who let the silver door close.

The card read, "Tiffany Saint-Pierre, Modelling, Acting, Escorts, Entertainment," with a phone number.

I stared at it, but Elizabeth knocked me back into reality. "See, you don't need me."

The issue between us, which had only percolated in our own separate minds, bubbled to the surface. "Why would you even say that?" My words echoed up the giant oval staircase where people turned in our direction. I slid the card into my waistband and pushed her over to the gift shop, whispering down into her, "I hate it when you talk like that," emphasizing the 'h' in hate. "I just hate it."

***

Driving the coastal boulevard, huge ocean bay on one side, a line of mansions on the other, I couldn't help wondering if one might be Tiffany Saint-Pierre's. Tiffany. Hah. I looked forward to telling Grayson. His Tiffany paled in comparison to this one, although who knows what Grayson's Tiffany would look like if she wore that tiny little outfit. To be honest, I forgot exactly what his Tiffany looked like, just that she was hot, no, not hot, more like elegant. This Tiffany was hot, sexual. Grayson could easily stand toe to toe with this Tiffany's consort though, and the next time I see her, if I did, I resolved Grayson would be at my arm, enhancing my presentation.

I mused, "What am I, a country girl, doing with these dazzling people?"

Elizabeth gazed out across the water.

"It's the look, Elizabeth. Like I said, everyone has her own."

Elizabeth said, "Do you think people see dolphins off this bridge?"

"Mine is not alluring like theirs. Mine's the young look, young, but old enough, barely legal."

"Help me out to the water today," she said, hand referencing the sea passing by. "I want to feel the weightlessness, walk in it."

I fumbled the rings on my fingers at the top of the steering wheel of our rental. "Everybody wants to hang around a bubbly, little petite, hoping the 'happiness' might rub off on them." I made air quotes above the wheel. "Makes no difference to them if the happy little petite is actually happy herself. She's just doing her part for them. Anyway, I'll give this Tiffany a call, see what's up."

"Time to get back to work soon," Elizabeth said. "I can feel it."

I glanced at her.

"I'm happy for you. I should have said that."

"Yes, you should have. This bridge we're on never seems to end. Eventually, we have to get where we're going."

After I had her taken care of and ready for a nap on the couch, I turned for the deck. Elizabeth said, "Coree, go on down to the beach. I'll be alright here."

"I'll sit in the hot tub and lay out on the deck in case you need me," I said. "And you do need me." I slammed the sliding door behind me with a bang.

36

Elizabeth

"I'm going to be ready when I return."

Coree rolled her eyes and said, "What, because you walked in the water?"

"And up from the beach."

"How long did that take?"

My teeth set to grinding, and when I began to speak, unbelievably, she cut me off yet again. "You can work from home for a while. Chelsea and I'll make it happen. There's no way the doctor will let you go back to the office yet."

"I find you irritating when you play mom," I said.

"And no fooling around with Michael yet, not for a longer while." I gave her a side eye. It broke the ice, and we were able to laugh. "So, what will you do?"

"Do? About what?"

"You know what I'm talking about. Don't play dumb with me, Ms. Elizabeth Ransom."

"The water is calm today, but do you see those tiny white caps that appear occasionally atop the little waves?"

Coree peered over the rim of the hot tub, shading her eyes from the sun.

"The French call them moutons, little lambs," I said.

"Have you been to France, Elizabeth?"

"Paris, for my honeymoon."

"Interesting. You have a lot of stories to tell me."

"No to that."

"Why not? Elizabeth, you hide things."

I nodded. "And I intend to go right on hiding them."

Coree splashed over, pushing the clean scent of chlorine ahead of her. She climbed out, and leaned against the railing, water drying fast in the hot Florida sun.

"You don't weigh much do you?"

Coree shrugged. "But this is what they want. The men want to do it, and the women want to photograph it in their clothing lines." She said it with no more emotion than if she had been giving the weather forecast.

"I don't like the way you are talking about yourself. I don't like it at all. And as for this Tiffany Saint-Pierre, what does she want?"

"We'll see."

"Be careful."

Coree turned. "Aww. You do care."

"Of course, I care. If you come down here with that Grayson and hang around with this Tiffany Saint-Pierre, you must be careful. You don't know either of them very-"

"That Grayson and this Tiffany?"

"My description sums it up perfectly."

"I'll be careful, Mother."

I conceded a tight smile at that. "I do not like the word 'escorts' on her card."

Coree plopped down on the wooden deck in her yellow string bikini, tiny triangular patches, all that stood between this girl's body and the world around her. "I think it means accompanying older rich men to parties and occasions. You know, for tips."

"I know damn well what it means, Coree. It was a rhetorical statement, and I do not like it. I don't like it at all."

"Chill, Elizabeth. It's probably big tips."

"That is not funny, if you meant that as a joke. I don't care what kind of tips it is. I don't like it and do not tell me to chill."

Coree shaded her eyes from the sun, squinting. "I noticed it too. How much do you think Tiffany Saint-Pierre would charge to escort a rich guy to a function?"

"I have no idea, and I don't care. It's an irrelevant issue."

"Take a guess, for fun."

"Oh, whatever." I said. "Five hundred, a thousand, more? I don't have any way of knowing."

"Yeah. She has no faults, none that I can see. A Landon-type guy, but one with unlimited brass...How much would it take for you?"

My mother jumped into my head again, and into my words. I hadn't seen her in forty years and she managed to make appearances when I least expect it. "Coree, why is this conversation continuing? You manage to distract me into these ridiculous tangents. It is not a relevant question for me. I have a comfortable income."

"Well, there's a number for me," she said. "I'm not sure what it is, but there's a number."

I was appalled. Casting a quick eye at her petite body, I knew there would be plenty of takers, and I suspected this Tiffany Saint-Pierre knew it too. "I'll protect you," I said, only I couldn't make myself say it loud enough for Coree to hear, and why did I even find myself thinking it in the first place? When did she become my concern, this little wisp? No, Coree Wysakee. There is no number, no matter how high. No, you will not involve yourself in anything like that. I need to take a bigger role in your choices. But, Elizabeth, your focus needs to be back on Landford-Smithson. What I finally did tell her was, "I need to conduct a face-to-face meeting with Michael today. I'm going to do it from the desk inside. I want you to be there."

"Why?"

"Just because...to make sure there are no interruptions."

"Oh, that's BS, and you know it. You think I'm stupid?"

"I had hoped. Unfortunately, you're not."

"You'll make sure he knows I'm there, so you guys don't go off into relationship land. You look like you just tasted a lemon. Don't worry, Elizabeth, I'll be your chaperone."

I conceded a nod. "We have important business and this 'relationship land,' as you call it, cannot get in the way."

"At some point, you two'll have to talk. Maybe not. Maybe you can pretend it never happened."

"How am I supposed to even have a serious conversation with you in that little swim suit? I mean, underwear covers more than that."

"You haven't seen my underwear," Coree laughed. "When I wear it."

"Why do I even try to have conversations with you?" I said, looking off.

Corrie laughed even louder.

"What is so funny?"

"I dare you, Elizabeth Ransom, to wear a bikini like this."

I looked up to the cloudless Florida sky.

"No one can see into our deck."

"Stop. How did we deviate off subject this far? Let's talk about the meeting. I texted him the time."

"Chicken? The girls are gone."

"The meeting, Coree, the meeting. Nobody wants to see a fifty-yearold woman in a little bikini like that."

Coree laughed even louder, and rather too obnoxiously. "Not only is that BS because you are an attractive woman, but I can name names. You want me to list them off, the men who want to see you in-"

"The meeting," I said. However, somewhere deep down inside Elizabeth Ransom, I did want to feel carefree like Coree, like I never have been allowed to, or allowed myself to, in my entire life, like the little moutons rolling free and curling playfully on the ocean surface.

37

Coree

Pulling away from the airport, Aubrey said, "My phone is busting out with messages. Jade is pissed, then pleading, then apologetic, then desperate sounding before going back to pissed again." Aubrey imitated Jade. "Why don't you answer me?"

Elizabeth reached back and jerked the phone out of her hand.

"Really?" pleaded Aubrey.

Elizabeth read out the words while she punched them in, Aubrey watching from the back seat, helpless and wide-eyed. "I didn't text u back because the bitchy lady who brought us down took my phone away. That being said, we r finished, and I am moving on." Elizabeth hit send and tossed it back to Aubrey, who juggled it around in the back seat to catch it.

"Your mom is mean," she said.

"Just do what you are told," said Elizabeth with bunched eyebrows and a wave of her hand. "That's all you have to do."

"Like you told Jo?" I said.

"Exactly," Elizabeth said. "It's just that damn simple."

"I love to watch you flex your tough swag." I reached for Elizabeth's hand, but she yanked it away. Her mind became more distant every minute. Her straight-ahead stare, I knew, attacked projects at Landford-Smithson, even as we spoke.

"What about you, Coree? What do you have going?" Aubrey called up from the back seat.

"Already on it."

"Yeah?"

"I texted her that I had someone for her to meet."

"When will I hear from her?"

"I'll tell her all about you at the next shoot."

"When will that be?"

"OMG, Aubs. Soon I hope, for both of our sakes."

"Let me know."

"No, I was going to keep it a secret. Can you go a day without a relationship, Aubrey, a day? Anyway, tomorrow, I'm going to a museum with Grayson. I'm going to contact this Tiffany and figure out what's up with that." I paused my words at an intersection until the little red Cooper ahead of us began to roll. "And I have to take care of my little sicky here a bit longer, right little sicky?" My pat on her leg produced zero reaction.

Without taking her eyes off traffic, she said, "Not much longer. I'm feeling stronger each and every day." She held the necklace, my birthday present to her as she spoke, the crown with her initials in old English type, E. R. plainly in view above her thumb and forefinger.

"Lily and the little girls will be happy to see us. It's going to be all fun with the kittens from now on. They'll have the zoomies. Aren't you anxious to see them, Elizabeth?"

"Oh, yes, I'm sure," she said, but her eyes battled the meetings and spread sheets awaiting her.

"Lily loves you. You know that, don't you?"

Elizabeth shrugged. "Cats can be distant."

"Or...maybe you're projecting. There's always that possibility."

She waved me and my comment away.

"Anyway, I think she'll be happy to see you." I tapped her leg again, though I may just as well have tapped the dashboard.

***

"You picked up some color down there, Coree. You look good."

"Where are you taking me today, Teach?"

"Twentieth century art again, my favorite."

"Any Dali?"

"A couple, I think. This week's lesson though, will begin with Jackson Pollock. I've made a couple of these myself."

"I want to make one. It looks like so much fun, so much freedom, in color and design. I want to do one, Grayson."

"Okay, okay, okay."

"It's lit. It's like participatory art, if that's a thing."

"Art is what you make it."

"Let's buy colors and frames today when we're done here. Let's go to the art store, so we're committed to next time."

"Did you need a commitment?

"I guess not. I mean, you haven't had this yet." I nodded down and gave my behind a little pat.

"You're funny."

"Is Tiffany funny, Grayson?"

"No, she isn't, but she has other qualities."

"Like what?"

"What's the point, Coree? What's the point in talking about her?"

"Grayson, I met a lady in Florida, a model, absolutely devastatingly steamy. Her name is...are you ready for this? It's Tiffany."

"Too funny."

"Even hotter than your Tiffany, I think. She wasn't wearing much clothing, so it's hard to compare. Is your Tiffany hot without clothing, Grayson?"

"Why, Coree? I don't ask you about men you've been with. It makes me wonder how much you like me, if you talk about her so casually. Do you have any jealousy?"

I shrugged. "Did you know I like to draw? I'm actually pretty good."

"And on to the next subject, just like that." Grayson shoved his hands into the bottoms of his tweed sport coat pockets.

"I haven't drawn or painted much lately. In my high school years, I drew for my escape."

"And now you want to draw again? Do you need an escape again?"

"No. Life is going well right now. This time I want to draw cause you got me back into art."

"I'd like to see your artwork."

I glanced around and motioned him into an alcove between two gigantic green marble pillars.

When I reached my hands up inside my untucked shirt, Grayson said, "What are you doing now?"

"I don't have a bra on, don't really need one, but anyway, I'm covering up with my hands, so pull up my shirt."

"What? Here? What are you up to, Coree?"

I glanced both ways. "Pull up my shirt."

Grayson hesitated, a deer caught in headlights.

"Quick. Do it. Before someone comes."

He finally got with the program and hesitantly lifted the front of my tee.

"All the way up to my neck. Hurry. See? This is my design, the butterflies, the vines." All that hung between Grayson and my art, my Elizabeth necklace, the crown with ER initials, brought a tinge of her disapproval. "What do you think?"

"I think I'm in love with-" He stopped, but my eyes widened.

"Come on, Grayson. I designed these tattoos myself, especially for myself. They are intricate. Did you even look at them?"

"They are incredible, but..."

"But what?"

"I want to see them again, when I can take the time to appreciate them."

Our voices echoing, we strolled the rest of the gallery holding hands, discussing the various pieces, taking extra time at the Mark Rothko, this time in shades of blue. He introduced me to his favorite, Joan Miro, and explained the symbolism.

"How do you know some of these artists aren't just bullshitting us?" I asked.

"Maybe some are. Art is subjective, right? I mean, there is as much great art being ignored than undeserving art being drooled over, more so, I'd say. What makes a great artist," he used air quotes, "is the simple fact that enough people think he or she is a great artist."

We stood before Dali's *Persistence of Memory. A*fter spending so much time with so much Dali art, seeing his most famous piece almost felt sacred, and I squeezed Grayson's warm hand.

I asked him about the clocks. "Time loses all meaning," he said.

I couldn't help comparing the feel of his hand to Elizabeth's. "What about the ants on the watch?

"Decay, against the permanence of the gold."

Though Grayson's hand enclosed mine in his warmth, Elizabeth's smaller hand had security of its own, different, but secure.

"What about the drooping face there?"

"It's Dali himself, a self-portrait. The background is the part of Spain he's from."

"This painting is me." Grayson said.

I turned up to him.

"Sometimes I'm lost, lost in life." We left his cryptic statement in front of *The Persistence of Memory*.

Back in his little car, I churned with the new artistic revelations and the man with me who knew and appreciated it. A whole new world opened. "What about the Dali Museum in Florida?"

"What about it?"

"You want to see it?"

"Of course. I never got around to it."

"Let's get around to it. Let's go down together. Can you manage it without Tiffany finding out?"

He rolled his eyes. "It's not like that."

"In case it is. Anyway, I have business down there. This Tiffany, Florida Tiffany let's call her, is a super model, and I want to find out what her interest in me is. You can go with me, be my wingman."

He nodded and reached for the ignition.

"Does Tiffany like art, Grayson?"

He tightened his lips. "Not so much. She likes to be seen liking it."

"Is she fun?"

"Not like you."

"Is she good in bed, Grayson?"

He ignored my question and said, "I'm lost in life, Coree, but you..."

"What?" I gazed up through my bangs.

"You seem sure of yourself, confident. I like that, I like being around that, around you."

I tilted my head, exploring these words and what they meant.

"You say you are just going where the story takes you, but I'm not so sure. I think you are on a path somewhere."

38

Elizabeth

"Coree, I will be alright now if you want to go back to your friends."

"I'll stay a couple more nights. Without me, you might over-exert yourself, do something stupid."

"Fine. You have a mind of your own."

"Do you have a hard time with people who have a mind of their own? What if you had children, Elizabeth? Would you allow them to have minds of their own? Would you want them to?"

"I don't want to talk about the subject of children." I nodded toward my laptop. "Let me do another meeting with Michael before you take off to your shoot."

"Chaperone time."

"Alright, Coree, I'll tell you something, and then I don't want to talk about it any further."

"Typical. Elizabeth makes the rules."

"Michael says almost the same exact thing." I petted Lily for a moment. "Coree, I don't like sounding indecisive or weak."

"Thanks, Captain Obvious."

"I hate it, and I don't trust myself around him. The more you are there, or at least someone is there, the better chance I have of not being weak." Lily laid against my leg on the couch. The three kittens crawled over Coree on the floor.

She said, "I try to imagine the secrets bouncing around in that head of yours."

I scratched Lily's belly.

"Do you meet with Michael one-on-one often?"

"He sometimes, more lately, waits for me in my office in the morning with issues and recently, he has been more personal, for lack of a better word."

"It'll be awkward when you return."

I nodded.

"It wasn't all you. It takes two. Don't put it all on you, Elizabeth."

"It does take two. Still, it is all on me. Michael never would have initiated it himself. Never. He followed my lead."

"To something he wanted," Coree pointed out.

"He never would have initiated it."

"If you did it again, would he be up for it?" she asked, lying on the floor, three mewling, tottering babies on her chest.

"Probably, judging from his reaction." I turned from Lily to Coree. "I said I didn't want to talk about it, and here you got me talking again."

"Talking about issues is what friends do, Elizabeth. We don't keep things bottled up inside. We help each other."

"I don't need any help."

"Elizabeth, why are you so stubborn?" Coree sat up, and the kittens tumbled into a little pile within her crossed legs. "You needed help through these difficulties, and it doesn't mean you're some weakling."

"I get your point."

"No, you don't, Elizabeth. I don't think you do get my point. Who helped you go to the bathroom and shower?"

"Where's my bag of gold stars," I said.

"I don't want anything. I don't need any credit. I just want you to be alright." Coree picked at the carpet. "Who's going to take care of you when you're old?"

"Are you saying you'll still be around when I'm old?"

"Why do you talk to me that way, Elizabeth?" By the end of her question, Coree's bottom lip poked out.

"I didn't mean it the way it came out. It's just, I suppose, I've never been in a long-term relationship, not with either husband and not with a friend, so what you said, whether in jest or not, just sounded...well, foreign to me. People come and go." I stroked the underside of Lily's chin. Peering at the girl with the kittens, I wondered for a moment who's going to take care of Coree when she gets old?

"Someone must have taken good care of Lily," Coree said. "They must have been nice because she's so nice."

"Nice shot, Coree. I caught that."

"Subtweet."

I blew out air. "Coree, doesn't it ever occur to you that Elizabeth Ransom is beyond hope. Why bother with me?"

"It occurred to me every time I helped you pee."

"You've weaponized my potty problems. I'm going to hear it the rest of my life."

"Are you saying I'm going to be around the rest of your life?"

I put my face in my hands and shook my head.

"I love you, Elizabeth Ransom." Coree laughed it out sing song, like friends do, but I kept my hands over my face until the echoes of her words dissipated into and out of my quiet house, like the echo in a canyon. "When are you going to tell me about your husbands?" she said.

I shook my head at yet another abrupt Coree Wysakee subject change and said, "Never."

"There must be juicy stuff. I know you. When you refuse to talk, it's emotional, and Elizabeth Ransom is not going emo."

"I did screw up, big time, and it is indeed emotional. Happy? Now, let it go."

"You can at least tell me their names, or how you met, or something about the weddings."

"No, no, and no."

"You just slam the door on whole parts of your life, your past."

"I do, but you keep prodding."

"I don't care if it's bad. I'll still love you."

I groaned at that.

"I've had enough," Coree said. She rose, holding the bundle of kittens in her arms. Placing them with their mother beside me, Coree settled in, and with them between us, reached over, and took me in her arms.

"What are you doing?"

"Group hug. Family hug." She squeezed around us, cats wrestling happily in the middle, me looking up to the ceiling. "You can't escape me, Elizabeth."

"Get off me, Coree."

"I won't."

"What did Aubrey call you, a Klingon?"

"That's right. I'm your Klingon." We sat in the quiet for what seemed like an eternity, Coree wrapped around me and four extremely contented cats within. "Elizabeth?"

"What is it?"

"I don't want you to move away from me," she said.

A bit of a knot formed in my stomach.

There were several answers I could have given to that, but none of them could I fully get behind, so I remained silent.

39

Coree

"Back to kid's stuff."

Sharon laughed. "It's the same color of green. Let's grab coffee."

As usual, I ran in my high tops to keep up with Sharon in her heels. Weaving through the busy sidewalk, I said, "Am I the only model you have coffee with?"

"You looked cute today in those tops and shorts, high school or not."

Why can't people ever give you a straight answer?

We stood in line chatting for a few moments, but when we settled at the little sidewalk table, she said, "No, I mean, the way you looked."

"Sharon."

"I'm just saying."

I tried to steer off the direction of our conversation. "I'm dating a guy right now, and sometimes I wonder if they date me because I look so young. You know?"

"A legitimate question." Her eyes made me feel uncomfortable. "Just own it, use it, like you do when you model."

"That's what my friend Aubrey says. Oh, wait, that reminds me. My friend, Aubrey, you met her at the birthday party. You remember her?"

She nodded behind her latte.

"She wants to meet you."

"You mean modeling, meet me?"

"No, like date, meet you."

Sharon frowned and looked down.

"Aubrey's my best friend, and she's coming off a rough break up."

Sharon looked away now.

"She's great. We've been friends since we were little."

She sighed and said, "Sure. Give her my number."

"Well, don't say it like that. She's my best friend. She might not have 'that thing,'" I said with air quotes, "but-"

"You know I have a partner."

"You give the impression you still window shop now and then."

"It has to be worth the risk," she said, eyeing me again.

I deflected. "She's twenty-three. Is that okay?"

"I like that age," she said, and I realized my deflection boomeranged.

"Let me tell you one more thing about her, and if you tell her I said this, I'm going to have to kill you." I glanced both ways for dramatic effect and leaned forward. "She's super passionate."

Sharon narrowed her eyes. "How do you know?"

"She's been my friend forever, roommates for years. I'll tell you something else, and Sharon, please, please don't repeat this stuff to her, okay?

Sharon nodded.

"Well...about Aubrey, she's like, how do you say it, kind of submissive.

She's attracted to take-charge partners. You know what I mean?"

Sharon threw her head back in laughter, her earrings and bracelets dangling again.

"Tell you what?" I said, raising an index finger. "Let's do something spontaneous. Let's go up to my place and totally surprise her. She'll be just hanging around all casual and down. Oh, hey, listen to this. I ran into a lady in Florida, who wants me to come down and see about doing some work there. See her card? What do you think?"

"Worth checking out, but the 'escort' thing might be a red flag. Ask a lot of questions."

***

I arrived in time to observe the Sharon Blaze version of parallel parking, jabbering on the phone and waving her free hand around for emphasis. I couldn't figure out how she even controlled it, but in one violent movement, her red Cadillac SUV lurched back, missing the vehicle in front by inches, the trash bin on the curb by millimeters, and the two ladies next to it by a prayer. Coming to a bouncing stop, she powered down a window. "What up, little sister?"

"TSC. I don't know how you made it in clean."

"That's the way I do everything, fast and furious. Better warn your Aubrey." Her laugh probably deafened the person on the other end of the call.

"Too much information," I said.

"I got someone on the line here. I'll be right up."

"Sounds good, 2C."

"Hey Aubs, I'm home." The single lonely beam of light from the kitchen streaked across the entrance hall. Passing that kitchen door, I had no time to react when a dark figure slammed me sideways against the passage wall. The cement block construction made no sound when I hit it and gave nothing against my impact. "You little bitch," growled the familiar voice in my ear, the side of my face squashed against the concrete. "I thought you were Aubrey? Where is she?"

"I don't know. I thought she was here."

She pulled my head away from the wall with a firm grip of my hair, and squashed it.

"Jade, please."

"Shut up, little bitch. You told her to break up with me, didn't you?"

"You're hurting me, Jade."

"Just shut up and let me think. Where's Sammi?"

"On her way up." I had no idea where she was, but no way would Jade ever risk tangling with Sammi.

"I didn't expect to see you." She turned me around to face her, pinning me to the wall, so close I could smell the sour of stale coffee on her breath. The dim kitchen light behind silhouetted Jade and her eyes glowed within the darkness of her face. The sound came first, my head jolted to one side, and a sting warmed my skin. My fear turned to panic, but our door swung open and now it was Sharon's silhouette, that stood, backlit from the outside.

"What are you doing?" Sharon said. She pulled Jade away from me.

"Who are you?" Jade said, in actually more of a snarl.

Sharon, who must have wondered what she'd gotten herself into, faced Jade in the passage, me in between, against a wall I wished I could disappear into. "Who are you?" Sharon shot back.

"I'm Aubrey's girlfriend."

"What a piece of work. No wonder you guys broke up."

Jade narrowed her eyes, and as the three of us stood in a silent standoff, it wasn't lost on me that my spot between these two in our narrow hallway wasn't the best place to be.

Sharon stepped into the kitchen doorway giving Jade an out. "Maybe you better just leave."

Sharon and I retreated to the living room and the couch. "How'd you get in, Sharon?"

"You left your keys in the door."

I laughed a little. "Aubrey and Sammi are always yelling at me for leaving them in the door. 'We're gonna get jacked someday.' Well, I did it again, and it saved me."

"What's going on?"

We turned to see Aubrey. "Not what you might think," said Sharon, taking her arm from around me. "Your ex just attacked little Coree here."

"Oh my God. Are you alright?" said Aubrey, running over to me. I fell into her arms and Aubrey said, "I'm so sorry, Sweet Pea."

"She hit me, Aubrey," I said into her chest.

"I'm so sorry, Coree. It's all my fault. I'm so sorry." She petted my hair. "We gotta get the locks changed, like now." She glanced up. "What are you doing here, Sharon?"

"You. Coree thought it would be fun to bring me over and surprise you. She said you wanted to meet me. Well, surprise! Here I am," she said, spreading her arms wide, bracelets jangling.

Old TV jumped onto the couch, oblivious to everything not involving him. With three people, he had the possibility of six hands, six chances of being petted. It made me think of Lily. "I gotta go."

"Elizabeth?" Aubrey said?

I nodded. "Can I leave you two here without a chaperone?"

Sharon looked Aubrey up and down. "I don't want a chaperone."

Aubrey just stood there with her stupid demure smile. "Oh, God." I said. "I'm outta here. I'm so totally outta here. Sorry to throw you under the bus, Old TV."

"Old TV? What's up with that?"

"He's black and white." The thunderous Sharon Blaze laugh rocked my apartment, the last thing I heard.

40

Elizabeth

"In here, Coree." I navigated around the kitchen with, I thought, fairly capable mobility. I can do this without Coree, at least soon, and if Lily would stop winding around my ankles, I might make it back to work instead of back to the hospital.

Coree appeared in the kitchen doorway, wide eyed, disheveled hair, and a red cheek. "What happened?" She ran to me and fell into my arms. Her shoulders shook within my embrace, and words, unfamiliar words, tumbled out of me. "Little girl. It's alright. It's alright, baby. I'm here now. I've got you."

On my terrace, Coree scrunched into a ball, tiny on her recliner. I sighed and moved over on mine. "Coree, come here." She scuttled over. "This recliner is going to break under us."

"Is that a fat joke?"

"Do you hear a lot of fat jokes? Probably have to weigh you on a postal scale." A freshening breeze fluttered the leaves before it outside. "Did you call Tiffany Saint-Pierre yet?"

"Not yet."

"Tell you what, why don't you call her, get out of town for a day or two, if Grayson can go. Do you good."

"But I need to be here with you."

"I'll survive. Sammi can come over, or Aubrey, or Chelsea, if I need anything."

Coree said, "By needing to be here, I meant that I need you, Elizabeth."

Her words settled around us, around me. I wondered what it's like to be needed, wanted. Michael wanted me and it felt...well, good. "Check with your Tiffany Saint-Pierre. I wonder if it's her real name. Check with Grayson and see what is possible. Grayson would be with you. You wouldn't be alone."

"I need you, Elizabeth," she said into my shirt folds, powerful words that both filled and terrified me.

Lily worked her way in between us, kneading against me, motor running hard.

"We can move back up there," I said, pointing upward. "I know you're going to end up there anyway."

Coree further pushed into me. "Sorry, if I'm causing you to have feelings."

"I didn't say I had feelings."

"But I know. We both know." We sat in a few minutes of silence until Coree whispered, "Elizabeth, she hit me."

"She what? Who?" My eyes widened.

"She hit me. Jade hit me."

I felt the blood pump in my neck. My whole skin burned. I glanced around for my phone, but my eyes, they wouldn't work. Everything was a blur, a cloud.

"What are you doing?" Coree asked.

I forced myself to hold her, to comfort her and hide my fury, for now. It's what Coree needed at this moment. After long moments of silence, in which I fought to control my breathing, I forced a chuckle. "I think we both need therapy."

"Therapy?" Coree said. "No to that."

"I was joking, but therapy doesn't automatically mean you're weak."

"It doesn't mean your strong either."

"You're more like me than you think, Coree Wysakee. Be careful about that." She fell into a rhythmic breathing. I spotted my phone on the window sill, out of reach. For God's sake, how long do I have to lay here now with her sleeping, especially after what happened? Lily stretched one long luxurious front leg out within us and closed her eyes too.

A gold chain lay against the contours of Coree's collar bone. Curious what trinket she might be wearing, I slid a finger under it and drew on the chain, pausing when she snuffled and stirred. She settled back into her rhythmic breathing, and I drew at it again. The pendant caught at her tee shirt collar, a last resistance. With one careful tug, out popped the crown. My mouth fell open. This was no trinket at all, but the same ER crown she gave me for my birthday. This girl bought us matching necklaces. She is wearing my initials around her neck, my initials. She must be obsessed. It began right away at Billie Jean's, right at the first meeting, the odd way she looked at me, like searching into me, and scanning all around my face. Maybe she needs therapy after all.

I slid the crown back under the collar of her tee and peered out the window. Perhaps her relationship with Grayson will blossom. If it did, maybe I could rebuild my walls. And maybe I could have a fling and get it over with, pacify myself. Oh, what in God's name is the matter with me? If anyone needs therapy, it's me. I'm lying here with this girl who loves me like a mother, and all the while, I'm thinking about myself. "Coree, help me."

Eyelids still closed, she said, "What? Did you say something?"

"Um no, baby. Go back to sleep."

"It's cold out here," she mumbled, pulling into me. Lily never stirred.

***

I watched and listened to Coree across the kitchen island. When she set her phone on the marble countertop, I said, "So, Coree?"

"So, what, Elizabeth?"

"So, you're on birth control, or have it?"

"Elizabeth."

"Answer me."

"That's personal."

I raised an eyebrow.

"You don't know what's going on. Who says we're going to have sex?"

I rolled my eyes.

"Okay then, who says, we haven't already had it."

"Somebody has to bring it up."

"I didn't just crawl out of a cave, Elizabeth."

"Neither did Sammi."

Coree slumped at that.

"And mind your tone when you talk to me. I've told you that countless times."

Coree bit her bottom lip.

"Keep Grayson with you, and don't do anything or agree to anything your mother wouldn't have agreed to."

A little late for that. My last six or eight years have been littered with the things I did for the sole reason that she wasn't there."

"Perhaps it's time to bring your mother back."

Coree, screwed her face up at me and yelled, "How the hell can I do that?" She stomped out of the kitchen.

"What's this? What's this? Don't you yell at me and walk out. I'm talking to you. You come back here right now." I found her collapsed on the couch, face down.

Coree asked, voice muffled by a pillow, "What does that even mean, what you said?"

"Well, keep her in your thoughts, her support."

She shook her head and turned away.

I put my hands on my hips. "Are you kidding? Tell me you're kidding, Coree. You are blaming your mother for dying and leaving you?"

She shrugged.

"Oh, my God, Coree. Stop that." I stood over her. "Don't you blame her.

Don't you ever blame her."

Coree mumbled into her arms. "I took care of her and she still-."

"Don't you think your mother would be here for you if she could be?"

She turned her back to me, but she jerked around quick enough when I jabbed my finger into her ribs.

"Ouch. That hurts, Elizabeth."

"Well, listen to me. I'm talking to you, girl. If she's looking down, watching, it would kill her to see you attach any blame to her, absolutely kill her. Sit up and look at me when I'm talking to you."

Coree tucked her hair behind an ear on one side. "Leave me alone, Elizabeth."

"I will not. What mother wouldn't want to love her daughter?"

"Why are you getting all extra on me?"

"Because you need to understand the point I'm making? Do you understand it?"

"I understand that you're getting all crazy."

Coree started to rise, but I blocked her. "You sit right there."

"What the hell, lady?"

"The name is Elizabeth, not 'lady.' Now talk to me. What's going on in that head of yours."

Coree slumped.

"Talk, Coree."

"You always get your way?"

"Pretty much, and I'm going to get it right now, so what's going on?"

She sighed into the floor, "I don't know. Sometimes I just feel like she left me stranded in life."

"I know the feeling. I know that feeling too, but you also need to understand, you need to put yourself in your mother's place, what a terrible feeling it is to lose your baby. Can you even imagine that?"

Coree shrugged.

I stroked her hair.

She took my hand in hers and pressed it against her cheek.

"You are being self-centered, Coree. It's an understandable reaction, but it's immature, and you need to stop."

"It's not that easy."

"I am telling you, not asking you? I'm no shrink. I just tell people to get their shit together."

"And they usually do?"

"Mind your tone to me."

"I didn't mean it disrespectful like, but you can't always just boss people and expect results. It's not that simple."

"I do expect results from you."

"But this is emotions. It's not work."

"Emotions, work, either way, I'm telling you, Coree, to get it together. Anyway, my mother, see that's different. She up and left us. Yours, Coree, it wasn't her fault, and you can't blame her."

Coree peered up at me through her bangs. “Elizabeth, do you miss her, your mom?”

“I don’t want to talk-”

“Why?” Coree let go of my hand and waving her arms helplessly, cried out, “Why? Why? Why? Why can’t you talk to me, Elizabeth?

“Alright,” I yelled. “Alright. Yes, I miss her. I miss her every day, every God damned day of my life, but she doesn’t want me. She doesn’t want me, doesn’t give a shit about her own daughter and that’s why I just have to push it back, constantly push it back, out of my mind, all the time.” I squeezed my head with my hands. “For forty years now.”

“I’m sorry, Elizabeth,” Coree said. She jumped up and took me in her arms. “I’m sorry I brought it up.”

I regrouped and pulled away. “But you, Coree, you need to bring it out, think of her, remember her, remember what she would say to you, what she would think of you, what she would want for you.”

Coree pulled her hair behind an ear. “You’re lit.”

“No, I’m not lit. I’m pretty awful.”

“Awful? Why would you say that about yourself?”

“Never mind. Just remember to always honor and remember your mother. She loved you, and didn’t want to leave you.”

“You would’ve made a great mom, I bet. I mean if things would have worked out differently.”

I shook my head at her and turned.

“Where’re you going, Elizabeth? What’s the matter with you? You flip out on me and then just stomp out of the room.”

41

Coree

I interlaced my fingers into Grayson's as we approached the blue, transparent geodesic dome. "Are you excited? I'm excited." Grayson smiled down to me and I felt his calm. "We couldn't take the oval staircase last time because of her wheelchair and good thing. If Elizabeth and I had taken the stairs, I never would have met Tiffany."

We started at the ink headshot drawing of the high school girl with all the eyes, the commentary on the pressures of teen years. "Is high school and middle school tough on boys' self-image too?"

"I suppose."

I fell deep in thought back on Elizabeth's latest rampage, the first and hopefully the last time she turned it on me. You're right though, Elizabeth. I'll take my mother with me from now on...and I'll take you too, Elizabeth. Grayson's comfortable voice barely echoed on the hard, marble walls, whatever it was he was rambling on about.

"What were you like, Grayson?"

"Coree, I hate to tell you, but I attended a prep school."

"Big surprise."

"Everyone..." he hesitated, "lots of us, anyway, we thought we were really something."

"And were you really something, Grayson?"

"I just floated along aimlessly, still do, going where the story takes me."

"Hey, you can't have my line."

"It's the truth." He hesitated. "No, it's not. I'm not going where the story takes me. I'm not going anywhere at all. I float along, not aspiring to anything because I don't need anything. Coree, your 'going where the story takes you' is like meandering down a river to new places. My going where the story takes me is more like floating around on a lake with no oars or motor, never going anywhere. I'm adrift.

I joined in his metaphor. "What if you sink?"

He looked down at me. "You see, there's the problem. You wouldn't think it is, but there's the problem. I can't sink. They won't let me."

"Must be nice to have that," I said.

"I suppose."

A tiny dot of annoyance appeared inside me. "Do something." I said it softly but it did not cover the echo of Aubrey's words in my head, "Somewhere in that boy's future is a broken heart."

Grayson looked at me, no, not at me, but at the two words I had spoken, hanging and disintegrating between us. He threw them a wan smile.

I thought of the mother I had lost, the incessant partying to forget losing her, and then, my search for her, the idea of her. I thought of Elizabeth and clenched my fists, not in anger, but to grasp her, to grab hold of her and not let her shake free of me. I thought of those things in the split of a second, before looking back at this man, this beautiful man, whose beautiful eyes became like clouds, indefinite shapes, passing and changing. Within the clouds, I envisioned the geometric forms of buildings definite in the space they took up, Elizabeth's art, her stupid buildings and cityscapes. I contrasted them with Grayson's Rothkos and Miros, Pollacks, and Dalis. "Are you sad?" I said.

"Sad? No, not at all. I'm content."

"Content," I repeated. I pictured myself with him in that boat, content...and adrift.

"Are you content, Coree?" Grayson asked.

I pursed my lips and shook my head, slowly at first, then more vigorously. "I've never been content in my life. I've been happy, sad, miserable, angry, but I don't know about content." I shrugged out of our funk and grabbed Grayson's hand. "Let's check out the Van Gogh bedrooms the school kids did. See this one down here? Doesn't it look like Mark Rothko painted the walls, like his colors? I want to make a painting of my room or maybe Elizabeth's."

His response was a smile that bordered on condescending.

"What's your apartment like, Grayson. I picture it with a view, floorto-ceiling windows with a view."

He smiled again.

"I already judged it, when I met you in the club."

Grayson raised his eyebrows.

"I ended up crying, thinking about it, and I stormed out of the club."

"How did I make you cry?"

"You didn't make me cry. My jealousy and my messed-up life made me cry. My life isn't as messed up anymore. I have a lot to be thankful for, but maybe the die is cast. Once an emo, always an emo." Stopping in front of, *Girl with Curls,* I said, "You like her behind, Grayson?"

"I've seen better."

"Good answer."

"Seeing this one is so evocative," Grayson said, wonder in his eyes.

"You know, after seeing *The Persistence of Memory* with you just a few days ago? It's like that's the beginning of the Dali experience, one bookend. *The Disintegration of Memory* is the other." This time, he squeezed my hand. He squeezed my hand the way I squeezed his in front of *The Persistence of Memory*.

"I'm glad we came here together," Grayson said. "I'm going to remember this, always."

"You look happy, Grayson. You look more than content." We walked back to the oval stairway and I said, "Check out the floor, Grayson. Parquet, right? That's what it's called?"

"Yes. Sort of a herring bone."

"I like it. Elizabeth needs this on her kitchen floor. Speaking of Elizabeth, let's go to the gift shop and find some art prints for her house."

"Do you live with her?"

I considered his question. "Sometimes." Elizabeth's answer would probably be different from mine, or even Grayson's. The parquet floor went out of focus, replaced by the four-way stop and the changes it symbolized. Deep within Elizabeth's neighborhood, hidden around a bend of imposing brick homes and under the canopy of old oak trees, her driveway approached between rows of vertical cedars. Rows of flowers, organized in rows, guarded the front of the house. Inside, you followed the hallway, dark, timber-beamed living room, a bit less dark. From there, a stairway led up to her bedrooms, lighter, and a door to the kitchen, lighter, led finally, out to the terrace, bright and airy, but secluded, hidden. "It needs changes," I said.

"What does?" Grayson answered.

42
Elizabeth

When not wrapped around my ankles, Lily kept a sharp eye out for the first appearance of my lap. If I lifted her close to me, she rumbled like an old refrigerator, pushing two soft paws against my chin. "Don't even pretend to act like you don't want my affection. I know." I considered her a moment. "Will you go with me to Chicago?" Do I take anything at all from here? Starting life all over has its attraction, no Michael, no little sisters, no George, no...Coree? When the mewling sounds escaped my closet, nails replaced soft pads. "You're such a good mom. Here, go to your babies." I set her on the floor and off she trotted.

Could I have been a good mother? Doubt it. I couldn't even manage to be a good wife. Perhaps if Raymond and I had had children right away, some kind of positive maternal instincts would have magically kicked in, maybe magically changed me. I contemplated my marriages, wasting parts of two perfectly adequate men's lives. I thought about the parenting I was forced into as a girl. Hopefully, Jo and Allison are not too scarred. I frowned. Oh, whatever. They need to face up to the world like everybody else.

***

Exhausted from the drive and the walk up, I sat behind my desk, feeling proud of my accomplishment of arriving before anyone else. Chelsea, appearing not long after, completely surprised me with an ambush. "Ms. Ransom! What're you doing here? You're not supposed to be here yet."

"I want to make sure the ship is running smoothly."

"Ridiculous. The ship is running fine. Where's Coree?"

"She's out of town."

"So, the minute she's gone, the first thing you do is come to work, against the doctor's orders."

I furrowed my brows. "I intend to take progress reports from my executive staff today, surprise them. You are to call them in one by one. I want a return to some sense of normal."

"This isn't normal," she said, "but whatever. You're the boss."

"I am displeased with your tone, Chelsea."

"You think everyone's trying to get away with something? You think everyone is having a party when you're away?"

"Listen here-"

"Just take this into consideration." She held her hands out to the side, palms open to me. "Try to keep these short, and I would suggest using them or making them appear at least, as a way to say thank you for their hard work and for coming to your birthday party and for the flowers and so on, rather than coming on like you're accusing people of misusing their time in your absence."

"I don't, at all, like this, as Coree would say, this 'tude' you are throwing around." Ever since Coree started this nonsense of talking to me any way she pleases, there seems to be an infestation of it. I sat back in my chair and took a deep breath.

Chelsea waited, across the desk, never giving me a let up from those deep brown eyes, before adding, "And here's another thing, Ms. Ransom. You absolutely need to be healthy for the Board of Directors. The quarterly finance report is not going to change much because of these last few weeks. The profit numbers are pretty close to already in the can."

"As I said, I am displeased with your tone, but you are giving me straight talk about the timing of the numbers." I clicked my nails on the desk for a moment and said, "When I am promoted, will you come with me to Chicago?"

Chelsea gave me a tight-lipped smile. "I take that as a compliment, Ms. Ransom, but no, my husband, you know, but thank you. Perhaps, you could take Coree."

"Why would I do that?"

"Oh, I don't know," Chelsea said, shaking her head at me a little too much like I had asked a stupid question. "She's extremely loyal to you...a personal assistant, something."

I deflected back to the work at hand. "Alright. Thank you, Chelsea. I may be charging ahead without considering all the factors." I scanned the room, my props. Having been gone for weeks, I looked to my familiar surroundings for my bearings. "We'll begin with Mr. Kent. I would like you to be present, perhaps take relevant notes."

"Again, I would respectfully disagree on that. The presence of your executive secretary might give the meetings a more formal appearance than you intend."

"I get that, but there are other factors to consider."

She narrowed her eyes at me, and I hoped there were limits to the perceptiveness of my secretary. "Can I go get him for you?"

"Whatever," I said and turned to my computer. After she left, I looked up and asked her empty seat, "Go get him for me?"

"The meetings were productive," I said to Chelsea on the way out. "Not only on a business level, but on a social level as well. Rather than seeing me as the usual nagging boss, perhaps they came out seeing me as caring, along with a bit of the usual overbearing, which can't be helped. Thank you for your advice this morning." Chelsea's face transformed as if Santa Claus just walked in the door. "I stepped out of character on that, didn't I?"

***

Driving my Lexus gave me the sense of control I had been lacking, however the empty Starbucks glass in my cupholder and wadded-up fast-food bags in my passenger seat floor, tempered that feeling. By this time next week though, Coree will be back in her apartment, and my life will be close to a semblance of normalcy. When I think back on these last couple months, I have to wonder what the hell happened. Coree, and a lot of other people, have tried to turn me into a needy old milksop. No more. We are all adults and we're going back to acting like it.

On my terrace, the outside light fell over me on three sides, four, if one includes the sky lights. The crisp air cleansed my skin. "Remember when you sat on the stone wall, Lily?

Remember when you lived on your own?" Lily evidently lived in the now, going where the story took her, because, despite my reminiscing, she rubbed her head against my hand, indicating the location in need of scratching.

"Who will take care of you when you are old?" It's what I said. I studied the cat, warming my lap. "Lily, I guess I'll be taking care of you when you are old, but I'm not home much, at least when my life returns to normal. Perhaps Coree can come over and visit you. No doubt, she would want to. Coree. I haven't thought about her much today. If she knew, she would be all, in her words, butthurt, and those green eyes all round as saucers. I imagine, she wants to be the one to take care of me when I'm old. Why? Why would anyone? She needs to build a normal life, be a better wife than me, but I have to admit, I have grown accustomed to her company.

43

Coree

"Thanks for coming with me, Grayson. I have no idea what I'm getting myself into, but having an eye-candy wingman has to be a plus."

"You're the one with the thing, the look," he said with air quotes.

"It's not classic. You're classic, like in a magazine."

"Whatever. You've been in magazines. Not me."

"It's because I have the thing as you say, the look. It's not real beauty."

"That's stupid," Grayson said. "You're so cute, so beyond cute, I could just eat you up."

I unbuckled. His words themselves almost unbuckled my seatbelt. I stood on my knees in my seat and kissed his neck, just below his ear. "Maybe we should blow off this meeting," I whispered.

"Are you serious?"

After a last kiss, touching my tongue to his skin, letting my breath settle around his neck, I said, "We have time." I plopped back down on my behind. "No. We can't come all the way down here and not find out if this is my big break."

"Are you hoping for a 'big break?'"

I surveyed the flat blue water of the bay. "See those little white caps popping up here and there? Elizabeth calls them moutons, little sheep in French, lambs. See the lambs, Grayson?"

He nodded.

I sank deeper in my seat. "I'm not looking for a big break. I mean, if something opened up, great, but I'm not leaving Elizabeth, at least not too far and too long." The thought of the Chicago thing made me cringe.

"You two that close?

I nodded.

"Why? What about me?"

"You gotta have me all to yourself or what, Grayson?" I peered off into the endless highway, as if the answers to my life unfolded with the miles. Huge homes rose ahead of us. "You think they're nice, or you think Tiffany Saint-Pierre lives in slumville?"

"It'll do."

The horizontal branches of a live oak extended over her front yard like muscular arms, creating a cavern of sorts. "This is like an old plantation house," I said. Angular slices of sunlight sliced across, and vertical lines of mint green Spanish moss draped down over the red brick drive. I climbed out of the rental BMW, eyes on the brick steps to the portico with its five white pillars, a long, long way from Richville.

"I'm a little mouse looking up at the gates of a palace. I'm glad you're here, with your imperturbable demeanor, Grayson."

"She's going to have to do more than this to grandstand me," he said. "Whoops. Did I come off as snobbish?"

"Coree. Great to see you." In her cranberry workout tights, so snug to her skin, so perfectly fit, Tiffany's perfection announced itself.

"This is my friend, Grayson."

"Hi, Grayson. Come in you two." She called into a side room as we passed, without ever taking her eyes off us. "Harold, bring us something out on the veranda. Surprise us, something fun and colorful." Tiffany took my hand. "Come on you two. Let's sit out back." We swept down a wide hallway, past a curving marble staircase, past marble busts of who knows who, past fronds of little palm tree plants, and past rooms, each with its own color scheme.

We surrounded a white cocktail table, where we were nearly surrounded ourselves, by a curving aqua blue pool, all within a courtyard of two stories of balcony. I tried not to let my touristy amazement show. A waterfall, cascading over rocks, flowed into the pool. "Jack," Tiffany called happily to the man skimming the surface. "Can you finish later?" He disappeared without a sound.

We chatted about the trip down and so on, fussed over our colorful cocktails and a white pomegranate candle. Tiffany confirmed it to be the scent I noticed when we entered. I tucked that info away for when we returned up north to a certain scent-free environment.

Tiffany said, "I knew the second I laid eyes on you, you had the look."

"That's what I tell her," said Grayson, even though I had clearly asked him to just be there for me, be eye candy.

Tiffany ignored him and trained her complete attention on me. "So, to get to the point, we're involved in many different business strategies. Modeling product lines, of course, is that what you're mostly into?"

I nodded. "I've done a few commercials, but for the most part product lines."

"You're cute. Smile for me Coree, a cute young smile." She reached over and fluffed my hair down over my eyes. "Those sparkling emerald eyes, through your bangs...keep smiling. My God, you're hot."

"That's the way I feel," said Grayson.

Coming from Aubrey or Sharon, the candor in her own pale blue eyes would have made me uncomfortable, but this was all business. "We do all kinds of things, the sky's the limit, modeling, cabarets, escorts. We look for all opportunities to monetize beauty. That's what we're all about." After we discussed more about their work, she said, "You know what? We have a party tonight. We try to have two or three a week here. Can I put you two down on the guest list? You can meet some of the girls and regulars, have a great dinner, and get to know us, ask questions. You don't have plans, do you? Come on then. I'll see you out." She took my hand again, completely ignoring the Grayson.

We passed the little marble statues on marble pillar stands. She stopped, turned to me, and reached out to my hair. "Blond," she said. "No, not blond. Caramel. Change your hair to sort of a caramel. I think to bring out the shades in your complexion better, and still keep your youthful look. Perhaps a little tanning, maybe even some sexy tan lines. How old are you, Coree? And that name works it for you, by the way."

"Twenty-three, almost twenty-four."

She looked me up and down. "That's so perfect because you could go for eighteen, easy. You could be making a lot of money in the right situations. You are straight up dollars and cents hot, or you will be by the time we get done with you."

Once we had put distance between the house and us, as if to get out of her hearing, I said, "In modeling, you hear BS flattery all the time, but coming from Tiffany, I don't know what to think. Has she cashed in her incredible looks to that extent, that success? I mean, she's filthy rich, nothing basic about her lifestyle."

Grayson nodded his head.

"Where is she on the one to ten scale, Grayson?"

He hesitated.

"It's alright. You can say it."

His eyebrows raised.

"It's okay. What am I on a one to ten scale, then?"

"Don't ask me that."

"I know where I am. It's just looks, Grayson."

"Looks are subjective," he said.

"It's just a simple question, oh, and by the way, I told you not to talk."

He turned to me in surprise and after a moment of silence, he said, "I uttered like five, ten words the whole time we were there."

"Still."

"Still what?"

"All you had to do is do what you were told."

"Are you being serious right now?"

I looked straight ahead.

"You are. You're serious, aren't you, Coree?"

I decided not to fight it, but not give any ground either, so I changed the subject. "We have some time. Let's go to the ocean."

With our pantlegs rolled up, the water lapped around our ankles. We walked along feeling the sun on our faces, the breeze on our skin, and the sand between our toes.

"I like you, Coree," Grayson said. "I like being around you. You seem like you know what you want."

"And you don't?"

Grayson looked out to sea. "I'm just floating along, Coree, just floating along."

I let the moutons run through my fingers. "So...blond hair, caramel highlights?"

"Whatever you think."

"Grayson, can't you give me a simple answer?"

He shrugged.

44

Elizabeth

"Hey, can I talk to u? I know it's late, but I want to talk." I didn't see the text until I woke up at two. Hmm. I sat up in bed, so as not to disturb Lily and messaged back, "Sure, anytime." Mama cat, stretched a long arm across my leg and sighed, never opening her eyes. The call appeared.

"Is everything alright?" I said, scratchy voice.

"Why are you still up?"

I rolled my eyes. "I wonder."

"I think it's because you miss me."

I rolled my eyes again. "Coree, what's going on? Come on. You didn't call me at two to pass the time. Is everything alright?"

"Elizabeth, I didn't call you at two, originally anyway. I wanted to tell you about my day, and you texted back at two so here we are. You're unemployed. We can stay up and talk all night."

My eyes reached into the depths of my dark bedroom. "Then you better tell me about your day before I fall asleep."

"I had a great day and a great night. Seeing the museum again, this time through Grayson's eyes made it different, and Elizabeth, listen to this. We held hands. We held hands the whole time."

"Please tell me you didn't call me in the middle of the night to tell me you held hands."

"Oh no, there's more, lots more. That's just the low-key. We visited Tiffany Saint-Pierre. She lives in a mansion, not really a mansion, but pretty close to it. Actually, yeah, it's a mansion, with an incredible pool, a staff, artwork and statues."

"So, what happened?" I tried to lead her along to the point, if there actually was a point somewhere. My body slid back down into the sheets, flat on my back.

"Tiffany seemed to be checking out Grayson at first, like right in front of me. I got a little torqued, but now, after considering it,

I think she was just judging me based on my accessories, and she approved because she turned her buzz on me and ignored him after that."

"Oh good."

"Sarcasm? Was that sarcasm, Elizabeth?"

"Can you get to the point here? I feel like we are at a slumber party."

"Did you go to slumber parties?"

"A couple. You think I never had any fun?"

"Having trouble seeing it, to tell you the truth. Elizabeth, I just want to tell you all about my day. Don't you want to hear about my day?"

"Of course, dear." I held the phone up to Lily, who stretched her front legs out and yawned.

"She had more clothes on this time, but she still looked steamy. Grayson is so imperturbable though. He agreed she is in the ten to eleven range and I'm in the eight and a half range. I mean, he didn't say that, but I think that's what he was thinking. But he said he liked me, liked me for what I am, how I act and my look, which always makes me suspect because I know I look like I'm in high school. Why would an almost thirty-year old want that? Speaking of what I am..." I dropped the phone on the bed and stared at it, the voice going on and on like some kind of chattering children's doll. "Tiffany said I should be blond, not bottle blond, but like honey or caramel. What do you think?" Before I could answer, Coree plowed on again. "I'm going to consider it, maybe ask Sharon and Aubrey too."

"Coree, where are you right now?"

"I'm on our balcony, with the slider shut, so I don't wake Grayson. The dark out here is decorated by twinkling lights from everywhere, shimmering lights of the bay and sparks from a campfire on the beach lifting up to the stars in the sky. It's lovely, a gorgeous night and in the moonlight, you can even see moutons."

My eyes closed.

"We hit the beach for a while. How romantic, right?"

Coree chattered in one ear and Lily purred in the other.

"We checked out a party at Tiffany's house in the evening. She said they have them all the time, so we should come back and talk to her girls and get a feel for what they do because a lot of them would be there."

My eyes opened straining to see her in the darkness. "And Coree, tell me what is it they do?"

"People, mostly men, but a couple of women too, pay to come to these parties, to eat and drink and hang out with these hot models. Tiffany said with my look, I could make a lot of money, like a lot of money, her direct quote being, I'm 'dollars and cents hot,' but Elizabeth-"

"What?"

"She understands the monetization of appearances."

"Corcc, stop. What actually is going on there?" Lily's ears twitched at the edge in my voice.

"Lots of stuff. You should have seen the pool, especially at night. Colored lights inside it and above it, and a waterfall. Elizabeth, the pool had a waterfall with boulders and plants. We need a waterfall, Elizabeth."

We?

"At one point, a light rain came down. With the colored lights, it twinkled and sparkled the different shades. It was a warm, passing sprinkle, not cold and harsh like back home. Everyone watched and talked under the canopies and table umbrellas...so lovely. Plus, a few people were sitting around a fire over in an alcove. The beautiful smell of wood smoke wafted out into the whole place, delicately, not overpowering, just like a campfire would, you know, if it was off in the woods somewhere. Speaking of smells, she had pomegranate candles. That's what we need."

"We," I silently mouthed.

"So many hot ladies there, flexing it," Coree said. "Some of them didn't have much on and some of them might even have been hooking up, I think, in rooms surrounding the pool, because they would disappear for a while."

"For tips, no doubt."

"Big tips, Elizabeth. Most of these guys, men, and in a couple cases, women too, were your age and seemed like they had plenty of money to throw around."

"Coree-"

"We left after a while, after Grayson had his eyeful, I think. Remember you said to consider what my mother would think, but, Elizabeth, a lot of money changed hands and just to hang out with hot, young ladies. I could do that. No harm done. Tiffany is rich, super rich."

"Coree-"

"I can see the lights of the city skyline in the distance, kind of glamorous."

"Coree-"

"I told Tiffany I'd stay in touch. I mean, I could always go down for a weekend, hit the beach in the daytime, be seen at the party for some green, and come back home tan and flush. We'll see."

"We'll see, alright," I grumbled, but she cut me off, yet again.

"I didn't call to talk to you about Tiffany Saint-Pierre though."

"Well," I slipped in, "we are going to be talking about it, Coree. You can bet your ass on that."

"I called you to tell you..." She interrupted again. I swear, Coree has interrupted me more than I have been interrupted in the last twenty years, maybe my whole life. Her voice dropped to a whisper. "Keep this low key, Elizabeth. Grayson and I made love." Her words stopped for a little giggle.

"Coree. Again, I feel like we are at a slumber party."

"I had to tell someone. I had to tell you." She paused and I braced myself. "Elizabeth, I might love Grayson. What if I love him?"

I do not have these conversations. I just do not have them, except possibly when I have excoriated Jo for one of her behaviors. I considered my own past and Jo trying to criticize me, but my life is none of her concern. Jo has no business in it whatsoever. Her life, on the other hand, needs guidance, and often corrections.

"Are you there?"

"Yes, I'm here." I texted while Coree rambled on. "Leah, I want u to have someone checked out."

"What do you think? What if I love him? Is it possible?"

"Anything is possible." I pulled the phone away from my ear to punch keys. "A Tiffany Saint-Pierre. She lives and works, modelling or something, in the Tampa area."

"Lovemaking with him, Elizabeth...such a beautiful experience. He told me he loved me and with the sunset from our room, reds and oranges glinting off the water, the whole scene, the whole experience..."

"I'm on it," the return text said. "And also, I took care of that other situation. Coree will never see or hear from her again."

I lowered the phone, nodding to myself, but then, for the first time, the quiet that is my house, that Coree had pointed out to me, oppressed me, weighed me down.

"Are you there?"

"Yes. I'm here. What did you tell him, Coree? What did you say?"

"I said it's a big step, and I feel like I'm there too, but it's a big step saying it."

"Good line."

"A good line? Elizabeth, is it a line? Did I give him shade?"

"Honestly, Coree, you probably have as much experience in love as I have. I'm sure more."

"You've been married twice. Didn't you love them?"

"I think I did, at the time anyway."

"What do you mean?"

"It means, at the time, I said I did, but I don't know, even now, if I know what love is, or what it feels like. Maybe I've never loved anyone."

"That's sad, Elizabeth."

At the time, I thought I loved George and I told him so, however, no Coree, Jo, or anyone is going to know about the weak moments of Elizabeth Ransom. I don't even want to think about them myself, so I said, "Let's go to a Tiffany Saint-Pierre party together next time."

"Elizabeth. I don't think so. What those older women are doing there, I hate to-"

"For God' sake, Coree, I'm joking."

"Oh, you caught me there. You're always so low key when you joke, I miss it."

"So, where do you two go from here, you and Grayson?"

"I'll let you know tomorrow, and the next day, and so on. I'm just going where the story takes me. You know me."

"You better get some sleep."

"The way I'm feeling, I can run on autopilot."

"On love?"

"Maybe."

"Be careful, Coree. I don't want you to get hurt."

"That's so sweet. You sound like a mom."

I scratched Lily around the neck and thought about what it means to be a mother, and I hung on to keep from sinking. "Moms say a lot more. You can ask Jo and Allison."

"I will. I want to hear all about your parenting."

"I'm not proud of it. You're lucky you're not on the receiving end."

"I think I felt some of it the other day," she laughed. "I'm good."

"It's not my place."

"Your place? What about with your sisters? Was that your place?"

"I had to do what I had to do, and they had to suck it up."

"I would have taken whatever you did, Elizabeth, still would. I didn't have a mother at all, I mean after fourteen. I had to wing it."

"You did pretty well."

"You don't know some of the things I've done."

You don't know some of the things I have done either, I almost repeated to her, but I did say, "I'll remind you of my two failed marriages...and..."

"And what?

"...and nothing."

"Tell me the 'and,' Elizabeth."

"No. There you go again, going places I don't want to go. Back to you. Come back home and keep it going as long as you can, because in my limited experience, you have to get love while you can."

"You thinking on following that philosophy with Michael?"

"I'm going to bed now, Coree. I'll see you tomorrow or actually today."

"It was a rhetorical question, as you would say, and the answer about you and Michael is a hard no."

"Are you the boss of me? No, you are-"

"The answer is no, Elizabeth. Stay away from him, at least in that sense. There are tons of other men out there."

"It's none of your business, Coree."

"Look, Mr. Kent is extremely hot, and I know, or I figure he makes you feel, well, I don't know exactly how he makes you feel, but you need to make good choices. I'll be home soon Elizabeth, and you behave."

"That goes for you too."

"Grayson isn't married, or working for me."

"Enough. I hear you."

"Love you, Mom," she laughed.

I peered a few moments in amazement at the light of the disconnected phone before dropping it into the deep folds of my white duvet. Pulling Lily up into my middle, I stroked the top of her head with the tip of my index finger. In the dark, I felt around for the phone and when I found it, I flung it out and across the floor, taking satisfaction in the thump against the baseboard. If she only knew what you really are. After all these years of burying the past, this girl, she drags it up again and rubs it right in my face.

The phone across the room sprayed a dim light up the wall. I climbed out of bed, picked it up, and stepped out the bedroom door. At the top of the stairs, I flung it down into the darkness of the living room, but I could still make out my phone down there, light spraying up the back of my high-back chair, refusing to die. I sat on the top step, shoulder and head against the wall. In my white silk nightgown, I pulled my legs up into a ball, and I covered my face with my hands. "I love you too, Coree," I whispered into those hands, and into the darkness of my empty house.

45

Coree

My keys skated across the old kitchen table, and off the other side, a rude crash on the floor in the silence. I had no right or expectation to find anything in the fridge, yet a neat row of Snapples in their various, bright colors saluted me from the top shelf. Tons of other fun things filled all the shelves, top to bottom. I hit the jackpot, bigtime. For once, the rattling, rusty exterior of our fridge belied a treasure inside. They must have just grocery shopped, but none of us ever bring home this much. We either don't have the green, or only part with it in dribs and drabs. I opened the freezer above, to find it so jammed that a bag of pizza rolls slid out and slapped the floor between my feet. When I bent to pick it up, a figure in the doorway caused me to flinch. "Holy shit woman, you scared me."

She flipped on the overhead light and the room took on a cheap yellowish hue from our sixty-watt bulb. "My bad," said Sharon Blaze.

"Give you flash backs?"

"What're you doing here?" My question trailed off to the obvious, her curvaceous figure skin tight in Aubrey's sweats.

"I had the day off, so Aubrey and I went shopping. I've been chilling, waiting for her."

"Sounds like you two hit it off," I said, nodding at her casual, in-myapartment, in-my roommate's-clothes appearance.

She plopped herself down at my table. "You have a good trip?"

I slid in across from her. "We had a great time. We hit a museum and a beach."

"And the modelling?"

"I don't know how much modeling they do, but they do a lot of escorting."

"There's different kinds of escorting. I'm sus to that."

"I think they do it all. I think if you wanted to model, escort, go to parties and keep men, or even women company, you could, and if you wanted to do some other things, the sky's the limit, if there even is a limit."

Sharon frowned. "Honey, you don't have to go all the way to Florida for that."

"Am I going to be seeing more of you these days?"

"Could be." She smirked. It was the first time I had seen her without lipstick. She wore none of the bouncy, loud jewelry I had become accustomed to, but her laughs and words animated the room like never before.

"I'm glad you're both happy," I said pulling my hair behind and ear. "Can you not hurt her, though?"

"I'll try not to. You know how it is in love though. You got to just follow where the story takes you."

"People keep taking my line."

"What about you? You and Grayson getting serious?"

"It seems that way. We're following where the story takes us too."

"It's all we can do in love."

"How's biz?"

"Good. I have some shoots for you."

"Elizabeth's healthy and heading back to work, so I'm soon free, free as a little wave on the ocean."

"Coree, I have a shoot in Atlanta, of all places. You want to go down there with me? I'm going to use local talent, but I could always use your look in a few shots."

"What is it, back-to-school?"

"It's a catalog for a local big box chain. They liked my bid. Tell you what, let me figure it all out. I'll give you free room and board if you can put up with me. I'll figure out all the finances. You can do a couple shots, but mostly I can use help running it. Be my assistant, set ups, break downs, calls, etc. I'm going to need help with all the logistics."

"I'm safe with you down there?"

"You're safe. I'll admit, I'm kind of taken with Aubrey."

"Aww, that makes me happy. What the...?" I stood up, glaring at my phone.

"What's up?"

"Oh, I got a text from Elizabeth's secretary. My Elizabeth pulled a fast one on me. She sent me off to Florida so she could go into work early. She thought she would slide it by me." I shook my head. "We're going to have a coming-to-Jesus talk about this."

"So," Sharon said. "Just wondering, which one of you is the mom?"

46

Elizabeth

"Are you going to be back at Billie Jean's soon?"

"Never mind about Billie Jean's. You didn't tell me you went back to work."

We faced off across the cold marble of the kitchen island. "Number one, I'm feeling strong and number two, it's none of your business."

"Number one, the doctor said no and number two, it is too my business."

"I don't see how. I'm almost back to normal and it is time to move on. You have Grayson now, so I guess I have Landford-Smithson. Your hair is different. I like it."

"Nice subject change."

"It makes you even cuter than ever." I scrutinized her mood and said, "Coree, seriously, I'm going back to work, and I felt the itch to get moving. We both need to get moving. Now tell me something else, anything. Tell me what's new." The light of my terrace reached in to brighten the side of Coree's face.

"Grayson and I are getting serious," she said with a frown that contrasted her words.

"Don't overthink it, the future. You'll only ruin what you have right now."

Coree looked me over and said, "Working your ass off, building a fortune, and living alone in this cold, empty house."

"That's not me."

"No? Which part am I wrong about?"

I turned my back on her statement to search in the fridge and find a way to get back on offense.

"Oh, and I forgot, have an affair once in a while."

I whirled around. "That's uncalled for. If you were Jo, I'd-"

"I'm not Jo. I'm not Jo or Alison or Chelsea or even Michael. And that's what you need, Elizabeth, but you have to be the big boss all the time, don't you? That way you don't have to hear anything you disagree with."

"You have a bit of alpha yourself, Coree, or some-"

"How's your blood pressure?"

"What? My blood pressure?"

"Yeah. Is it getting under control."

I just shook my head at the head-spinning randomness of Coree's attacks.

"Would you tell me if it wasn't? Elizabeth, you need someone to check on you and keep you honest."

"I'll be sure to let you know next time I get it checked."

"Not a good enough answer, but I'll let it go for now."

I raised my hands in disbelief.

"Don't you ever use this stuff?" Coree said, glancing around at my state-of-the-art cooking gadgetry.

Her gear-changing required me to reset yet again to keep up. "I'd like to, someday."

"When you aren't working eighty hours a week?" She turned. "Look at your kick-ass terrace, the wicker chairs and couch, and loungers."

"I like it."

"No shit. The lattice work and molding alone are insane. It must have cost an arm and a leg, and all for just you. Am I the only other person who's ever been out there?"

The question, though simple, challenged me.

"It should be a place to live, not a place to die."

I bunched my eyebrows. "A place to die?"

"Or sitting there alone, waiting to die." We faced off across my cold marble island again, Lily rubbing at my ankles until Coree said, "I better go. Can I come back and visit the cats and help take care of them or are they all independent too?"

"Coree, you can visit anytime," I said to her disappearing back.

***

A text came from Sammi. "Good news, my little friend came for a visit today. Never thought I would be so happy to have it."

"Congratulations, from someone who is never going to have one again."

"Sorry. Bad Timing."

"I'm dealing with it. What now?

"Here's more good news. Joey is sidelined with an arm injury. Well, that's not good for him, but good for us. We're seeing each other all the time."

"Be careful."

"I learned my lesson."

"Tell me how Coree is doing," I said. "I haven't seen her much lately."

"She's spending a lot of time with Grayson, so sweet, and working with Sharon."

"Tell her I said 'hi."

***

"U don't have to tell my friends to say hi to me! U can do it yourself!" If the long middle-of-the-night phone conversation a while back sounded like a slumber party, this text read like a snippy middle school note.

"Trying to be polite."

"Thanks for being polite, Elizabeth."

"Ouch," I told myself, but she has Grayson now. She doesn't need me anymore.

Lily and I watched a couple furballs streak across the living room. "Little Aubrey and Little Sammi are becoming so independent." I said to momma cat, but Little Coree leaped halfway up the couch and tenaciously clawed the rest of the way, wild-eyed in determination and settled onto my lap. "Baby, what are you trying to tell me?"

I texted, "Can u help me find homes for the kittens? I think I might want to keep Little Coree though. Mom and daughter would be happy together, since I work all the time." I tossed the phone away from me in disgust again and felt the satisfaction of hearing its thump on the carpeting.

When I finally picked it up, Coree's reply awaited me like a sledgehammer. "R u taking them to Chicago? What about me, Elizabeth? R u just going to up and leave me?!?"

I frowned at her question, but the emoji she added moments later caused another knot in my stomach, a broken heart.

47

Coree

"Surprise!" My roommates, Joey, a couple of his friends, Grayson, of course, Sharon and a couple of my model friends jammed into our tiny living room. When my eyes scanned the crowd, Aubrey leaned in, "She couldn't come. I'll talk to you about it later." I opened a few presents, ate cake and made a toast. We tipped our glasses back, and when I searched the faces again, Aubrey quickly ran over to me. "No, Coree. No. Don't emo out now." Too late, I jumped up and ran to my room. The tiny apartment made it easy to overhear Aubrey talking about me. "Here we go. You want to deal with it, or you want me to?"

Grayson's voice said, "What's going on?"

"It's about her Elizabeth."

"Sweet Pea. Everyone's out there. They came for you."

"Not everyone, in case you didn't notice."

Aubrey moaned.

"Where is she? Did you invite her?"

"Yes."

"Well, where is she?"

"She didn't think you'd want her here. She said you have Grayson now and all your young friends and all."

I rolled my face into my pillow. "Why does she treat me like this?"

"I don't know what to say. You love Grayson, don't you?"

"I suppose."

"And the rest of us. Come out to the living room and hang out. It's your birthday."

"You sound like my dad," I said. "It's always, 'We gotta move on, Coree. We gotta move on.' Well, I don't wanna move on. I want my mom."

That silenced the living room conversation, but the TV came on, and loud. Aubrey said, "Uh oh. They think something's going down in here."

"Nothing's going down in here, especially with you, Aubrey, ever."

"That hurt," she said with a laugh. "Coree, seriously, not to sound like your dad, but your mom is not coming back. It's been like ten years."

I laid there a few moments, buried under those words I'd been told so many times. Finally, I whispered, "Can I tell you a secret, Aubs?"

"Of course. You and I are so full of secrets, we're 'bout to burst."

"Right?" I whispered to her, "Grayson and I are, well, even though we have been," I paused, in search for a tactful way to say it, "getting kind of busy lately-"

"Go girl."

"What I want is Elizabeth. I want her support. I need her, Aubrey."

"Didn't I tell you she'd break your heart? I told you a long time ago."

"She's not like that. I swear she's not like that."

"She's a corporate man. You tried to change her. It's just not there."

"You're wrong. There is something, and she needs me too."

"Plus, you've been spending all your time with Grayson," Aubrey said. "Let me tell you a secret back, Coree." Aubrey glanced back and forth in my little bedroom for effect and whispered, "Sharon and I are getting serious, and, low key, we've been at it like rabbits too, but even though my bestie is in here crying, I would totally rather be with her right now than listening to your incessant little whiny ass." We laughed and laid there on the bed, staring up into the faded gray ceiling. Aubrey said, "It's getting tight. She's all me."

"Good for you, Aubs. You deserve to be happy. You so deserve to be happy. It's been so long for you."

"Like maybe never. You know Coree, this is the first time we're all in relationships, solid relationships."

When I didn't respond, she said, "but there is still a hole there, in your heart."

I nodded one slow nod.

Someone above's plumbing whooshed down through the walls.

"Shade," we both said together.

Grayson appeared in the doorway. "You guys come and hang out."

"We were just about there," said Aubrey. "Had to deal with Ms. Ransom, or rather the lack of Ms. Ransom." I looked at both of them with pursed lips to one side.

"You know," said Grayson. He picked at the door frame for a moment.

"What, Grayson?" I said. "What do I know?"

"It's just..."

"What? You got something to say to me, say it."

"I'm the one who loves you and-"

"Aware," I said looking away.

"Well, I'm the one who's here for you. Can you, at least, throw me a bone or something?"

I didn't, and he retreated to the living room.

Aubrey feigned fanning herself and said, "Okay, Earth to Coree, that is the hottest man on the planet, and he loves you. If I was straight, I'd, oh, man, I might anyway."

"Aubrey, just shut up."

"Why do you have to make everything difficult?"

I picked at my rings and felt the receiving end of her disapproving glare.

Aubrey squinted an eye at me.

"What?"

"You're going to dump him, aren't you?"

"No, I am not going to dump him, Aubrey," I said with singsong sarcasm.

"Yes, you are. I know that look. You don't even know it yourself, but I know it. What is wrong with you, Coree? What in the hell is wrong with you?"

Sitting around in our little living room again, Sammi said, "Joey and I have an announcement."

"Oh no, not again." We all laughed.

"Joey, you spill the tea."

"I've had an offer for a job, a real job, and I've decided to take it."

Someone said, "You mean give up baseball?"

He frowned, "I have this recurring injury, but even without it...hey, I'm twenty-seven. I played through high school, college, five years in the minors. I'm so over the travel. It's time to put down roots and after all this time, I'd be fooling myself to think I'm going to make it to the big show." He turned to Sammi. "I love this girl. We're going to get a place together and see where it all leads."

Grayson said, "Where're you going to work, bro?"

I rolled my eyes at Grayson's "man talk."

"Here's the thing. Sammi has a friend, Senior Vice President at Landford-Smithson, pretty sure you know her, Coree, almost like a mom to you. She's bringing me into the marketing department under one of her directors."

"Dunning," I said. "Dianne Dunning."

"That's her. I'm excited. I'm going to be a real grown up for the first time in my life, doing adult stuff, adulting. And, well you guys know Sammi. I mean she's beautiful and all, but..."

He took her hand and their arms together struck me. His, muscular and tanned, hers a combination of caramel and ebony anyone would die for. "Can you stop already," I said. "Sammi would have to take several steps down to be considered beautiful."

He laughed. "But she's smart and driven."

"We get it. We get it." Aubrey said, laughing. "We know we all suck compared to her."

I said, "Joey, you better not be a slob."

"She's the mom in this house," Aubrey said. "Without her-"

"It'll be a dump," said Sammi.

Joey laughed. "She'll have her masters soon. She's good at everything. We'll be a power couple." Joey turned to me. "Coree? I want to thank you for hooking us up with Elizabeth. She is an incredible woman. You're lucky to have her."

I forced a smile, mulling his words, "like a mom," and "lucky to have her."

Sharon broke in, "I'd like to make an announcement too." I checked Aubrey, who shrugged. "Coree recently worked with me in Atlanta, not only as a model, but as an assistant. I'm going to put you on the spot, Coree, in front of everyone, so you can't let me down. Will you come to work with me, an assistant, partner whatever? I've got way more than I can handle? What do you say? Do you want to go into the business end of it?

All eyes turned to me, "I don't know. You think I can do it?"

"What do you mean?"

"I mean, there's a lot to it. It seems complicated."

"Coree, you're not dumb. You can learn, can't you?"

"Step it up, girl," said Sammi. "It's a great opportunity."

I nodded to Sharon.

"Good. That's settled. Like they said, you got the connections. Aubrey and I are getting tight. Sammi and Joey are tight. Coree, it's your birthday, but you've done so much for everyone else."

The happy talk of bright futures became a loud blur and in an off moment, I typed into my phone, "I miss you." I glanced up to see Aubrey watching, and I erased it.

48

Elizabeth

I stood before the mirror, dark navy business suit, white blouse, dark stockings, business heels. You look good, Elizabeth, strong and tough, of course, maybe you are even lit too, as Coree would say. "Don't you think I look good, Lily? The yawn tells me you're not impressed. It's fine. You're wearing the same outfit you've worn all week, so what can you say?" Little Aubrey and Little Sammi ran across the bedroom, leaped on the bed, back down again, and out the door, ears back, tails straight up. "Where's Little C?" As if to answer the question, the orange kitten, the striking image of her mother, poked her head out from under the bed.

"Now, you girls will have a long day without me...or Coree. You have plenty of food and water, and this huge house all to yourself. I turned back to my reflection in the mirror and noticed a lapel turned in. "Now you have me," Coree had informed me. "And now you don't have her,"

I said to myself in the mirror. "She's in love." I made air quotes, more mocking of the concept of love than mocking her.

Little Coree followed me down to the front door. "You want to go with me, help Elizabeth kick some butt?" I stepped out over the threshold and Little Coree watched me leave.

Off the elevator, I strode purposefully down my hallway, Chelsea at my shoulder, rattling off my day schedule, adding wind to my sails. "Call Mr. Kent in here as soon as he arrives, Chelsea," I said taking my coffee from her.

"He's in his office, ma'am."

"Well, what are you waiting for? Get him in here."

"Yes, ma'am. Good to have you back, Ms. Ransom."

"Good to be back. Now, make it happen."

"Have a seat, Michael," I said, from the security and authority of my desk. "Chelsea, you are excused."

I scrutinized his notice of her leaving and brought him back with my words. "You did a good job while I was away. Now, I want to be brought up to date on a couple things that happened in my absence."

"How do you feel?"

His interruption caused me to hesitate. "I am fine, and we might as well go there first. I made a huge mistake before I left, and I apologize. I take full responsibility. The most important thing is, I want to put it behind us and be able to work the way we did before, the effective working relationship we had."

"Your desk is between us."

"Thank you for your observation of the office geography. I don't know what your point is. I don't know, and I don't want to know."

"We all missed you."

I peered over my glasses.

"Did you miss us?"

"I am trying to speak here, and I find it perplexing that when all you need to do is listen, you don't do it."

Chelsea appeared and pulled the door closed. Evidently, Ms. Ransom is raising her voice again.

"How is your girl doing?"

I let out a deep sigh, looking to the side. "Fine, I'm sure."

"You're sure? Don't you know?"

"She's in love. She spends all her time with him."

"Good for her. Do you miss her?"

"I am doing fine. Michael, will you please?" I rapped the palm of my hand on the desk.

"A blind man can see how much she dotes on you."

"We have work to do," I said. "Why do you insist on going way off point? What is wrong with everyone lately?"

"Elizabeth, it's okay to have feelings," he waited until my eyes met his again... "and to let them show."

"I can't believe I'm having this conversation." I took note of my cityscapes on the walls, so organized and predictable. Michael rose, that damn grin on his face and approached along one side of my desk. "What are you doing, Michael? Why are you coming over here?" Without moving a single muscle in my body, I followed him out of the corner of my eye. He proceeded around the desk and sat against it, right next to me. "Why are you so close?"

"Elizabeth, there are people who care about you." He rose and stepping behind me, placed his hands on my shoulders, long enough for me to feel their weight, their strength, and finally, their warmth. He continued to the other side of me and around to his original seat in front of my desk. I furrowed my eyes at him and looked down at my folded hands.

In answer to the question Michael must have seen in my expression, he said, "I had a desire to trespass into your zone, see how it feels, and so, I walked behind you. I touched you. You can scald me with that look, but we both know your anger is with yourself."

"You don't know me like you think you do. You don't know my life. You don't even have any idea just how angry I am at myself, Michael. Nobody does, no idea, years and years and years of anger, but that is none of your or anyone else's business."

"And now you're angry for what you won't let yourself do."

"Michael, you don't know half as much about me as you think you do. Nobody does. Just leave. I have work to do and so do you."

On my phone, I spotted a text from Coree. "Can I come over to your house while you're at work and see the cats? I miss them."

"Sure," I typed in and hit send. She didn't say anything about missing me. She comes over when I'm gone. I slammed the flat of my hand down on my desk.

Chelsea popped into my office. "Is everything alright, Ms. Ransom?"

"Wonderful. Just wonderful. Close the door behind you." How did my much-anticipated return so quickly degenerate into this misery I'm feeling?

***

Home seemed bigger and colder than ever when I returned after that first day back. A note lay on the kitchen island. "I think I found homes for Little Aubrey and Little Sammi. I'll let you know. Your dinner is in the fridge. I stopped at Billie Jean's and selected you a takeout. All you have to do is warm it up."

"Coree and Michael," I said. "What are you doing to me?" The cats scurried out of the room at the timbre of my voice. "I just want to live my life." I laid the top of my body down onto the cold marble, head in my arms.

Rising and wiping a finger under each eye, I said, "George and Raymond. You two can also take a bit of responsibility for what..." I hesitated, "this Elizabeth has become, and Mom, but we've been over it and over it." Little Coree poked her head around the corner at me. "It's mostly me," I said to her. "No, it's all me at this point in my life. I can't keep blaming everyone else. I did this to myself, and I need to get my shit together." After a deep sigh, I said, "Been saying that for a long time." I raised a hand to my mouth and peered out into my comfortable, but empty terrace. It wasn't empty at all, until you came along, little Coree Wysakee. You had to come along and stick it in my face.

49

Coree

Back in his huge bed with the floor-length windows overlooking the city, I snuggled into his arm and in the placid afterglow, I said, "This is what I feared, the first night I met you."

"What's to fear?"

On the wall opposite me, the dim evening light made the dog and the moon the only discernible parts of Joan Miro's painting *Dog Barking at the Moon*. "Remember the night at the club? We watched you there with lovely Tiffany."

"Stalkers."

"Yep, and I turned all emo. I told Aubrey, you'd bring me up to your apartment to make love to me, and I'd do it because while I'd ride you, I'd get to gaze out over the city lights...just for one night. It turned out to be wrong. I mean, about it being one night. You did turn out to be a trust baby, and I thought we wouldn't have much in common. We fell in love anyway, and I've been here night after night after night." I slid my fingers among the sandy curls on his chest.

"I'm happy," Grayson said. An occasional car horn or siren rose from the street far below. "Now it's your turn to say, 'I'm happy, too.'"

"I'm happy too," I said, listening to the sounds in his chest, the breathing and heartbeat, and moving with the rise and fall.

"I love you, Coree."

"And I love you too, Grayson." Again, we listened to the faint city sounds below and I breathed in his scent. "What are you thinking about?" I whispered.

"You guys were right, though, in the end," he said. "We don't have a ton in common when you think about it."

"I suppose," I said. "But we have love, Grayson."

"Is love enough?"

"That sounds like a song."

He nodded.

"Love always has to be enough, doesn't it?" I said. "Where does anyone go with their life if love isn't enough. I mean, love just has to be enough."

"I suppose."

"You suppose? Okay, here's your choice. You can either live in a ratty little place with the love of your life or in a mansion with a person you hate." After too long a silence, I said, "Isn't that a no brainer, Grayson?"

"Not necessarily. Why does it have to be someone you hate? What if you lived in that mansion with someone you liked instead of hated? Lots of people probably live contented-enough existences with people they like, instead of love."

"Like Tiffany?"

"Her name is Alexis."

"What?"

"You've been calling her Tiffany all this time. Alexis is her real name."

"Figures. Alexis, Tiffany, it's basically the same name. It doesn't matter." Again, the sounds of a few car horns rose up to us, and I asked, "Do you ever see her?"

"Not anymore, I just want you."

Those right words just didn't have the right effect for some reason.

Grayson said, "I suppose we had things in common though."

Those wrong words didn't have the right effect either. I said, "Like what?"

"Oh, I don't know, our background."

"Money, trusts, prep schools?"

"Maybe."

"Straight fire, what are we talking about here?" I said, leaning up on an elbow. "We just made passionate love. You told me you loved me, and we're lying in bed together afterwards talking about this other woman who you have so much in common with, this Alexis, Tiffany, whatever."

He sat up on his elbows and peered vacantly at the glittering skyline.

"This is a good time to say something reassuring to me, Grayson."

"What do you want me to say, Coree? What can I say to make us more compatible?"

"Compatible?" My face warmed. "What does compatibility have to do with it? What are we doing here, picking out a dog breed? We just made love. We've been making love like...I don't know, like lovers do for...I don't know, a lot. Did it even mean anything to you?"

"Of course, it did. You mean the world to me, Coree."

I narrowed my eyes at his calm and his "You mean the world to me." Grabbing my clothes, I stomped off to the bathroom, and yelled back at him, "So, I got it right after all. I'm just a piece, a cute piece of ass, your model. You had me and now it's back to your rich girlfriend, who you like." I used air quotes for the word "like" as I regarded myself in the mirror, glanced at my butterflies and yanked down my tee shirt. I took a deep breath and opened the door to see him still gazing out at the city skyline. "You sit there all calm and impassive. Your life is so permanently comfortable, you aren't even capable of throwing any shade, are you?"

"What are you so worked up about, Coree?"

"You've never known any reason to be anything else. It's your family, isn't it? You could've never stayed with me. You knew it all along. They own your weak little ass...your millionaire trust-baby ass, floating aimlessly on your lake."

"What's going on? You're going back to the girl at the cafe. Chill." Grayson ran his fingers through his luxurious hair.

"Does she love your hair too and your dimples and your body? Oh, it doesn't even matter, does it, because she's the one. She's always been the one. She's compatible with you. You just detoured to have a fling with a hot little commoner."

"Coree-"

"Put some clothes on. You can't argue that way, laying there naked. Oh, wait, you're not arguing, are you, because you don't even know how to argue."

"Coree, please. What are you mad about? Can't you be rational?"

"Always rational. Always calm. Sorry, I thought we had love. We did have love," I corrected myself, "but relationships are supposed to be rational for you, Grayson."

"What is wrong with you, Coree? I love you. What do you even want from me?"

For just a second, I wondered what was wrong with me too, but my mouth blasted along on auto pilot, pushed on a wave I couldn't get off. "Couples are supposed to be compatible. Is love enough? Clearly not. Later, Grayson."

"You're acting more like your Elizabeth every day, all headstrong and muscular."

"If that was supposed to be shade, it wasn't. I take it as a compliment."

"Run off to your mom then."

"That one didn't score either, not even close."

"Is there such a thing as a mommy's girl? You talk about Alexis. Well, I never had a chance with you against Elizabeth."

I stood there lost in his words. I wanted to run to him, hold him and pretend everything was alright, that I was normal, but my bottom lip just quivered.

"Coree, I noted the effervescence in you when we met, but the resolve, well, I completely missed the resolve. No, I didn't. I saw the resolve too, and I adored it. I've wanted to attach myself to it ever since, but you won't let me."

His words kept crushing me, and I ran out the door.

Descending the floors on the gold elevator, I read his text. "Coree, I love u."

I hit the wall with the bottom of my fist and at ground level, stormed out. "This place sucks."

"Thank you, ma'am," said the doorman. "Have a good day."

On my way home, I read one last text. "I don't know if anyone can ever fill the hole in your heart." I had pulled over to read it, and after I did, I rested my forehead on the steering wheel. You think you know me, Grayson? You think you know me? I sat up straight again, jammed my car in drive, and cut across three lanes of angry traffic to take a left for Somerset.

50

Elizabeth

"Thanks for letting me come over."

"You are always welcome here," I said evenly, watching Coree stretch out on my couch and throw off her high tops.

"Tomorrow, I'm going to take Little Sammi. I found a home for her, a girl who models for Sharon. I guess now you could say, she models for Sharon and me both. She and her husband have been on the lookout for a kitten. After we find a home for Little Aubrey, we should have the other two spayed."

I nodded. "Little Coree wants to stay with me." How do I begin to unpack everything in that statement? "Thanks for the dinner the other night."

"You're welcome. I don't know why I do nice things for anyone."

"Because you are such a good person, Coree."

"Yeah, good people get screwed over."

"What's going on? What's the matter?"

"Grayson and me."

"Not going well?"

"Coree is stupid."

"Did he say that to you?" I felt a spark of anger rise inside.

Coree shook her head. "It's just the way it is. Relationships are just a huge, complicated puzzle...that I can't do, that I can't figure out."

Her statement hung there in the quiet of my living room, and I considered my relationships and the memories of them. Bad memories take time to sink out of view, but even then, when you least expect it, someone like Coree comes along and they surface again and pull you under with them.

"Cats are good though, aren't they," Coree said. "They love you unconditionally."

I nodded, one slow nod. "When Lily came here and had the kittens, you and I were around all the time. Now they spend a lot of time on their own."

Coree dragged her eyes from the floor. "I hear you. Our apartment is lonelier without Sammi and Old TV."

"Will you find another roommate?"

"I don't think so, at least for a while. Aubrey and I'll try to cover it. It'd be hard to replace Sammi. She's been with us, well, the three of us have been a squad since high school, before that. How do you find someone compatible? There's that word. Grayson said his Tiffany is more compatible than me. What a stupid word for a relationship." Coree looked up to me. "Were you compatible with your husbands, Elizabeth?"

I pursed my lips and said, "I suppose. Yes, now that I think about it, we were quite compatible."

"But it didn't work. That proves love is more important than compatibility."

"It is evidence, not proof. There are other factors."

"Like what?"

"Coree, I don't want to talk about them. What's going on with Grayson?"

"I'm so messed up. Aubrey'll blow a fuse when she hears." She mimicked her friend's voice. "What the hell is wrong with you, Coree?"

"Is it over? Did you two break up?"

She shrugged. "I walked out, and I don't even know why. I guess I'm moving on."

"You said from the start, it wasn't going to work. Remember? Was that a self-fulfilling prophesy? I'm going to play devil's advocate here, but, Coree, how many guys have you moved on from?"

She shrugged again.

"You are handling it well. You are strong, Coree, and getting stronger, just in the time I've known you, I can see it."

"Maybe the Elizabeth affect."

"Possible, but don't let too many of my attributes rub off on you."

"I could do worse than be like you."

"Not much worse. We both have the same number of relationships now."

"Not true. You have a married guy hot for you."

I nodded.

Corry glanced around. "Have you ever even used your fireplace? It's so clean and cold. If I lived here, I think I would have a fire occasionally. It would be so cozy in the winter, and maybe romantic, if you ever had a man over. The smell of wood smoke is just what this room needs."

From the loftiness of my straight-backed chair, I studied the field stone and mortar as if for the first time. I admired the rough-sawn beams across my ceiling. "Perhaps it would be messy."

Coree waved my objection away. "This place is so earthy, like off-thegrid, but right in the hood."

For some reason, I visualized, at that moment, sharing my house with Coree and all the compromises such an arrangement would require. "I'm proud of you for being so strong." My comment made me uncomfortable. Why? What's wrong with giving compliments? This girl needs confirmation once in a while from someone older and, Elizabeth, you just hate yourself when you do it. What a piece of work. Michael is right. And Jo. I hold my confirmations so few and far between with her and Allison, particularly Jo. I keep a fist over her rather than a heart and make her grovel for my approval. And what about this girl? She doesn't receive the confirmations a mother gives at all. I rose. "Excuse me a moment." In the bathroom, I peered at the face in the mirror. What a piece of work you are. You feel something inside, and you run away. I turned to the cabinet and banged my head into it, hoping to feel something, anything. Peering at myself in the mirror again, what I beheld did not please me. Come on. Get your shit together, Elizabeth. Toughen up.

When I opened the door, I found Coree standing right outside. "Are you alright? I heard a bang."

"I...banged my arm against the wall. Coree, you don't have to worry about me all the time." I passed her into the kitchen and feeling her close on my heels, I braced myself.

She wrapped her arms around my waist from behind, resting the side of her face on my back. "Do you feel anything? It doesn't matter. I do. Elizabeth, I lost Grayson."

She kept rambling on with the conversation while holding me. Unbelievable.

"Well, I lost the idea of Grayson, the idea of me and Grayson. Okay, the idea of me with anyone."

Coree held me long enough for me to feel her warmth. "I've got you. You may not have me, Elizabeth, but I've got you, and even if you tell me to shove off, I'm not going to. I'm going to cling, metaphorically and physically too."

Coree laughed at her little joke and let me loose.

"Thanks for the hug...or standing still long enough for my side of the hug."

I never took my eyes off the outside window the whole time, and I changed the subject. "Coree, why have you never done any college?"

"How am I going to do that? It's all I can do to stay afloat."

Elizabeth waited somehow knowing there was more.

"I screwed it up in high school, wrong priorities. It was a tough time. And anyway, I just don't know if I can do it, you know, if I'm capable. I don't even know if I could get in, anyway."

"There are ways around that, but first you have to decide that you can do it, have the confidence."

Coree changed the subject, yet again. "I love your house. I love how its set up, but you use it like a fortress instead of a home. You have the door, then deeper, the hallway, deeper still, the living room, and the kitchen and finally your supercool terrace, your favorite spot, mine too, but instead of doing some serious entertaining here, it's deep into your layers of protection, like the center of an onion."

I peered out into the lightness of my terrace and back into the earth tones of the living room, the "off-the-grid, right in the hood" as she put it and then at Coree, who had penetrated my fortress. I considered my office, down the hall from the receptionist, Leah's office, then Chelsea's, and finally mine, if you can get past them. Michael had penetrated my Landford-Smithson fortress and Coree, my home.

51

Coree

"This place seems empty without Sammi. You think Old TV is happy?"

"He'll be fine."

"I can't ever remember a time when this edge wasn't coming loose."

"And I can't remember a time when you weren't picking at it." Aubrey slapped my hand away from the table.

"Remember this table in our house?"

Aubrey nodded.

"My mom used to get after me for picking at it too." I ran the tip of my forefinger under it.

"And you keep doing it, Coree? You're so annoying."

"Hey. I have an idea. We already found a home for Little Sammi. What if we took Little Aubrey over to Sammi's. You suppose Old TV would like a little girlfriend?"

"He might," said Aubrey.

"Maybe she'd be his little Klingon."

"Kittens are relentless, like some people," she said, eyeing me and slapping my hand away from the edge yet again. "They keep at it and at it until the older one gives in."

My fingers went right back to the edge.

The door opened, interrupting my thoughts. "Hi, girls." The melodic, sing-song voice of the one and only Sharon Blaze echoed down the hallway accompanied by the wind chime of jangly jewelry.

"In here," we sang back together in imitation of her.

She dragged fingers over my shoulder as she passed, leaned down to Aubrey for a hug and kiss before collapsing into the chair between us with a breath. "Well, girls, what's the good news?" Before we could even answer, she chimed back in, taking each of our hands on the table. "Let me just say first how happy I am meeting you two? Aubrey has become the love of my life and

Coree, you are my business partner. I'm just ecstatic how it all turned out." She drummed the table to end her proclamation, took each of our hands, and looked at Aubrey. They glanced at each other and at me.

"What?" I said.

Aubrey's eyes darted back and forth between Sharon's and mine.

"What's going on?"

Aubrey studied the edge of the table I had spent a lifetime picking at. Looking back up at me, she said, "Coree, we both love you. We love you so much."

Sharon reached out to my hand again, and I said, "Why you two telling me you love me? What's going on?"

Aubrey peered at Sharon, and Sharon nodded to her.

"Alright, out with it. Spill the tea. I'm a big girl, metaphorically speaking."

"Coree, I love you so much. You know that."

"Cut it, Aubrey." I sat up straight. "What's going on?"

"Sharon has asked me, and I have said 'yes.' I'm going to move in with her."

My heart sank down to the bottom of my stomach, thinking of all the years I had known Aubrey, Sammi too, but Aubrey longer. We played together out in my yard, wearing down the grass under the swing set. She had been there for me when I lost my mom. I'd been there for her when she came out. We snuck around partying, lived together, and shared so many secrets. I thought of all of it, but watching Sharon and Aubrey with joined hands and thinking how much I loved them both, I made myself say, "I'm happy for both of you. You deserve each other, and you deserve to be happy together."

"Coree, I figured you'd be crying. I told Sharon about the times you'd showed up at my door, in an emotional meltdown, and I figured-"

"Elizabeth says I'm getting stronger."

"Seems like it. Sorry about the timing. Just when it all went south for you and Grayson, Sammi and I are finding love and you are-"

"Destroying relationships, as usual. I still have a lot to be thankful for, great friends, a job I like-"

"An old lady to cling to."

I nodded. "And I have to cling. She got no handles to hold onto," I said, clutching the air with both hands.

"Handles?" said Sharon. "Love handles?" She tipped her head back in laughter and grabbed her own sides. "I got those, love handles, but emotional handles, that's an interesting metaphor. I got those too."

"But some people don't have either," I said. "Or they don't let others hold them."

52

Elizabeth

Lily and Little Coree watched me get ready for work and made me feel guilty for leaving them alone yet again. At least I'll be home earlier than I used to be. Coree keeps dropping off food. It doesn't take a brain surgeon to figure it out. She's taking care of me, always taking care of me, staking some kind of claim. I glanced down to the cats. Lily busied herself cleaning her remaining little girl.

***

Stepping off the elevator, Chelsea met me like a wolf on a deer. "Good Morning, Ms. Ransom. "You have a full day, as always. The morning in particular is packed. There is an issue on the loading dock with some employees doing some stupid things."

"The loading dock? I'm a bit busy for that."

"The memo is on your desk. It's serious enough for your involvement, or at least for you to be aware of it. Also, Ms. Dunning wants a few minutes of face to face to talk about an employee you sent her way. You have a presentation at ten from a supplier. You remember?"

"Yes, yes, and yes." I acted annoyed, yet she and I knew fully well this is the kind of morning elevator-to-my-office adrenaline-powered walk I craved, as good for my energy as a jolt of caffeine and as good for my ego as a crown.

When I reached Leah, she started in on me as well about a call from one of the lower vice presidents. "Not now, Leah." Chelsea waved her away. "I'll help you with him when I'm done getting Ms. Ransom settled in. We passed from Leah's office through Chelsea's and into mine and everything stopped. All the predictability, all the hard-core testosteroneladen planning for the day, all the over-blown self-importance deflated with the sight of Michael sitting at my conference table.

"What?"

"We have a problem."

"You help yourself into my inner office. That problem? Don't you think I have my own problems to deal with?"

Michael displayed his apologetic look.

"Seen that before and don't need it."

Chelsea stood back for a moment to let us work out our morning battle. "Your coffee is on your desk. Would you like coffee, Mr. Kent?

"No, Mr. Kent would not like coffee as he will not be staying."

Chelsea turned to leave, and it wasn't long before I heard my two secretaries going at it on the issue of the junior vice president, strained annoyance in both their voices. This must be what it's like listening to Michael and me arguing. I also knew the junior vice president, older than me, much older than Chelsea, and a man, would be annoyed with the possibility of my senior secretary resolving his issue rather than an audience with me, whatever his issue was. I reveled in it all, but before I could reach my desk, the sound of my office door closing prompted me to freeze. Still in my morning power mood, I took the offensive, albeit, with my back to him. "Michael, why did you close my door?"

"I want us to be alone for a moment."

"It is eight o'clock in the morning, for God's sake."

"At least you know what this is about."

"Did you not hear Chelsea when I came down the hall? I am slammed."

"The morning Ransom power walk? Who's that show for?"

I felt a soft touch on my neck and reflexively brushed it off like a mosquito. "Stop it."

The touch returned and my body gave away some of its rigidity. Warm breath replaced it and I pleaded, both with myself and with Michael. "We can't do this. Did you lock the door?"

"Yes, I did," he breathed into me.

"I need to get rid of that lock."

"Funny. The great and powerful Elizabeth Ransom made a joke."

Save me. Somebody save me, from Michael, from myself.

We both jumped when the intercom sprang to life. "Sorry to bother you from your morning argument with Mr. Kent, but Vice President Emery, is in the outer office with Leah. He's in a state. He has some life and death issue which he will only talk to you about. He won't even sit down."

Some of my rigidity returned and Michael pulled away, but not before letting his light touch trace a line down my side, not breaking contact until it had just passed over my hips and paused there a moment. An electrical charge went through me.

"Work calls," he said, "Work always calls."

I turned to the door, finding myself face to face with him.

"I'll tell you what," he said. "I'll try to wind my day up early, say four? I'll pop down to see you. We can resume our argument and you know what would be nice?"

He touched my hip again and helplessness descended over me.

Imagine it, me helpless. "What?" I mumbled, not like the dignified, powerful fifty-year-old executive I am, but like some flattered fifteen-year-old.

"If you would send your Chelsea on an errand or send her home early, anything. What do you think?"

"There's still Leah."

"Oh yes. Well, maybe you can send your hitman home too."

"Don't get overconfident."

Michael blinked.

I pushed passed him and taking a last glance, yanked open the door. "Chelsea, tell Leah to send Mr. Emery in and let's see what his deal is."

"See you at four," Michael said.

"That was a shit show, an unnecessary shit show," I said to Chelsea, across my desk. "Every rumor, every bit of information about me and my promotion has become, 'How does it affect me?' I haven't even left and he's trying to stick a foot into this office."

“Not to sound like everyone else, but... will he actually be the one moving into this office, Ms. Ransom.”

“I don’t mind hearing it from you, Chelsea. You have been the picture of efficiency and loyalty. Until I am officially promoted, we can’t address my replacement, but since you will not be coming with me, I will assure you, you will be taken care of.”

“Thank you, ma’am.”

We both looked at the phone light when it blinked. “What is it, Leah?”

“The quarterly earnings report is online. I forwarded it to both of you.”

As I brought it up, Chelsea said, “She wants to go with you.”

“Who?” I said.

“Leah, of course.”

“I’m aware. Thank you.”

Chelsea studied my face. “Who did you think I meant?”

I gazed past her at my geometric buildings on the wall.

“Did you think I meant Coree?”

I shook out of my trance and turned to my computer.

“At least you won’t have to deal with Mr. Kent anymore.”

That statement drew my eyes from the screen back to her.

“You know. All those morning arguments.”

“Oh, yes,” I said. “Those morning arguments.” I turned back to the numbers on the screen.

Chelsea sat in front of me, bringing the report up on her pad, and she broke the silence. “If that’s all they were waiting on, for a last bit of political cover, or economic cover, that’s it then. Great report. Congratulations. Will they make the formal offer today, do you think?”

“It is possible. Or they may wait a day or two in a show of decorum...or to make me squirm one last time.”

“Ms. Ransom,” she asked. “Would it be okay if I leave a bit early for an appointment this afternoon?”

I struggled to make words.

53

Coree

After a working lunch within the perfumed walls of Sharon's little office, I continued on my kitchen table, call after call after call, scheduling on my laptop. Perhaps there is something exciting to this, a smaller version of Elizabeth's work. When I closed a deal or lined up a model, I wondered what huge deals and decisions Elizabeth might be making right now, or what "asses were being kicked," at this exact moment.

Our once happy apartment had become my office. My faux Jackson Pollack canvas I made with Grayson on our painting date livened up the living room. Leaning over the couch, I ran a finger along a red enamel line nearly as thick as my pinky finger.

My Andy Warhol soup-can print boosted the energy of the kitchen, but with no Aubrey, no Sammi, and no Old TV either, the place lacked spontaneity. The fact that I couldn't afford the rent on my own hung over me like a ticking clock, adding to the Chicago ticking clock. I'd have to make a decision soon, figure something out. I lit a white candle on the end table, maybe its last burning because I had to reach the match way up inside the bottle to light the wick.

Back in the kitchen, despite being covered with papers, I found the ragged edge of the table. I ran that same finger under it, but jumped about a foot in the air when four loud bangs on the door echoed through the empty apartment. The memory of Jade rendered me immobile. Another four hard raps, loud and insistent, sent chills into me. "Police," a woman's voice, deep and booming said, "Are you in there, Ms. Wysakee?" The banging commenced again. When I didn't reply, the voice commanded, "Open it up," and the rattling of the landlord's dozens of keys commenced.

While hastily unlocking the chain and the deadbolt, I peered through the peep hole at a frowning woman in a dark uniform and the little hairy man in his white undershirt peeking around her shoulder.

"Sargent McKenzie, I need to talk to you. Can I come in?"

"Am I in trouble?"

"No." she said. "I have news for you." She walked past, turning back to the landlord. "This doesn't concern you. You can go now."

He nodded and scurried down the dim hallway.

Following her into our little living room, actually just my living room now, I felt so small, her in her menacing uniform and hat, shiny black leather belt with all kinds of mysterious equipment hanging from it, and heavy boots, me, barefoot, in shorts and a tee shirt. She turned on a lamp, and in the jaundiced light of it, directed me to a chair, one of my own chairs, as if I was her guest. I was right about the candle. It had already burned out.

Perched on the edge of my chair, my mind raced, thinking of what this cop could be here for, all the people I knew, the relatives, the friends. I tried to read her eyes with the bizarre idea that if I figured it out, the reward would be making it go away, making it not happen. She sat straight across from me. "It's my father, isn't it?"

"I'm sorry, ma'am. He passed away about an hour ago, a heart attack. I don't know the details. I've only been told to pass along that he didn't suffer, and he wasn't alone. That's all I know. They thought you would want to know that."

My eyes fell to the not-so-clean wood floor of my desolate apartment. Sammi would be all up in my ass about it if she saw it. "Where is he?"

"He's at the Richville Hospital. I'm sorry, ma'am." She took my hands in hers. They were large and strong, much darker than mine. "If there is anything I can do..."

My old house, the dogs, the cats, the family pictures on the walls, the gullies under the swings, those things seemed so far away now and so abstract. The cracked cement front steps and Daddy standing inside the screen door came to mind, the last image of him I could remember. "He never recovered after Mommy died," I mumbled.

"I'm sorry, ma'am. Do you have someone you can call?"

I peered down at the frayed edge of the rug.

"Someone to be with. Someone who can drive you? You shouldn't be alone or driving."

I cast an eye around the room.

"I noticed all your work in the kitchen. Is it in there?"

"Yes...yes," I said.

"What do you do, ma'am?"

I paused and tried to remember what it is that I do. "Modelling agency. I'm a model, and we have an agency."

"Of course. I can see it," she said. I ignored the compliment that seemed pointless now, and I wandered across the room, down the hallway, and into the kitchen, followed by the sound of boots, heavy on the wood floor. I avoided all the familiar squeaky spots. The officer stepped on them all. There it lay, next to the frayed table edge. I punched in the numbers and raised the phone to my face. "I need you. Please come get me." My head fell into my arms, onto the papers on the old kitchen table.

"This is Sergeant Suzanne Mackenzie. I'm with Coree Wysakee. Who is this?" She stepped out into the hallway with my phone, but her voice was clear and strong. "Her father passed away...about an hour ago. She called you first. Yes, ma'am." The officer reappeared in the kitchen.

"What have I got now?" I said. "What have I got now?"

She handed me the phone.

54

Elizabeth

"Do not go anywhere, Coree. Do you hear me?"

"Yes, ma'am."

"Stay right where you are. I'll be right there. Tell the officer not to leave until I get there. Do you understand me, Coree?"

"Yes, ma'am," Coree said. I remembered all the times she said 'yes ma'am' to me in the restaurant before I came to know her, before we came to be friends. We were past that, but events seemed to rekindle in both of us the need for me to take charge again.

I glanced at my watch. "Three forty-five and I'm out of here, Michael," I said to the empty room. "Coree has saved me. She doesn't approve of this business with Michael anyway, and she saved me from myself. Now I must save her."

"Emergency," I said, hustling through Chelsea's office and finding it strangely empty.

***

Silence filled my Lexus to bursting on the way back to Richville. Coree peered straight ahead or down at her hands, cried in short intervals, wiped under her eyes, and sat quietly again for a time.

She indicated an exit, one of those ramps in which nothing appears to be there at all, save an unfamiliar town name and an arrow pointing somewhere off into the countryside. When I had made the turn and headed in the direction of the arrow, I reached over and took her hand. Coree clutched at it like a lifeline, laced her fingers into mine, and covered it with her other hand. On buff-colored country roads, I visualized little Coree bumping along in a big yellow school bus, a cloud of dust rising behind.

"I want to show you where I grew up."

"Mm, hmm," I said, taking in all the wide-open spaces, the red barns, and the white or brick farmhouses.

"Someday, Elizabeth, can we see where you grew up?"

"I suppose." Today stretched my mind in so many different directions. The call from corporate had come barely an hour before Coree's call, but I said, "Coree, that doesn't matter right now. We need to take care of you." She pulled our hands up to press her lips against the back of my hand and pressed it against her cheek. At a four-way stop, within four fields of crops unfamiliar to this city girl, we were the only car that seemed to exist.

"You're what I have now, Elizabeth. Everyone has left...in one way or another."

I hid an eye roll in my mind, but chastised myself for being unreachable? Where did it all come from. Jo isn't like me. Allison isn't like me. Did my parents find me on the doorstep?

"There it is. Way up there. The little white house on the right. See it? I hope you aren't judging me, compared to your house."

"Coree..."

She squeezed my hand. "I'm glad you are here, Elizabeth."

The two-track driveway caused us to bounce in my Lexus. "Coree, I grew up in a house similar to this, in the city, yet very similar."

"How'd you end up in your mansion?

I considered that. In our nineteen-sixties ranch house, the neighbor's houses, exactly the same, were only a driveway's width apart. Now I live in my sprawling comfortable home, what Coree calls a mansion, but quite alone.

"Come on. I'll show you where I grew up."

"Coree?" Whatever my words were going to be, they floated away on a silent country breeze. She held the screen door, and my eyes wandered to the field next door where a gray donkey stood in the shade of a stunted apple tree, flapping long ears and wagging a long black tail at a circling army of flies.

Coree turned to look in the direction of my glance. "That's Peggy. She's a guard donkey."

"What does she guard?"

"The calves there."

"Like a sheep dog?"

"Not exactly. The calves go where they want, but if something, a coyote or dog bothers her little ones, look out."

"Does it work? She looks, well, occupied, for want of a better word."

"Oh, she might look like it." Coree laughed. "One time we had company and their young boxer went in there, approached some calves. Peggy came thundering over from the other side of the field, sounded like a cavalry charge the way those big old hooves were slamming the ground. The race was on, and that dog ran like his life depended on it, which I suppose it did. Peggy get's kind of irrational when her calves are threatened. They don't even know it, but they got nothing to worry about under her protection."

I watched Coree disappear into her empty house and took a last glance at Peggy before following.

Within the screened porch, Coree kneeled within a dog and two cats, comforting them with her touch and calming words. She said, "We had two dogs but lost one recently. I don't know what to do about these guys. I'll ask around."

It made me think about Lily and Little Coree. What happens to pets when they lose their master? I took leave of her to explore inside, and her soft words fell away into the background. A paneled hallway, covered with various-sized pictures in various styled frames, drew me into it. What happens to family pictures when the family dies? What will happen to these? I suppose Coree could take over the house and leave them up. What would she do out here though? Work at the grocery store and marry one of the locals? Is this how our friendship ends then, me in a Chicago high rise, and Coree in her old family house in Richville?

The dozens of pictures in the narrow hallway were interrupted by bedroom doors, into which I took passing glances. Dust along the spaces not commonly used, baseboards, ceiling corners, shelves with the knickknacks of the former lady of the house, easily identified it as the home of a widower. The scent of an old library came to mind.

All the faces, dozens of unfamiliar relatives, seemed similar, as family pictures do, and Coree, the only child, appeared everywhere, baby Coree with adoring mother, toddler Coree, grade school Coree, and so on, the star of so many camera shots, parents in their supporting roles. In a picture of a whole lot of what looked like ten-year-olds, maybe a birthday party, there they were in the middle, Coree, Sammi, and Aubrey, so much life, so much unknown still ahead of them.

A quick glance at one particular photograph nearly caused my knees to buckle, the first of three bombshells within a few short minutes that would send my entire life reeling. I grabbed for the nearby windowsill for support. Squinting, I read words scribbled in pink marker, "Me and Mommy, backyard." At a picnic table, Coree looked to be eleven or twelve, the cutest preteen ever. She fit naturally within her mother's arm, and gazed up at her with love. The woman, deep hazel eyes, looked right into the camera and right into me. I gazed at her too, because we could have been twins, at least years ago. Did she look out at me from her picture as I looked at her and if so, what did she think? I traced over the picture's smooth surface with the pads of my fingertips, as if to understand her, to know her.

"Ellen at the lake," another picture said. Did we look alike? Not exactly, but quite similar? I easily identified her in various pictures, here in the kitchen, here at Christmas, and here in the garden. Ellen is her name. Ellen is Coree's mother's name. The picnic table picture captured the resemblance perfectly though. Is this what the whole thing has been about, that I look like her mother, why she searches all over my face with her eyes? But now my mind raced until I shook when I spotted a picture of the happy parents with their "new baby." My eyes darted around, crazy-like, my body having to hurry to keep up. I searched for maternity pictures, pregnancy, anything like that. "Oh, God, Oh, God," I whispered. I pressed my hand into the paneled wall, seeking support again.

"Sammi's family is going to take them."

"What? Who?"

Coree appeared at the end of the hall. "Salt and Pepper and Whiskey, the cats and the dog, of course. That's settled and what a relief."

I kept my back to her.

"They have a pile of kids. They'll be happy once they get used to the noise. What're you looking at?"

"You were such a beautiful child, Coree, such a beautiful child."

I could hear her smile form without even looking.

A huge piece of green farm equipment lumbered past on the dirt road, prompting Coree to peer out the window a moment. I took the opportunity to study her, to really observe her features. When the noise and shaking subsided, Coree said, "Maybe I should just go down to Florida and make a butt ton of money with Tiff-"

"No." My own intensity surprised me. I took in a long breath, straightened my business suit and said, "That will never happen."

Coree eyed me. "Maybe a fresh start."

"I said that will never happen."

"But you can see why-"

"Drop it, Coree."

"But if you go to Chicago-"

"It's not happening." My words came from some place I didn't know, and they didn't need thought. "You are not going to Florida. You are not working for this Tiffany. That is final, and the discussion is over."

In the absolute silence that only farmhouses can have, her shoulders slumped. Coree scrutinized me before turning back to the pictures. "My mother's so beautiful, don't you think?"

How could I respond to that? This Ellen and I have similar appearances, but it ends there. She's the loving mother, the loyal wife, the ray of sunshine. Me? I'm consumed by my success, an ambition which has eaten me alive from the inside. I felt like I was made of cement.

"Sunshine," she said. "Grayson would have used the word 'effervescent.' It's where I got it from, evidently, even though I was adopted. I told you that, didn't I?"

Number two. I flinched and my throat instantly turned to sandpaper. "I...don't think you did. I need to step outside for a moment. I need some air."

With a hand on my car, I peered out into the sunny, sloping fields, surrounding the shaded yard. She grew up here, played, had every childhood experience that became the Coree I came to know. And every one of those, every single one, this Ellen woman watched and guided. Leaning on my car and taking a furtive view of the house, two lines ran down my cheeks and this time I didn't even try to stop them, nor did I want to. I wanted to feel their course, experience them. One slid fast, the other, lingering, moving, lingering again, and finally hesitating at my jawline. I sucked in air, sucked it hard, right down to my diaphragm, hoping to fill my lungs enough to control my shaking.

And now I set number three in motion. "Leah. Drop everything else, everything. Absolute confidentiality on this. Get this done as soon as possible. Whatever it takes. Do you hear me? Whatever it takes. Get it done."

I turned to the house to see Coree inside the porch, fumbling with keys. She descended the cracked cement steps, an arm extended back to let the old screen door close quietly on its long steel spring, like she had, no doubt, done a thousand times. She peered into the neighboring field, affording me a chance to observe her again. Her jeans and tee shirt carried youthful energy, always. Her carefree hair let a strand cross her face, but her shoulders, the bearing of her walk, gave away to my familiar eyes, the burden that played on her usual effervescence.

I turned away.

"You ready to go? I've got to say good bye to Daddy. Thanks for coming with me. I don't know what I would have done without you." She slid an arm inside mine and hugged her head against my shoulder. Coree's narrowed eyes searched around my face the way she often did, and she ran an index finger along my jawline.

"You would have risen to the moment like you always do, like you always have."

Where her driveway met the gravel road, I said, "What is in that field?"

"Those are sunflowers."

"That's what I thought."

"They don't look like much now, lifeless and withered," Coree said, "but you should see them when they are in full bloom, an endless sea of yellow and gold."

I looked both ways, nothing, but vanishing point each way. Next to us, that rural icon, their black mailbox with the red flag, a vision materialized, a little girl waiting for the bus, this Ellen woman standing by her side, hand in hand, and a sea of golden sunflowers lighting their life. What was Elizabeth Ransom doing at that time? Rotting, self-absorbed, selfimportant, in some barren, cold board room.

I accelerated, a cloud of dust filling the rearview mirrors. In the field beside us, Peggy migrated purposefully across the pasture, a brown and white calf trotting close beside her.

55

Coree

The headlights stretched into the unknown ahead of us, and I suppose the various dashboard lights told us about our present condition. I didn't want to drag her down into my memories and Elizabeth, even if she wanted to, lacked the ability to talk a person through what I felt. No radio station played music appropriate for our mood, so we rode in silence. A block or so away from my apartment building, Elizabeth said, "I'll come up and help you pack. Follow me in your car. Do you think you can drive alright if you follow me?"

"Yes, ma'am."

"Do not call me that." she said, raising her voice and an index finger. When we stopped, she said. "I'm sorry. I had no right to raise my voice. "It's just..." She gazed at the rusty, green dumpster in front of her Lexus and sighed.

"Michael?"

"I don't want to talk about-"

"Over and over, Elizabeth."

"No. Coree. There are other things."

"How about you're wound as tight as a ball of rubber bands?"

Elizabeth scrunched her eyebrows at me, turned back to the dumpster ahead and scanned it like she'd never seen one before. "I am, of course, wound as tight as...but my problems are, well, I have no right to bring them up. And all my problems are self-inflicted. You, Coree, are playing the cards you've been dealt, like you always have, going where the story takes you, rising to the occasion. Me? Well, any problems I have, I deserve. I deserve my life."

"You need help, Elizabeth."

"Not from your energy, Coree, at least right now. You need help yourself. I need to put on my big-girl panties, for once in my life."

"Said the Senior Vice President of Berkshire White."

"Said a lonely and horny, fifty-year-old lady."

"An Elizabeth Ransom joke. I love those."

"Let's go up and get your things."

"Yes ma'am."

"Now who's being funny?"

I followed her Lexus across the four-way stop, the informal demarcation of entering the land of the comfortable, the secure. For me, the canopy of mature oaks symbolized coming under the protective wing of Ms. Elizabeth Ransom. We each climbed out of our cars at the same time, and she motioned me to the little couch along the front wall of the garage, as if the six steps we'd walked required a rest.

I sat, duffel on my lap. "Your garage is nice. It's all paneled and clean, like your car has its own den."

Elizabeth sat next to me, the sides of our legs pressed into each other's. We waited while the two garage doors rattled down to the cement floor, with echoes into the silence of her house.

"You'll move up to my room with me."

I picked at the top of my duffel, a loose seam, looked up at her, and nodded. "Tomorrow, I suppose, I'll be working on this business of my dad and the house." I laid a hand to my cheek. "Where do I even begin?" I returned my attention to the seam on my bag. "I don't even know what to do."

Elizabeth raised a hand with an outstretched index finger. "I'll have Chelsea contact my attorney. He will be able to suggest someone. Better still, I'll tell her I want his office handling it. James Wallingford."

"I've heard that name. Can I afford-"

"It's settled, Coree." She cut the air with her hand like a knife. "Look for their call in the morning."

I frowned just one side of my mouth and looked up at her. I think she could feel my gaze because she turned, reached an arm around me, and pulled me into her. She whispered, "I'm here now, Coree. I'm here now."

I had been about to cry within her embrace, but her words...I didn't know what to do with them, what they meant or where they came from.

"Something we have in common, Coree, is that you and I have to get back up and do it again."

"Do what again?"

"Life. It knocks us down, but we have to get back up and do it again."

I came from the bathroom in my signature sweatpants and oversize tee and climbed in on the other side.

Lily leaped onto the bed and pushed within the back of Elizabeth's knee joint. "She likes that spot. She likes to be against me, but just out of my reach."

Little Coree clawed her way up the side of the bed with wild-eyed determination and settled within Elizabeth's arm.

"Her regular spot too?"

Elizabeth nodded. "She's more openly dependent."

In the darkness, I rolled away from Elizabeth and pulled bunches of sheets up into my mouth. After a few moments to work up the courage, I said, "Elizabeth, I don't know what to say about this Chicago thing. I just...I just don't want you to leave me. Does that sound dumb?" I waited for her response with a mixture of apprehension and hope, fearful of the no-nonsense reply Elizabeth Ransom was known for.

"It is on my mind too, Coree," she said.

***

Thanks for bringing all my stuff over," I said to Aubrey and Sammi, "even though I didn't ask for it to be brought over." I directed those words to Elizabeth, who ignored me. My friends snuck curious glances, back and forth, at the two of us.

Sammi saved us from the ponderous silence. "Elizabeth, you must be quite the chef. You have everything imaginable in this kitchen."

"She doesn't cook," I said.

Elizabeth watched, mute, from behind the marble island.

"She wants to, but no time. Right Elizabeth?"

Her eyes moved from one to the other of us.

"You know, Coree," Sammi said, "it was your mom who really got me into cooking. Your mom could do everything, and she made it fun. I learned a lot from her."

"I just watched from the sidelines and ate what you guys made."

"I remember that part too, Coree. You haven't changed a bit." Sammi turned to Elizabeth, who still watched, from behind her marble island. "Let's cook, Elizabeth. You want to make something with me? You going to stay home today?"

Elizabeth glanced at her closed laptop and at me. "I'm not going anywhere."

"Do it, Elizabeth," I said. "Sammi knows everything."

"I don't have much here," said Elizabeth. "You know, my fridge and freezer are kind of empty."

"Bachelor pad," I said.

Elizabeth put a hand to her face. "There is too much to do, too much."

Aubrey said, "Why don't you two go shopping. Coree and I'll bring her crap in from the garage.

Elizabeth's lips narrowed.

"Then you can make us dinner," Aubrey said.

"Always," Sammi said to Aubrey. "How about Joey and I move in with you and Sharon for the rest of our lives, so I can cook for you every night, forever."

"Perfect," said Aubrey.

I turned to Elizabeth. "Be spontaneous. Sammi'll teach you."

Sammi rose, approached Elizabeth around the island, and urged her along in front of her toward the door. Elizabeth took one last cryptic look at me before disappearing.

"What's going on, Aubs? Why did she tell you to bring all my stuff over?"

Aubrey shrugged. "She was kind of vague about it...and bossy."

"Don't doubt that," I said.

"She said something about the lease running out pretty soon anyway," Aubrey said. "Did you ask her?"

I chuckled at the thought of that. "Elizabeth decides when she wants to give answers. The rest of her world is on a need-to-know status."

Getting to work in the garage, Aubrey said, "Us kids sitting around the kitchen with your Elizabeth...kind of like we did with your mom...too weird."

"Except Mom was like a camp counselor," I said. "Elizabeth's more like a, I don't know, a supervisor."

Sammi and Elizabeth appeared and climbed into her Lexus. Elizabeth said, "Leave the garage door open. There'll be a truck with your furniture coming soon." Aubrey and I looked at each other, but before closing her car door, Elizabeth said, "Aubrey, do not leave Coree here alone. We shouldn't be too long."

Watching them back out, Aubrey said, "What the F was that? When did you get so helpless?"

***

"I'm going in tomorrow for a bit." Elizabeth watched for my reaction.

"Why?"

"There are some things."

"You can't do them remote?" I said. "You've worked with your staff over the phone and face to face on the computer these last few days. Except Leah. It seems like you're all secretive with her."

She ignored my point and said, "A couple issues need oversight."

"Ass kicking?"

"We'll see. I'll try to get out early."

"I'll miss you."

Elizabeth gave me a deadpan look.

"Okay, that sounded dumb, but I've enjoyed this time with you, despite the circumstances." Enjoying the time with her was an exaggeration, because Elizabeth had been more distant and mercurial than usual in her time home with me.

***

After I'd seen Elizabeth off to work, I returned to her bedroom, and hearing a cat digging in the closet, I ducked in to clean. "Oh no, Lily. You've got litter everywhere. It's litter palooza in here. I considered ignoring it and letting Elizabeth find it, so she had to clean it, a ploy I often pulled on Sammi, but thinking of the ever-possible Elizabeth Ransom eruption, much more motivating than Sammi's griping, I said, "Everything out and let's clean up."

Within the boxes, a faded manilla envelope fell out, and the handwritten words, "Letters never sent," though tiny in the corner, caught my attention. Out in the light, a few crinkly sheets floated back and forth to the floor where I dropped to my knees, turned one around, and read, "Dearest George, I find myself writing about 'last night' after every time we meet." My behind dropped onto my heels on the floor, feet turning inward, one overlapping the other. "I've never had love like this before. I don't think I've ever even had love." I paused to scan the papers, a dozen or so. "My dream, of course, is someday we'll be together. However, you and I both know it will never happen, so we share each moment while we can. These words will never be read, but by writing them, maybe they live forever."

I pulled my hair back behind an ear and stared off in front of me. When my eyes fell to the paper again, I read, "Your weight presses against me and-" I dropped the sheets to my lap, remembered to breathe, remembered to swallow, and listened to confirm the silence of the house before glancing around, making sure Elizabeth's glare didn't magically appear like a specter in the doorway.

Everything back in its place, I sat on the edge of the unmade bed, shoulders hunched, hands clasped together between my knees. "My Elizabeth," I whispered. I slid a hand across the underside of the duvet.

Our visit to my old house came to mind. Despite keeping her cards hidden, and despite standing like a rock, unyielding and unbreakable, in the middle of her world, despite all that, at my old house, Elizabeth cried...so uncharacteristic. Was it for me, for my loss? No, that's not Elizabeth. Was it for something with Michael? No, he could never in a million years make Ms. Elizabeth Ransom cry. "Why won't you talk to me, Elizabeth?" I made her bed, and left.

My things, furniture and so on, everything I owned, my life, was stacked neatly in front of my car. I peered at them over my windshield crack wondering how everything came to this point. Without so much as a comment or discussion, Elizabeth brought everything I had, everything that is me, within her house.

I navigated my way around the curving lanes, past fortress homes, past oaks, standing like sentries, until the four-way appeared in the distance. You either lived in it or out of it, in my view, based on this intersection. I didn't know where I fit, in sometimes, simply because of my vague attachment to Elizabeth Ransom, out others, simply because, well, Cory Wysakee of Richville had little business in Somerset. My mind replayed, going backwards, all I'd experienced, Elizabeth's apparent affair, Daddy's death, my buds moving out, my breakup with Grayson. What else? It's one thing after another, crushing me down.

I stared across the intersection into life's unknowns. Why is my story screwing me over like this? How much can I take? And what if I lost Elizabeth? It would be the end. Or would she want me to go with her to Chicago? I could go to Florida and get myself a mansion like Tiffany. But Elizabeth told me no, about shouted it at me. Where did that come from? I tucked my hair behind an ear. And she cried. She'll never admit it, but I saw it. I definitely saw Elizabeth Ransom cry. I touched the tear on her face. What's she got to cry about? I'm the one losing everything.

55

Elizabeth

"So, there we are. With their startup complete, we'll begin receiving product in thirty days."

"Heard it before, Michael. You should have more details in writing."

"We wouldn't have gotten the deal."

"That's on you."

He frowned. "All we can do now is keep after them."

"And that's on you too. Stay on them, Michael. Make it happen." I spent a few days at home helping her attend to her affairs and to lend moral support. Now here I am, back to the office and for this trivial bullshit? One of my staff drops the ball, and for all intents and purposes, the only reason I'm here is to make sure he knows the responsibility for this project's success or failure is directly and completely on him. I glanced off at the window and said, "Why am I here?" I texted Leah and looking at her reply, I exhaled.

"What's wrong, Elizabeth?" Michael said.

"Nothing is wrong."

"You're fairly pounding holes in your phone."

"Is this meeting over, Michael, because it seems to me that it is?"

"You tell me?" he said.

"We have covered the status of this new project of yours, to my dissatisfaction, I might add, but it's your department and your problem. We both have work to do." I rose, collected my things, and retreated in the direction of my desk.

"Always work to do." He knew the words that pushed my buttons. I turned, midstride, jaws clenched to look at Michael still sitting at the conference table.

"How do you think I got to where I am?" He looked up to me. "By working, determination."

"Where do we go from here, Elizabeth?"

I glared. I had the strength to not encourage this conversation, yet not the firmness to slap it away either, so in reality, how much strength did I really have? Michael was unaware of the status of my promotion, ignorant of Coree's tragedy, and he especially did not know what I was texting Leah about. He did, however, sense the weakness in me caused by the weight of these pressures, evidently, intending to leverage this weakness.

And it always comes down to strength with you, doesn't it, Elizabeth? How much do you have? How much is displayed? How much are you using and keeping in reserve? I remember Coree telling me how exciting my power can be, maybe even arousing to people like Michael Kent. She also, several times, told me to stay away from him, yet here I was, standing in the middle of my office, like a ship without power, adrift, and waiting. I wished I could take a time out like they do at critical points in ball games, to talk to Coree right this minute, get her insight. I need her. I've always needed her, I realized that at her house, ironically when she was at her most vulnerable. Elizabeth, she has enough problems. She doesn't need your self-centered, self-inflicted issues. I need to get Michael out of here and focus on Coree, focus on Coree's needs.

He interrupted my thoughts, firing on that ship, adrift on the open water. "Is there a heart? Is there a passion? I know there is. You know there is. It may be locked up or hidden, but you and I know it's in there."

On my side table, Jo and Allison and their families watched me from their pictures. "Michael, you have a wife and family."

"Is that part of the attraction?"

"What on earth do you mean?" I asked, desperate to buy time for how and when I could get back on offense.

"That's it, isn't it?" he said.

Damn him. He knew his statements scored, and he sat there calmly watching their effect.

"I'm no threat to your organized life. You call the shots. You keep control...of this," he said, moving his hand between us.

"You are talking crazy," I said. I kept up the veil of my poker face, my boardroom persona, but Michael Kent possessed a boardroom persona as good as anyone's. No rookie to negotiations, he could pick up the minutest flicker to the effects of his words. He smiled, a knowing smile, perhaps even a mocking smile, and I recollected George, the only time I let my guard down. I've regretted it ever since, every single day of my life. "Sorry, Michael," I lied to him, but also to myself, trying to convince both of us that Elizabeth Ransom is indeed the heartless woman she pretends to be. "What you see is what you get."

"What about Coree? You two have become close."

"A friendship, nothing more," I said in a despicable attempt to retain the crumbling image of a cold woman I had spent decades constructing. Did Peter feel the same way when he denied Jesus?

"Not only is that a lie, it's cruel. That little child dotes on you like a mother and you know it."

That statement blasted my defenses apart. My thoughts and words became pointless and nonsensical. "She's far from a child." I took my lies to the window to see if I could fling them out or maybe better yet, fling myself out. The sound of his approach and the feel of his hands at my waist caused me to freeze. I could not speak, could not even open my mouth. I thought of his family, my lies to myself, my two broken marriages. His hands slid down just enough, not much, but just enough to hold my hips and they felt delicious...to be wanted, to be desired. I thought of Coree. I left her alone when I should be there with her. I'm sorry, baby. I'm so, so sorry. But again, I thought of myself, my own needs.

The heat of Michael's whisper behind my ear said, "Tell me what you want, Elizabeth," and he paused long enough to let me drown. His body pressed against mine, and all I could do was consider the terms of surrender to the passion and affection of which my life was so devoid. I whispered, "Michael, lock the door."

The heat of his touch withdrew and when I turned, I saw in my peripheral vision, the blinking of my phone.

Michael nodded to it.

The comedic irony of the moment hit me. What a couple of corporate losers we were. Despite such a palpable rush of passion between us, like trained monkeys, work always came first.

I furrowed my eyebrows.

"What is it?"

"Aubrey."

"Who's Aubrey?"

"Coree's friend. Why would she text me?"

My lips moved as I read silently. "Coree had an accident. They took her to Bay Hills-in critical condition."

My breathing stopped, and I stared up past the phone into the blur of my life, the complete wreckage I'd made of it. I deserve everything that has fallen upon me, every miserable moment, but Coree, what about her? Why do these things happen to her? I knew the answer, so simple. It's because of her connection to me, to Elizabeth Ransom.

Approaching from behind again, the weight of Michael's hands returned to me, to my hips, grazing lower, and around. That touch, so warm and sensual just a moment ago, now felt grotesque. "Get your hands off me," I said, and my brain clicked on like a struggling car finally starting in a scary movie when the guy with the ax has nearly caught up. With handbag and brief case, I hustled to the door. "Why in God's name is this door locked?" I said, struggling to get it open.

Storming past Chelsea, I burst into Leah's office. "Coree has had an accident. Get your things and meet me downstairs. Get everything we might need."

Turning to the man in the doorway, I said, "Michael, I don't know when I'll be back." I took a step or two, glanced back at Leah, shoving materials into a brief case and then back to Michael. "I lied...about myself, about Coree."

He nodded. "If Coree, or anyone for that matter, could choose their savior, you would be the one."

I stormed down the hall, vaguely aware of an altercation erupting behind me, between my two secretaries.

The elevator's unhurried indifference infuriated me. Despite my head start, the door next to mine opened just after I exited, and the telltale clicks of Leah's stilettos hustling to catch up echoed in the parking garage. "Get Wallingford on the line," I called over my shoulder.

"I'm going to want to talk to him as soon as we are under way."

"I'm on it."

"Tell his secretary it's an emergency and do not take 'no' for an answer. I want him on that phone within minutes, Leah, within minutes. Make it happen."

***

Across from the surgeon in a tiny conference room, I prepared, as well as one does, for the worst. Leah moved methodically, selecting a document from her brief case and sliding it the short distance to him. He gave it a cursory glance and pushed a few errant strands of black hair back from his damp forehead.

"Doctor, I appreciate all you have done and the fact that you must be exhausted...six hours, was it?" My words were caring. My tone, agitated.

He nodded. "What is your connection to her again?"

"I'm her...friend." I heard the shift in Leah's chair. Under the table, my hands opened and closed wildly on my lap. Leah took them both within one of hers and clamped them still. If her hold on me could have spoken, it would have said, "Do not lose your shit, Ms. Ransom, not now."

"All the damage is on the left side, arm, ribs, hip, leg, really top to bottom. Her cheek is fractured, just a hairline. We need scans of her brain, but first she needs to be stabilized. She is under heavy sedation and will not be conscious for..." He shrugged.

"When can I see her?"

"Perhaps a few hours." He hesitated. "Ms. Ransom, I don't know how close you are to her, but you need to prepare yourself." I closed my eyes to that.

After the long, unpleasant rundown, the surgeon left us to ourselves. Leah and I rose to leave, but my body would not move and truly, where was there to go? Hidden away from the world, in that little room, the woman of power and control crumbled to pieces. Leah, took me in her arms, where I cried into my hands, spasms shaking my body, eyes and nose running. "I never should have left her alone. I never should have let her drive in her condition. I never should have come to work. I should have been there for her, but that's me. That's always Elizabeth Ransom. That's why I'm CEO, because I can't do anything else. Never could. Let go of me, Leah." I tried to pull away from her, but she hung on, wrapped around me. I growled and pushed at her, but she hung on, not letting me go until I had cried myself out. Years and years of pent-up regret and guilt culminated in one final horrifying catastrophe. Finally, she guided me back down where I slumped in my chair. We sat in silence. Me, I stared, alternating between straight ahead or into my lap. Leah occasionally worked her phone or tablet, sitting, standing, taking a few steps in the little room, or stepping out to speak.

***

Pulling a chair to the side of her bed, I took Coree's right hand, her good hand, so fresh and young, mine, similar, but showing the stresses of my life. I tried to focus on the right side of her face, what was left of her fresh, youthful beauty. Tubes and cords seemed to sprout from her everywhere. The room beeped. Lines on screens bounced under the vigilant eye of a nurse. In the center of it all, Coree lay peacefully, so peacefully, in fact that I fought the urge to shake her awake.

After a check of all the connections and screens, the nurse eased out the door. I leaned in, her hand within mine, pressing my lips against the back of her hand. "Coree," I whispered, but paused. "Would you leave us for a moment, Leah?"

"Yes, ma'am," she said and turned to leave, but at that very moment, her eyes drew to her phone. I watched her turn directly at it, as if gazing deep into a crystal ball. She read something, lips moving, glanced up, and looked back at the phone, as if to confirm what it said. Leah turned to me now and handed it over. "Here, Ms. Ransom. Here it is. Read this message." Leah's charcoal nail polish surrounded the screen.

Though short, the message consumed all of me. I squeezed my eyes shut, tapping my forehead with the ends of my fingers in effort to activate my brain.

Having spent half a lifetime practicing for this moment, why did I feel like I was ad-libbing now? My eyebrows furrowed and quivered when my gaze up to Coree closed the lifetime of distance between us. "Honey, I don't know where to start. I'm so sorry. I love you so much. I've always loved you, and I've missed you, and I'm just so sorry." I looked her all over. "I ruin everything I touch." I took a deep breath. "If we can get through this, if you can stay with me, get through this...please stay with me, Coree. Don't leave me. Don't leave me now that I've finally found you. I know I don't deserve you, but we can still have a whole lifetime. I'll take care of you, and when I'm old, you can take care of me. You have to recover, baby. I'll just die if you don't. All will be lost. There will be nothing left. The sliver of hope I clung to all these years will be gone."

I glanced up at the incomprehensible monitors in a vain attempt to see good news flashing on the screens. Leaning into her face and hair, I took in her scent. "Coree, I can change. I can." I searched for everything that needed to be said. "You're the only one who could have saved me." I scanned her other side, the injured side of her body. "But first, I need to save you."

Leah's heel scraped on the linoleum floor outside the door, prompting me to glance in that direction and then back to Coree. "My work, Coree. I need to pull back. I can do it for you, for us." What would my promotion to CEO, my dream, the goal of my lifetime, mean now? Studying her hand again, I touched the freshness, the youthful vitality of it. Mine looked like that once, exactly like that. Can I let up on my work to be with her? Can I take time to love her? "I'll turn it down, Coree. Or whatever you want me to do, so we can be together. Or you could go with me to Chicago. Whatever works for you, for us." I thought of Allison and Jo and my father. "You need to be closer to them. Actually, I need to be closer to them, myself. You can help me with that too. There's so much you can help me with, Coree. You're the only one who can save me."

Thinking of Landford-Smithson made me turn to the door. "Leah." When she popped her head in, I said, "Contact Chelsea, make sure everything is under control, Michael, the day to day. Have her deal with the Board of Directors somehow. Figure it out, Leah."

"I've already taken care of it, Ms. Ransom. I have everything under control."

I turned back to Coree and realizing what I had just done, I said, "I'm sorry. It will be hard for me, but I swear I can change." When I finally rose, my stiff body resisted movement. Not taking my eyes from her, I once again called upon Leah.

"Yes, Ms. Ransom. I'm right here."

"Contact Dr. Everett Woods at Somerset Hospital. Here's what I want you to do."

57

Coree

Hearing that voice, unyielding, commanding, I struggled for just a glimpse, but my eyelids refused, so heavy, I couldn't even begin to lift them. The familiar unrelenting machine gun blasted away, and even in my muddled state, I wasn't surprised.

"Ma'am, he is with other patients. He'll be in later."

"I'll wait."

"You'll have to do that in the waiting room. You can't stay in ICU indefinitely."

"Somerset Hospital? This is Ms. Elizabeth Ransom. I am with a patient at Bay Hills, in ICU, whom I have power of attorney over. Today is the day we are transferring her to Somerset. Forward my call to the office of Dr. Everett Woods. Make it happen. Leah, take over this call. I'll be right here if they need to speak to me."

"Ma'am, you-"

"Are you still here? I told you to find the doctor."

"You cannot stay in-"

"We all have a job to do. Get on it."

I so couldn't control myself and fell back into darkness for who knows how long. When I woke again, I momentarily won the battle with my right eyelid, forcing it open a crack and there she stood, black power suit, back as ram-rod straight as I remembered her from the first time I saw her at Billie Jean's. Framed in the doorway of my hospital room, she stood toe to toe with a man in a white coat like an angry manager going at an umpire. "Who are you?" he demanded.

Elizabeth's arms flailed wide. "I don't understand for a moment and actually, I don't care what your resistance is about." He looked over a document while she bulldozed on. "This afternoon, Miss Wysakee will be transferred to Somerset Hospital."

"Impossible. She is in no condition to-"

A finger immediately stabbed at his chest. Not more than a molecule of air could have separated the end of it from his white coat. Elizabeth's eyes bulged and it appeared for a moment she might take his head off or her own might explode. "It's at three, exactly, so you and your staff have work to do. The people from Somerset will do everything else."

"Ma'am-"

"I don't want to hear another word from any of you here unless it's about how you're going to make this happen. Ahh, Leah. This is my secretary."

"Another person? You all can't be-"

Elizabeth gave the "stop" hand to the doctor's objection and said, "Leah, take a seat there. I may be tied up with this situation, and I want you to be here, just in case."

"Yes, ma'am."

"I'm calling security."

At those words, Leah spun around on the doctor. "I'll call Mr. Wallingford to let him know what is going on. James Wallingford is her attorney, Doctor. I'm sure you've heard of him."

The doctor found himself double teamed.

Leah said to him, "You or security or whoever will be able to speak with him directly if necessary."

He hesitated and turned back to Elizabeth. "Just who are you again? What is your connection?"

"Elizabeth Ransom. You have the paperwork."

Leah said, "Ms. Ransom is CEO of Landford-Smithson Data."

Elizabeth said, "It is no matter here what I do." With slaps on the heal of her hand, she addressed the little medical throng collecting around her, "Three o'clock," she said, voice becoming strained. "Three o'clock. The transfer happens at three o'clock."

Leah edged between the two, forcing Elizabeth back a step, and she, herself, faced the doctor at extremely close range. She had the same corporate presentation as Elizabeth and Chelsea, conservative blazer and skirt, blond hair and makeup tightly under control, but her height, strong shoulders, and square jaws added a physical force. In another world, Tiffany might have found Leah an asset to her business, but Elizabeth evidently accessed other attributes of Leah's. Her own voice, more even and controlled than Elizabeth's current raging, carried unmistakable authority. "Ms. Ransom is going to want a verbal briefing on the patient's condition before she leaves at three, accompanied by the patient. I, myself...I will not exit this building without a complete, hard-copy status report on this patient in my possession." My eyelid became too heavy to hold open and the sound of the brawl receded into darkness.

58

Elizabeth

"She's been under so much medication, it's been days, but we are finally having conversations, although it mostly consists of me talking and Coree nodding her head."

"That sounds like your kind of conversation, Elizabeth."

"Amusing, I suppose, but Michael, I'm going to want updates-"

"Ms. Ransom," Leah interrupted me from across the room. "Mr. Kent is fully capable. You need to put all your focus on this situation right here."

I hesitated at her words and nodded. "You'll have to pick up the slack, Michael," I said, glancing back at Coree, "my slack."

"I'd be honored. You take all the time you need."

"Don't go hiring a bunch of new people on me."

"I won't. Listen, Elizabeth-"

"Michael. It's over. Period. You asked where we go from here. You have a family and I have..." I glanced at Leah, realizing what she overheard, but observed no reaction at all. I might as well have been reading my shopping list.

I disconnected before he could respond and laid my head in my arms on Coree's bed. A few moments passed until a light touch on my elbow brought me back to life.

"Well, hey, baby. How are you doing?"

The corner of her mouth raised only slightly, but enough to brighten the room.

"What happened?" she said, her voice a dry whisper. "What's the matter with me?"

"You've been asleep every time the doctor has been here. Perhaps next time."

"Can't you tell me?"

I sighed. "A car hit yours...on the left side. I guess they call it a T-bone accident."

She gave a roll of her hand, palm up, as if to say, "Get on with it."

"Coree, it is difficult. I'm not a professional."

Allison and Jo poked their heads in.

"Hi, girls."

Coree repeated the little grimace of a smile.

Allison said, "Coree, you couldn't have a better person in your corner than our big sister. She has the resources-"

"-the tenacity," chimed in Jo, "and-."

"Mostly the balls," Allison said, "to, what do you always say, Elizabeth... 'make it happen?'"

They rambled on filling the space with as much happiness as possible until the doctor poked his own head in the door.

Allison said, "We'll get out of here now, but we wanted you to know we're thinking about you."

"Thank you for coming," I told my sisters in the hallway.

Jo hugged me, an embrace that somehow replenished some of my diminishing strength and resolve. "Elizabeth, I'm sorry I wasn't more supportive at first." She still held my arms. "But I didn't know."

"Nobody knew."

"And you're my sister after all, my big sister."

"Jo, you don't have to explain," I said.

A nurse pushed a cart by us, rattles approaching, then disappearing. When the sound receded, Jo leaned into me and whispered, "Elizabeth, is Coree going to be alright? Is she going to recover? I don't know how to say it, but lead a normal life?"

"I think so. It's going to be a long haul, though."

Allison leaned in close now too. "Libby, does Coree know?"

I shook my head.

"What's the hold up?" Jo said. "I mean, when will you tell her?"

I took a deep breath and shrugged. "Girls, this is not something I say or admit very often, but I'm scared. I mean I'm terrified. How will she react?"

They both watched me with the large eyes I remembered from when they were little.

"The right time will come along and you'll know," Jo said. "Take good care of her, I know you will. I love you so much, Libby."

"Everything is going to work out, big sister," said Allison. "If there's anything we can do, anything."

I wrapped my arms around them. "My girls. My little girls. Thank you. I love you too."

When they pulled away, Jo said, "Stop that crying, Elizabeth. You stop that crying right now."

I chuckled. "You sound like Mom."

"And you," Jo said, "but what I mean is, do not let Coree see you cry. Be strong and positive for her."

I wiped an eye and took a deep breath before reentering the room.

"Doctor, Coree wants the lowdown, and I didn't feel I had the credentials to give it to her."

He turned to Coree. "First of all, Coree, you have the best support you could ever have."

"Exactly why I transferred her here. I wanted the best."

He waved my words away and said, "Thank you, I'm sure, however, I'm talking about you, Elizabeth."

Coree made the circle motion with her hand prompting the doctor to turn back to her.

"Coree, the other car hit yours on the driver side making a T when you missed a stop sign. All the damage is on your left side. You haven't looked in the mirror, and I don't suggest you do for a while." He smiled, kindly. "You have a black eye and a lot of swelling from a fractured jaw, but it won't require surgery or wiring, thank goodness. Also, there is zero head or neck damage, extremely welcome news."

His attention dropped to her midsection. "You have fractures in your shoulder and your humerus. They are serious and will take time and physical therapy to heal. Six of your ribs have fractures, two serious and four, not as much." Coree closed her eyes and waved him away. "He looked from her to me and then down to her pelvis and leg. "I'll run along. Coree, you're making remarkable progress. Each day gets you stronger." He disappeared out the door. A nurse passed through, checked vitals, and disappeared as well.

When I took her hand and kissed it, Coree pulled it away. Tough words fell out of me, almost instinctual. "Don't you ever pull your hand away from me, Coree, ever. You are not going through this alone." Moments passed and a tear escaped the corner of her closed eye. It rolled slowly over her cheek before picking up speed down to her jaw. Her hand dragged back across the white cotton and into mine.

59

Coree

"You really do have connections, don't you? They released me early, and we brought half the hospital with us."

"I wanted you here...with me."

"Why? You don't want me here. You want to be alone. I know you."

"You thought you knew me, Coree. I thought I knew myself." Elizabeth plopped Lily on the bed with me, glanced out the window, back at Lily, and finally at Little Coree on the floor. She took in a breath and her mouth made the subtle click as one does when preparing to speak, but Elizabeth hesitated and stroked the top of Little Coree's head with the back of her first two fingers. When she had taken in yet another breath, she said, as if about to divulge some great testament, "I'm going to try to...try my best...I'm going to try to be a...real human being." She swallowed after she said it and put a hand over Little Coree's body as if to feel it's being.

I frowned. "Kind of a low bar to aim for, isn't it?"

Elizabeth watched Little Coree, as if the kitten was doing something interesting. It wasn't. Again, she took a deep breath. "It means what it means. I don't know how I could say it better."

I frowned again and this time my impatience didn't let the words sit as long. "It's vague, Elizabeth."

"It means, I'll take care of you, Coree."

"You told me that, lots of times, and I'm grateful, but you're on edge. What's your deal?"

Elizabeth's eyes darted about the room. "What do you want from me, a written proposal, a contract?"

"What are you even talking about? What's going on? A written proposal of what?"

"I don't know. It's the way I am. I'm sorry."

"What are you apologizing for?"

She stroked Little Coree's soft ears between her finger and thumb. "I love this little kitten," she said. "I'm so glad we kept her. When I'm seventy, she'll be twenty, if both of us live that long."

"And the two of you will have great times," I said. "This is a stupid conversation. This is the stupidest conversation I've ever had." We communicated in meaningless short sentences, which evidently required contrasting long breaks to consider the meanings. Sentences hung in the air like slow-moving clouds in the sky. When she didn't take her turn, I said, "Tell me about the power of attorney in the hospital."

Elizabeth blinked. Again, I waited. She took in a breath and said, "You have been doing great work with Sharon, I understand. I want you to go to college and move forward when you are better."

I just stared at her in wonder. "I'm broken to pieces. Do you see me? I'm literally broken to pieces, and you're talking about college." I paused and looked into her unyielding eyes. "Elizabeth, I am so grateful for you, and all this, but I can't even walk, and I can't afford to go to college even if I could and then, I don't even know if I am capable of doing college work."

"I'm paying for it, and you're going, and that's the end of it."

I slumped. "Yes, ma'am."

"I told you not to call me ma'am."

"Well, what else can I say, Elizabeth, when you lay down the law?"

"You can say, 'Thank you.'"

"Alright, thank you. It's incredible of you. I never said I wanted to go."

"You're going."

"If you give me no choice, then the only thing I can say is, 'Yes, ma'am.'"

"Coree, you have to want to change."

"College sounds hard, kind of scary."

"If you want to be successful, Coree, you have to push yourself, take on challenges. I'm going to make sure you do that."

"Like your mom did you?"

My comment didn't slow Elizabeth down one bit. She said, "Going where the story takes you is no longer an option."

"You could use a little more of that," I said.

She waved my comment away as usual. "It's decided."

"Yup, just like your mom."

Alright then," Elizabeth said. "Like my mom. What of it?"

"I didn't have a comeback for either her challenging statement or the tone with which she delivered them so I said, "You realize then you'll be stuck with me for a while, years?"

"I'm aware," she said. "I'm not dumb."

"I didn't say you were dumb. Lighten up. You're sure uncomfortable with being nice, downright angry."

Her eyes darted to me and away and she said, "And you will live here, where I can keep an eye on you."

"Oh, Lord. I'm not Jo." I watched her hand wringing. "Can you chill? You do generosity with an attitude."

"I'm trying to, as you say, chill, but Coree, you need to understand where we are going here."

"It's nice to have someone who cares again, who wants me to succeed. I just feel like I might let you down. You're kind of hard to measure up to."

"You will succeed, Coree. Believe me. You will succeed."

"See, you're scaring me, Elizabeth, but I'll try, if you believe in me."

"I do believe in you, and you will do more than try."

"You're lucky I can't get up, or I'd hug you, you know, to calm you down."

Elizabeth's line of sight gradually rose from the kitten, to the bed, and finally up to mine. "I forged your name."

"What?"

"On the power of attorney. I forged your name."

"I figured you must have, but why'd you do it? It's like you are taking over my life, moving my stuff in and everything. Why'd you do it?"

"Decisions had to be made. You needed the best care possible. I had to have the power to make those decisions."

"You needed to make decisions, decisions about me?" Elizabeth's eyes held mine until I had to break off for a moment.

My mind hurtled in a hundred directions. "Do you know something I don't know? Am I not going to recover?"

"Why would you say that?"

"You're sending me to college. Is it because I might never model again, never walk again?"

"The doctors are optimistic, given time...but, regardless of whatever happens, you cannot rely on your youthful looks forever. None of us can." Elizabeth forced an awkward smile which I didn't join her in.

"What do you get out of it?"

Elizabeth glanced at me out of the corner of her eyes.

"You're transactional. You admitted it yourself. What do you get out of it?"

"Perhaps you can take care of me when I'm old," she said.

I chuckled. "You're old already."

"I still have men after me."

"True, but you're limited to single men from now on."

"How fun is that?"

"One of those low-key Elizabeth jokes? Hey, what is this?" I said, feeling Lily's belly. "She feels like she is getting bigger again. It's too close to having had her kittens and she hasn't even been outside."

60
Elizabeth

"I want her working while she's home, if possible, Sharon. She needs to be busy. She needs a purpose. Can she make calls, scheduling, logistics?"

"Is she up to it? I'm swamped"

"She is. Can you help me on this? Can you make it happen?"

"Absolutely. I can use her back on board."

"Good. The busier the better. She will be starting college at some point, but she will continue working for you then too. As I said, the busier the better."

"You know," Coree said. "I'm sitting right here. I'm twenty-four. I can talk too, especially about my own life and future."

I considered her a moment, before turning back to Sharon. "She is somewhat immobile for the time being, but her mental acuity is excellent, so-."

"Hey!" Coree waved. "I'm right here. Do you see me? I kind of think I should be part of this conversation."

I turned back to her. "Coree, I sometimes have a propensity to...I sometimes tend to be..."

"Bossy? The word is bossy," I said. "Another one might be controlling."

Sharon smiled at both of us, before breaking out into one of her huge bouts of laughter, setting her body shaking and her bracelets jangling.

***

"The rain is coming down so hard you have to 'bout yell out here," Coree said, dropping into a lounger. "I love it though. The two of us sit here all cozy while water rolls down the windows in sheets."

A small branch, with its leaves attached, fell against the glass and then down. "I feel good today. It'll be nice to lose this sling but you know, it's hard to model when your face frightens small children."

"You look fine. You're hypercritical about your face. It's much improved. The black eye is gone, the swelling down." Outside, the raindrops danced high on the surface of puddles in the grass.

"The left side of my face is not functioning right. When will it? I feel like I've had a stroke." Coree peered at herself in her phone camera.

"It's not noticeable. The doctor said there is a good chance for a full recovery."

"A good chance," she groaned and glancing at Lily, she said, "We need to take her to the vet for whatever is going on there."

"Agree."

"Can I take her? I haven't driven in forever, and I feel strong now."

"Let's both take her."

"Good idea. She might turn crazy. Have you ever taken a cat to the vet, Elizabeth? Like little kids. Some behave and some don't. Some get all crazy, scratching and biting. We had one that the vet had to wrap in a blanket and shove into the corner just to give it a shot."

The rain let up and finally became a mist, steamy on the flagstone walk.

Out of the blue, Coree jolted me. "Want to tell me about George?"

I sat perfectly still, but she dragged my eyes to hers as if controlling them. My first instincts, deny or pretend ignorance, died a quick death, against the knowing look I saw on Coree's face. All that was left were the terms of surrender. I swallowed and said, "Not really."

"Do it anyway." Coree's eyes bored right into me, straight on now, like a prosecuting attorney who already knows the answers to her questions.

I turned away in escape. Jo said I have to do it, if anything, for my own sanity, but that's easy for her. She's not in the middle of it. "Coree, I don't want to lose you, what we have."

"What does that mean? What do we have?"

Her question had a weight to it, so I let it hang there, stalling for time, the only thing I had left, but she quickly yanked that away as well.

"Talk."

I took a deep breath. "I was young, your age."

"Oh, cut the crap, Elizabeth and don't play victim. There's enough victims to go around, and that's not your M.O. anyway."

This is what my employees must feel like when I pin them to the wall. "Coree."

"Stop it. I asked you a question, Elizabeth."

I stroked Little Coree.

"And gimme that kitten." She yanked Little Coree out of my hands, causing it to cry out. "I'm not going to sit here all day and watch you pet a cat."

Through gritted teeth, I said, "It's all true. Everything you are thinking. It's all true."

"Nice non answer. You're the best at those. And what is it I am thinking, Elizabeth?"

"I can only imagine," she said.

"Another non answer. Get on with it. You had an affair. Am I right?"

I gave no answer, made no reaction, and by doing so, I affirmed her suspicion without having to say it.

"Both of you were married, married to other people, right?"

I used the same tactic.

"An affair is bad. It's not unheard of though, and I hate to say it, but I've done my share of fooling around. It's not the end of the world as we know it, not enough to have caused you such stress or depression or whatever it is you have."

Words burst out of my mouth. "You want me to admit it all to you, what I did, what happened? Is that what you want, Coree?"

"Well, there must be more, way more and yes, I do. All of it. It's eating you up inside."

I hoped she couldn't hear the pounding of my heart. "Coree," I pleaded, shaking my head.

"Stop it. You're being a big old wuss here."

"I've never been called that before."

"I don't imagine." Coree rose with a groan, leaving Lily in her spot, and she brought Little Coree back.

"What are you doing?"

"I'm climbing onto the recliner with you. Here. You can have Little Coree to pet if it will help you tell me what happened. You need to talk about it, get it out."

With my eyes closed as tight as they would close, I pressed my face into the softness of the little kitten and whispered, "I got pregnant." I paused and listened to the screaming fallout of my words within the deafening quiet of my house, but Coree waited. She didn't help me at all. "I got pregnant by him, by George...while married to Raymond, while my own husband was on this long business trip overseas." I paused. "And I loved him, George, that is."

Coree waited again, and the inertia of the silence pushed me on.

I looked off, out the window, and into the memories. I said to Coree and to myself, "You're so happy, supposed to be so happy to have this new life inside you."

Coree's quiet drew out my story, but I could still slam on the breaks, still hold back the worst, if I sensed telling her about it, the whole, complete story seemed like a mistake.

"A baby, a time filled with happiness, hope, and optimism, or should be, turned into a nightmare, an absolute nightmare. We tried to make it work, as if anything can work at that point. How can you make a marriage work when you are carrying someone else's baby? I loved George, but I swore off our love to try to keep my marriage. We quit seeing each other, no contact at all. But you can't do that? How do you even do that?

Coree finally spoke. "What did you do?"

"Right after birth, they took it away, adopted." I shuddered, as I've done a million times, reliving the moment, and Coree reached out for me. "Can you imagine living with that the rest of your life? Can you?" I swallowed, trying to bring moisture to my mouth.

"That's what's been haunting you. I figured there must be something else besides your mother leaving. You've been carrying a lot."

"Somehow, Raymond and I thought we could put the pieces of our marriage back together. What a joke. What a sad, sad, joke." I sucked in a breath. "There's no way. We never even slept together after the birth, of course, not during the pregnancy either. He didn't want anything to do with me, wouldn't touch me, like I was contagious, would barely talk to me or acknowledge me and could you blame him? Could you even blame him?" she said louder. "He hates me, hates the ground I walk on, still to this day, I bet."

Coree watched my eyes.

"We slept in separate bedrooms, and it wasn't long until we landed in divorce court, him bitter, me alone and traumatized." Little Coree stretched out a front paw toward my face. "And it was all my fault, all of it, no question about it. Unlike me, George did manage to put his marriage back together. Me? I ended up with no husband, no love and worst of all, no baby, totally alone."

"You married again, then, later?"

I gave a little swish of the hand. "A quick and forgettable foot note, not even that...on the rebound and desperately looking for...well... I didn't know it then, but what I wanted was my baby, and over the years, I came to the realization that I couldn't have anything else until or unless I found my child. Jo always told me that too." Little Coree's warm, spongy pads pushed up on my chin, and I sucked in a jagged breath.

"So, you're making up for it all by helping me, somehow paying a penance?"

I could feel my eyes dart around. I was at the precipice, looking into the abyss. Who'll take care of me when I'm old? I could lie one more time, hold back, and carry on, but Jo spoke to me, gave me the courage to go on.

61

Coree

"Coree, I'm sorry. I'm so, so sorry."

"Sorry for what?"

"It's been twenty-five years."

"That's a long time to carry your burden."

"Ellen, your mother may have been the most loving and caring, the most virtuous mother you could have ever had, and I was or have been a piece."

"You're not."

"I am nothing compared to her, absolutely nothing."

"I don't agree, but why compare yourself to her anyway?"

For the first time, Elizabeth looked right into my eyes. What I saw were the soulful, brown eyes of my mother, like the first time I met Elizabeth, but a weariness weighed on them. She swallowed, shook her head, and said, through a hand over her mouth, "Oh, Coree, Coree, Coree. Don't you get it? Don't you understand?"

"Don't I get what?"

"I gave you up just to keep my husband, my marriage."

I sat up.

"Please don't leave me, Coree. Please don't hate me. I'm sorry. I'm so sorry. I was young and stupid and..." Elizabeth sucked in a rough breath.

"What're you saying? You're my mother? Are you saying you're my mother? You're my real mother, my bio mother?"

The floodgates of Elizabeth's words continued to flow. "Don't leave me Coree. Please, don't leave me. Don't hate me. I was young and stupid and oh, my life has been a living hell, and I deserved every bit of it, giving up a piece of me, wondering about you, where you were, if you were alright, and that I couldn't know and couldn't help you or take care of you if you needed me. I don't even know if I could have helped you, I turned into such a piece of shit over all these years."

I heard her speaking, now an open flood of words, but at the same time, wheels turned in my head, and realization overcame my brain, a feeling almost palpable. I touched my neck and became aware of my racing heartbeat.

"Coree, I should have been there for you."

"I'm alright, Elizabeth. I survived. I ended up okay."

She blew out a long sigh. "It all probably worked out for the best for you. I would have messed it up, messed you up. You turned out wonderful and it's all because of Ellen. If I would have kept you, you might have, probably would have grown up to become a cold, calculating bitch like me."

"Oh, wow," I said. "Don't say that about yourself. I suppose, maybe when my mother died, if you could have found me, you could have saved me from myself. I fell into some dark places."

"Everyone of those dark places were my fault."

"How were they your fault, Elizabeth?"

"The whole thing was my fault, and I don't even know if I could have helped you, I've been such a mess myself." She reached out and pushed a strand of hair from my cheek. "I probably would have made you weak and dependent, or you would have rebelled from me and broken away, angry. At that age, you might have hated me for what I did. You probably hate me now."

"Why would I hate you?"

"Well, my words came back to haunt me a while back when I told you I never wanted to see my mother again as long as I live. You remember? When I heard those words come out of my mouth, they struck fear into me. She left her children and I hated her for it. I just figured you might feel the same way."

"I don't hate you. I love you."

Elizabeth swallowed and said, "And I love you too, my daughter, so much. You can't even imagine."

I melted into her, within her arms, and I fit perfectly, just like my own mom, all those years ago. I said into her, "Elizabeth, do you need my forgiveness? I never blamed you for giving me up, never resented that real mother out there for giving me up, maybe because I had such a happy childhood, but if you need it for your redemption, Elizabeth, I forgive you for what you did.

What you really need to do, though, is forgive yourself. We can't choose our past. You can't change your past, Elizabeth, but now there is a future."

Thinking more about it, I said, "Elizabeth, you carried regrets your whole life, but here's something to consider. Without your affair, you and George, there would have been no me, no Coree. The one time you loved, Elizabeth, the only time in your life, Elizabeth Ransom really felt love, I am the product of that love. It's beautiful. You loved once, Elizabeth, only once, and I came from it. That's so legit."

I felt Elizabeth's subtle nod.

"I'm from that. I am from your love. I don't care if it was an affair or whatever. I could give a shit. It was love, my mother's love, and I'm what came out of it. It must mean something."

"Coree, you were the only one who could save me. I just never dared to hope that I would have the chance." Elizabeth lay back, exhausted and spent, looking up into the sky lights and beyond.

"Are you sure about this, Elizabeth? How can you be so-?"

"I am sure," she said, in her unique level tone, her tone that carried so much power and finality.

I studied on that in the ensuing silence, until things popped in my head. "Leah." I whispered it, the epiphany, the realization so palpable, I almost felt another physical shift in my brain. The fact that Elizabeth so easily ignored my realization both confirmed it and made me marvel about her power, her strength, and capacity. Had I only seen the public part of it, the tip of the iceberg? I found it not only intimidating, but intoxicating.

"Leah is your...your..." I trailed off, unable to find the right word.

Elizabeth tightened her lips, and with cold, sober eyes that gripped mine, she said, "Coree." After another pause with tightened jaws, she said, "In my world," again she paused. "Coree, you have to understand that in my world, there are things that have to be done...sometimes...things that just have to be done."

Maybe she has some 'cold, calculating bitch,' in her after all, but that doesn't necessarily have to be a bad thing, maybe...if she's my own mom, on my side.

Almost in answer, she said, "I'm not Ellen. I can't be Ellen. For all her loving...well, I'm not...I'm just not..."

"Being a mother isn't just being loving, is it? Be you, Elizabeth. Just be you, for me. Be my mother."

"You are twenty-four, a grown woman."

"I lost time having a mom, and I want it back.

"I'll try to be the mother that you missed."

"I'm sure we'll have our moments. I can already envision that." I chuckled, thinking about her college expectations. "We'll have to fight it out sometimes, like everyone else, I suppose. Elizabeth, I'll try too. I'll try to be the daughter you wanted."

The distant chime of the doorbell resonated in the interior of the house. Elizabeth picked up her phone to view the porch camera. "That's strange."

"What?"

"Leah. She's here. She's here at my house."

"So?"

"It must be serious. Excuse me while I meet with her."

"Can't I be there?"

My mother shook her head. "I have no idea what it is, but, as I said, it must be serious."

So, was this going to be it then? Sitting around chilling with the cats while my mother, my new mother has separate issues and secrets from me?

"I wanted you to hear this directly," Leah said, "no paper trail, no electronic fingerprints."

"Go on." Elizabeth said.

"I discovered a rat." After a pause, she continued. "I intercepted electronic messages from Chelsea to the Chairman of the Board."

A silence followed until Elizabeth said, "And?"

"She tried to sabotage your promotion by implicating you in an affair with Mr. Kent."

"Evidently, she was unsuccessful," Elizabeth said.

"As I said, I intercepted them. She doesn't know her messages were never received by the-"

Leah's voice stopped abruptly. After a pause, Elizabeth said, "Coree, come in here."

I froze, a little child caught. My body, in its current condition, couldn't run for the terrace, so I stood like a statue in the kitchen.

"Coree, come here. I can see your shadow in the doorway."

I eased out into the living room, head down.

She pointed to the far end of the couch from where Leah waited. "Sit down there and be quiet."

"Sorry," I said.

Elizabeth sat in her leather high-back across from us, legs crossed, arms folded. Her gaze leaving me with a sigh, she turned to Leah and said, "Go on. What is her motive?"

Leah glanced down the couch at me and back to her boss. "I dug back into her messages. She had an affair with Mr. Kent, right before he moved on to you. Her motivation was that she, shall we say, still has feelings for him."

"He's a player," I said.

They both turned to me as if a house plant had joined in the conversation.

"Well, he is. Just saying."

"I told you to be quiet," Elizabeth said.

"You thought he had feelings for you, but he's just looking for hookups...in the offices of Landford-Smithson of all places."

She raised her hand for me to stop. "Please continue, Leah."

Leah looked at Elizabeth, then me, and then back to Elizabeth.

"Go ahead."

"She wasn't able to implicate you, but in the process, she did implicate herself, to us. I have all the documentation." She laid a thin stack of paper, held perfectly neat by a black binder clip, on the coffee table.

Elizabeth regarded that neat stack and pursed her lips.

"It's the only copy," said Leah. "All her communications. No others exist."

Elizabeth pondered them again as if this physical evidence might add significance, while Leah and I watched and waited. She tightened her lips, raised an eyebrow, and finally said, with the same emotion one would have in discarding a piece of old furniture, "Get rid of her."

Leah nodded.

"And what is Mr. Kent's role in this?"

"He is aware of her...her..."

"Butthurt," I said.

Leah's pause acknowledged my comment. "He doesn't appear to be aware of her schemes against you. As your daughter here says, he seems to just be out there chasing women, and Chelsea was-"

"Butthurt," I said. "How many other Landford-Smithson women do you suppose he's done?"

Elizabeth turned on me. "What did I tell you, Coree?"

"He doesn't seem to have broken any policies, any written policies," said Leah.

Elizabeth gave it a moment of consideration as well before saying, "Start a paper trail." The three of us sat in the cool, quiet of the living room for a moment until my mother sucked a deep breath into her nostrils, let it out through her mouth and said, "Are we all set here then, or is there anything else?"

"That's all."

"Well done, Leah."

She left us alone there without as much as a glance at me, or a nod at Elizabeth.

"That was legit," I said.

Elizabeth turned to me. "Don't sneak around. I don't want you to be a part of-"

"I'm your daughter, your grown daughter. I'm not some ditzy kid."

"Still, there will be things-"

"Let me help you, Elizabeth. It's what families do." I rose, and moving down the couch, I sat in Leah's spot, directly across from Elizabeth. "You just carry everything by yourself, and it's not good for you. Let me help you to carry the weight, the weight in your life."

She squinted at me and my words as if I spoke a foreign language.

I approached and kneeled on the floor next to her. "Elizabeth, will you please call Leah back?"

"What? Why?"

"Because I want you to do this differently." Elizabeth's hand rested on the arm of her chair and I took it with both my hands. "Please, Elizabeth? I think there's a better way."

***

"Even the ceiling crushes out here," I said. "Look at the lattice work and skylights, but you lived here all alone."

"According to you, and you were pretty much right, waiting to die."

"Hey, what's that doing in here?"

"I figured we could use a little breakfast table," Elizabeth said.

"It goes with, well, nothing," I said. "The chrome legs, the frayed edge, it doesn't go with anything.

"It's staying."

"You have a heart, don't you? You have a heart. My ratty-ass old family table in your beautiful terrace."

"Ratty?" Elizabeth said. "I love it. All I see when I look at it is you, baby Coree, little girl Coree, teenage Coree, and even grown-up Coree."

I got up and ran a finger under the edge.

62

Elizabeth

"Look here, Elizabeth, I want to show you something, an album of my family, uhh, my adopted family." Coree plopped onto the floor, crosslegged, back against my recliner. I had no choice but to move my legs to the side, and even then, her shoulder pressed against them. Evidently, Coree seemed to find this physical contact acceptable.

One by one, she explained each picture, who was in it, or where they were. On perhaps only the third or fourth page, my eyes flew open wide. I jabbed a finger over her shoulder. "Who's that?"

"That's me and Mom and Dad and some neighbors-"

"That one," I said." Who is that one right there, to the side?"

"Oh her. Yeah, that's the adoption lady, the one who put us together." Coree chattered on about the next picture, but my chest constricted.

The woman showed up again in a couple pages. "Why is she back? Is that what adoption ladies, as you called her, do?"

"I don't know. I only had the one. She came around to check on us now and then, and we all became friends. She was kind of eccentric, maybe a little off if that doesn't sound mean. We could go a month or a whole year without seeing her. She'd just show up out of the blue. Once in a while, we'd even notice her driving, just looking, which is weird, cause our house is kind of out there, you know."

"What's her name?"

"Sarah. Sarah Ward."

I collapsed back into my recliner. "Lord, I can't do this. I cannot do this anymore."

Without glancing behind her, Coree said over her shoulder, "Can't do what?"

"Life," I said. "I can't do life anymore."

Her back to me and my reactions, Coree dismissed my words with a wave of her hand.

"What was she like?" I said, peering up through the sky lights at the passing clouds, "She was nice. She'd stop by, and visit, see how we were getting on, bring me toys, or bring Mom something."

"When did you last see her?"

"Oh." Coree looked up and out the window a moment. "I'd have to think about that, probably back before Mom died. Actually, at the funeral, I think." Corrie tapped my knee." I'll tell you a secret, Elizabeth. Do you want me to tell you a secret?"

"Okay, dear," I said with sandpaper throat. "You tell me a secret."

Coree flipped more pages, mentioning a few details here and there. By the time she got to her secret, I had already received the response from my text. "I'll get right on it, Ms. Ransom."

"Dad told me, just a couple years ago, you know, after I grew up, he thinks the lady from the adoption agency might be Mom's mother, that she had given Mom up as a baby, always regretted it, and kept up on her. I don't know for sure if it's true. She kind of disappeared."

Coree continued through the album, pointing to this person and that. I heard little, but examined each picture over her shoulder, a hand covering my mouth. My mother appeared a few more times. My twin sister, my devoted and affectionate twin sister, the polar opposite of me, appeared over and over, everywhere, spreading her warmth throughout the album, as she had, no doubt, the family. "She has the same birthdate as me?" my mouth said, when Coree closed the album, but I remembered the answer.

"Who? My mother? Yes? Why?"

I stole glances at my phone. Though I might not hear back from Leah for a day or two, I knew. I knew, and I let out a long breath.

Coree rose, placed the album on her old kitchen table, the very kitchen table my sister used, the sister I just found out I had, at age fifty, and I never got to meet her. Sounds like my mother probably sat at it too, long after she abandoned me. And here it is, right in my terrace.

I watched Coree at the window, my daughter, my very own daughter. I observed her features, what was mine, what was her father's. As much satisfaction as finding her brought me, it came with a price, a new burden to carry, a sister I never got to know, a mother I didn't even know what to think about now.

***

"Elizabeth! This is a nice surprise." Michael flipped on his charming smile like a light switch. "Are you back, then?"

"I stopped in to tie up a few loose ends."

He glanced around. "Where's my Caitlyn?"

"I sent your secretary away so we could have a minute or two."

"Great."

"Michael, I want you to take an office suite nearer to your department, where your supervision will have more presence."

The smile dropped. "What's this about? You're dissatisfied with my work?"

I narrowed my eyes at him. "I am dissatisfied with your attitude toward Landford-Smithson." Glancing at the family portrait on the shelf and back to him, I said, "What you do with your personal life is your own business, but don't bring it into the office...anymore. Do not treat this place as your personal pickup bar. I'll be keeping a close eye on you."

He opened his mouth to speak.

"That'll be all."

I turned, and he said to my back, "Does that mean you are not taking the promotion?"

I ignored his question and walked out the door.

***

Motioning her to sit down with me at my conference table on the same side and with one chair between us, I laced my fingers together on my crossed legs. "I know about everything, Chelsea."

She raised her eyebrows.

"I'm going to cut through the shit and get to the point."

"You always do."

"Right. We are similar in that regard." I drummed my four nails on the table once and said, "Here it is. I am staying here."

"Not being promoted to CEO?"

"That is under negotiation, and it has nothing to do with your conspiring." I laid a hand on the neat stack of papers. "Your attempted conspiring." Now she blinked and glanced at them too.

She sat silently, a defendant awaiting her sentence.

"I'm not going to play cat and mouse with you, Chelsea. As I said, I know everything." The pads of my fingers slid across the papers, the evidence, and I brought my hand back to my lap. "But we're going to move forward. Mr. Kent's suite will be relocated down to his department, away from us. He is, as my Coree put it, a player. He played you, and he tried to play me as well. We are putting that behind us and putting him away from us. Ms. Dunning, she doesn't know it yet, but she will take his suite here in the executive wing. Chelsea, you are an outstanding executive secretary, and you will stay with me."

Guarded relief formed on her face, but I added, "You screwed up. I've screwed up myself, big time, and I've been informed...recently," I swallowed and glanced down at my hands, "that both forgiving and being forgiven are important. Evidently," I paused and swallowed again, "I'm not too old to learn new things."

Chelsea took a deep breath.

"Is everything alright at home for you, on the home front?"

She touched the fingertips of one of her hands to her forehead.

"If you need someone to talk to." I glanced off beside her for a moment and exhaled. "Chelsea, I know in the past I have been strictly professional, okay, aloof. Alright, let's be honest here, I've been, at best, indifferent. However one chooses to characterize it, I am now aware of what I have been." I reached out for her hand, but fell short of it. "If you need someone to talk to, well, I'm here for you."

She forced a tight-lipped smile.

"That's right. I'm trying to learn to be a real human."

She smiled at that too, but hanging her head, she whispered, barely audible, "He doesn't know."

I laid a hand on hers, covering the scintillations sparkling off the rock of a diamond on her left hand. "Chelsea, let's get back to doing what you and I do best, running this company."

Rising with me, Chelsea said, "Thank you, Ms. Ransom.

"You can thank Coree."

"I will do that."

"We can all thank Coree."

At the door, Chelsea took one of my hands in both of hers. She regarded our hands together and peered up at me. "Ms. Ransom, I'll be loyal to you."

I made an obvious glance at the little stack of documentation and back to her. "I know you will, Chelsea."

When the door clicked behind her, I turned my attention to my pictures of Jo, Allison, and their families. I retrieved a framed portrait of my daughter out of my briefcase, careful not to leave fingerprints on the glass and I placed it between my two sisters.

***

The morning sun, finding a few openings through the oak canopy, dappled patches of light on random places in the garden. Coree stared down at Lily's little grave at the foot of the wall under the lengthening shadows and said, "I hope the lilies of the valley we planted survive."

"They will," I said.

"You don't know that." Coree's tone startled me. "Everything dies. Everything in my life dies," she said, glancing over at the album and back to the little mound of dirt. She turned to me with an icy glare that sadly, I knew she had inherited, not from my sunny sister, Ellen, but from me, her biological mother. "You'll die someday," she said, an accusation.

"That's a happy thought."

"It's true. Just like Mommy and Daddy, and just like Lily."

"Coree, stop it. I'll try not to die, okay?" But I knew I had lost her. "You...you and me, we have to build something bigger, more permanent. We still have 'Little Coree.' And you can't have this forever. Nobody can."

"But I want this forever." She motioned her hand between us. "This is what I want."

Her demand hung around us in the terrace, accompanied by Little Coree's whistly snores. She drew near my recliner.

"What?" I said, but, of course, I knew. "Oh, for God's sake, come on then. One of these days, this lounger is surely going to collapse under us." She curled into her little ball within me, laying a hand on the kitten's round and fuzzy middle.

I reached over and opened the drawer on the side table. "Coree, I missed about everything in your life, but here. I have something for you."

"What is it?"

"Hold out your hand."

"What is it?"

My fingers opened just enough to allow a gold chain to suspend above her open hand. A little gold heart hung at the bottom of it. "Happy Birthday, Coree. I've missed them all, including that last one, but I won't miss any more. I swear to you. I will never miss another." I opened my shirt collar enough to show her the heart I wore, exactly the same as hers, but larger and with a heart shape missing within it.

Coree's green eyes followed.

"See the smaller heart there on your chain? It has been stamped out of mine. I made sure it's the same piece." I leaned in and whispered, "Yes, I even sent Leah to the jeweler to witness it. See how it fits perfectly? It's from the exact same piece of fourteen karat gold, the exact same piece, Coree."

My daughter's eyes moved from her necklace to mine and back to hers again. She swallowed and after a quick glance at me, snapped her fist shut around it, sliding it off my fingers. After another quick glance at me, she pulled it close to her face, and opened her fingers to examine it again.

"I haven't been a real good person, and certainly not a good mom."

Coree pulled her closed hand, containing the heart, against her own heart. "We all had to play the cards we were dealt, Elizabeth."

I nodded. "But I'm going to change. I know I've probably scared you with my expectations and so on, but I may also spoil you. Yeah, I'm pretty sure I will spoil you." With two fingers, I pulled a few strands of Coree's hair off her cheek and tucked it behind an ear, as is her habit.

Curled into me, Coree closed her eyes and whispered, "This, forever."

Made in USA - Kendallville, IN
66543_9798385523429
03.13.2023 1340